FROM SHADOWED PLACES

13 DARKLY TWISTED TALES

By

Jeremy M. Wright

The characters and events in this book are fictitious. Any similarity to real persons, living or dead, is coincidental and not intended by the author.

Copyright © 2021, 2011 by Jeremy M. Wright

Cover design by Lance Buckley

All rights reserved. No part of this book may be reproduced in any form or by any electronic or mechanical means, including information storage and retrieval systems, without permission in writing from the publisher, except by reviewers, who may quote brief passages in a review.

First paperback edition by Stone Gateway Publishing November 2021

ISBN: 978-1-7340887-8-6

Printed in the United States of America.

For my lifelong friend, Jason Neece.

Through the craziness of our youth, we grew even closer and somehow made it out of our bizarre adventures alive. Here's to us and our decades of mayhem yet to come!

Also by Jeremy M. Wright

<u>Fiction</u>

Chasing Daylight

<u>Young Adult</u>

The Good Ship

In the middle of the journey of our life I came to myself within a dark wood where the straight way was lost.

Dante Alighieri

CONTENTS

58 MINUTES ~1

FATE ALWAYS KNOCKS TWICE ~17

DOWN THE ROAD ~29

THE BATTLE AT DAYTON HILL ~45

SACRED ~63

PERFECT CIRCLES ~71

NIGHTLINE ~95

A DEVIL OF A DEAL ~113

DREAD 121

I AM DIMENSION ~151

IT'S THAT THING ABOUT DEATH ~183

RED HOUR ~193

FROM SHADOWED PLACES ~209

58 Minutes

"Please, please, someone help me," the man said as he pushed open the café door.

Six regular customers turned in their chairs to look at the man. Helen Westcott, the waitress, watched from behind the counter. Garrett Malone, the cook, lowered his head to peer through the small window where he placed the prepared orders.

The rain had soaked the man's clothes. His black, curly, wet hair plastered his head. His glasses had slipped down his nose, and he watched the small crowd over the rims.

In stunned silence, they looked from the man to the woman in his trembling arms. They seemed to wait for a perfect explanation to the evening interruption.

"It's my wife. Please help her. She got hit by a car on the road."

They watched, transfixed by the strangest Tuesday any of them could remember.

"Please!" he shouted, which shook several of them from their position.

"Oh, my heavens, hurry and bring her over here," Helen said as she met the man halfway. She cleared silverware from one of the vacant tables.

The man gently placed his wife on the table. As he backed away, he looked down at her as if trying to figure out precisely what to do.

"Is she still alive?" Garrett asked as he exited the kitchen and hurried to the table.

"I—I—I don't know," the man stammered as he pushed his glasses back in place.

Helen touched the woman's bloody throat. After a moment, she said, "Yeah, she's still alive, but her pulse is weak."

"She got hit by a car, you said?" one patron asked from the counter.

"We were coming down the highway, and we got a flat. I was changing the tire, and my wife was holding the flashlight. A car came down the road and got too close to the shoulder. We didn't even see it coming. I think it was a black or dark blue car. It hit her and my car and kept going. I don't know how it missed me, but my wife got thrown right over our car. The crash damaged my car too much to drive. I picked her up and ran down the road until I got here. I didn't even know this café was here. I couldn't see anything in the rain. I was pretty sure there was a town ahead of us, but I didn't know how far. I can't believe I even found this place," the man said, then began weeping.

Helen quickly moved behind the counter, shuffled through one drawer, and promptly returned with an armload of clean hand towels. She dropped them on the end of the table and began handing them out.

"We've got to stop the bleeding. Do you know where your wife's injuries are?" Garrett asked.

"I don't know. The car hit her right side and threw her down the embankment. I just picked her up and ran."

"All right, don't worry because we'll figure it out and patch her up the best we can," Garrett said.

The night outside briefly lit up like a stadium, followed by a vicious rumble of thunder. The café lights flickered but stayed lit.

"Helen, call 911 and get an ambulance and the police. Whoever did this needs to be caught and held accountable," Garrett said.

Helen went to the phone on the wall and removed the receiver. Her face went slack while listening for a dial tone. She rapidly clicked the disconnect button but found only silence for her efforts.

"The phone line is dead. The storm must have knocked it out," Helen said as she raced back to the table.

Garrett turned to the soaking, shivering man and said, "What's your name, mister?"

"Adam, my name is Adam."

"And her name?"

"Evelyn."

"All right, here's the deal, Adam. We're going to have to pick up your wife and get her to my car, and then we'll drive her to the emergency room in Stowell. It's the closest town with a hospital, about twenty miles from here. Does that sound okay to you?" Garrett asked.

"Yeah, whatever you think is best."

"I wouldn't do that if I were you," a man at the counter said as he dipped a French fry in ketchup and shoved it in his mouth.

"Why's that, Lloyd?" Helen asked.

"She's in awful shape. Moving your wife could do a lot more damage," Lloyd said.

"The guy ran with her all the way here," Helen countered.

"I know, but she could have serious internal injuries. One wrong move could make things a lot worse. If you want to try it, then go right ahead. I wouldn't if I were you. That's all I'm saying," Lloyd said.

"You seem pretty relaxed for seeing something like this," Garrett said.

"I've seen a lot worse during three tours in Iraq. I've seen stuff that would make any other person in here puke up their dinner," Lloyd claimed.

Garrett waved his hand as a way of dismissing Lloyd's comments and said, "Let's get going."

Adam grabbed Garrett's forearm and said, "Maybe he's right. I took a hell of a chance moving her. I didn't really have a choice. What if we make things worse, as he said?"

Garrett's shoulders sagged as he studied the unconscious woman. "You didn't have a choice before, and I don't think we have a choice now. If we don't get her medical help soon, she could die. I suppose it's your call."

Adam was biting his thumbnail. He ran his other hand through his wet hair and brushed it back from his forehead. His eyes scanned his wife and then the faces of the people around the table.

Adam said, "I don't want to move her, at least not yet. Let's get these wet clothes off her and try to see what we're dealing with here. We need to know where she's injured before we take a chance moving her."

Helen went to the counter again and returned with two pairs of scissors. Helen, Garrett, and Adam carefully removed her jacket and blue jeans as the other customers watched in shock. They saw blood seeping from a wound in her throat. As they cut away her clothing, they discovered a gash across the lower ribs, as well as the skin and flesh of her right thigh torn open. They used hand towels and applied pressure to stifle the bleeding.

"Helen, do we have any blankets around here to cover her up? She's as cold as a damn icicle," Garrett asked.

Helen looked over her shoulder to study the area. "No, I don't think so. I think a tarp we've got in back is the best we can do."

"Wait, I have a blanket in the trunk of my car. I'll go out and get it," Brandy Perkins said. She dashed out the door and into the storm before anyone could reply.

"This has become one hell of a situation," Garrett said.

The group nodded with confirmation.

A long, unsettling moment went by before Brandy returned. She looked like a drowned rat while holding a wool blanket and trembling in the doorway. Her eyes were horror-struck.

"Let's have it," Garrett said to her.

Slowly, she walked to the group, but her eyes never left the man at the counter.

Lloyd watched balefully in return. He slowly chewed the last bite of his ham sandwich.

Garrett took the blanket, unfolded it, and carefully draped it over the woman.

Helen watched Brandy study Lloyd.

"What's going on with you?" Helen asked.

Brandy quickly pulled her eyes from Lloyd and briefly made eye contact with Helen before lowering her gaze. She shook her head, droplets of water falling to the floor. She shrugged and mumbled something none of them could understand.

"Speak up, girl," Garrett said.

"It's nothing. Do you think the woman will be all right?" Brandy asked.

"Not if we don't get a miracle to happen real soon," Garrett said.

Helen pulled back the hand towel from Evelyn's neck and inspected the wound.

"Look, the bleeding has almost stopped," she said.

They pulled the blanket down and checked the other wounds.

"I guess you got the miracle you wanted. The bleeding has nearly stopped on these wounds as well. Let's keep the pressure on anyhow," Helen said.

"Thank God," Adam said and gently took his wife's hand.

A long flash of lightning scarred the sky, followed by a fierce rumble that felt as if Hell were breaking free. The diner lights flickered and then went out.

"I think you were a little too quick to thank God," Lloyd said from the counter.

"Agreed," someone else said.

"Everyone needs to calm down. I've got a few flashlights and a box of tea candles in the back," Garrett said, then stumbled into the darkness of the diner.

"You should have sprung for emergency lights," Lloyd said.

"It wasn't in the budget," Helen said.

Garrett returned with two flashlights and a small box of candles. Brandy and another patron helped him place candles on the diner tables and lit them. The shadows slightly receded when they finished.

One long minute ticked after another as the small group watched the dying woman. None of them could think of anything to say or do to bring relief to the unfortunate situation.

"Hey, can I talk to both of you for a moment?" Brandy whispered to Garrett and Helen when they were out of earshot of the rest of the group.

"Sure, hon, what's on your mind?" Helen asked.

"I don't want to talk here. Can we go in the back?" Brandy asked and headed for the kitchen before they agreed.

When Garrett and Helen entered the kitchen, they saw Brandy pacing and quickly rubbing her hands together.

"What's going on? You've been all worked up since you went outside," Helen said.

"I know something. At least, I think I know something. I'm not sure. I could be wrong about the whole thing. Maybe my mind is just full of tension, and it's inventing things to keep it occupied," Brandy said.

Helen gently seized Brandy's arms to halt her pacing.

"Just relax and breathe. Now tell us what it is you think you know," Helen said.

Brandy chewed on her bottom lip and eyed them both.

In a voice barely above a whisper, she said, "When that guy came in with his wife, didn't he say a black car hit his wife?"

"Yeah, it was black, or maybe dark blue. Why?" Garrett asked.

"Well, that guy Lloyd, he's got a black car," Brandy said.

"So?" Helen said.

"Well, I wouldn't think much about it, but the front fender is all busted in, and a cracked windshield, too."

Helen looked at Garrett in disbelief and said, "Lloyd came in, what, fifteen minutes before the couple? He ordered, and I put his plate down only a few minutes before they came in. Lloyd never looks at the menu. He orders the same damn thing every time, a fried ham sandwich with a large order of fries," Helen said, then looked over her shoulder at Lloyd. Her gaze shot through the order window and watched the group in the dining area.

Garrett held up his hands and said, "Just hold on for a minute. I've known Lloyd for nearly ten years. If he hit someone on the road, there's no way he'd drive away, come in here, and then order dinner without saying something about it. He would have stopped. He would have done something."

"He did something. He drove away," Brandy said.

"Okay, I'll be the first to admit that Lloyd is a little off, but he's not the kind of guy to do a hit and run. Did he seem shaken up or nervous to you?" Garrett asked Helen.

"Well, no, I guess not any more than usual."

"There you go. The guy won't run down a lady on a dark road and calmly sit at my counter and eat dinner."

"He sure didn't seem that worked up when that guy brought in his wife. He didn't seem surprised. He might have seen many injured or dead people in Iraq, but that was quite some time ago. He didn't seem at all concerned for the woman," Helen said.

Garrett said, "Lloyd is the one that recommended not moving her. I agreed with that."

"Maybe he's worried that she saw his car. Maybe he's waiting to see if she's able to tell her husband what kind of car it was," Brandy said.

"He wouldn't stick around if he was the one who hit her," Garrett countered.

"Maybe he's waiting for her to die," Helen said.

"Do you think it was him?" someone asked behind them.

Startled, they turned around to see Adam standing at the order window and watch the three of them speak in secret.

"Was it him?" he asked in a voice building with rage

"We're not saying that at all. Don't get yourself all worked up," Garrett said, but might have well held his tongue because Adam had already disappeared from the window.

The three of them quickly stepped from the kitchen in time to see Adam lunging for the other man at the counter.

"What did you do?" Adam screamed, and the entire diner stopped and watched.

Adam threw his arm across the counter and swiped Lloyd's nearly finished dinner plate across the room and against the wall. French fries took flight. Ceramic shards flew in all directions, and the wall caught a splatter of ketchup that eerily looked like blood.

"What in the hell is your problem?" Lloyd yelled and removed his massive body from the counter stool.

"Did you hit my wife on the road?"

"You're damn crazy, man. I didn't hit anyone."

"They said your car is all busted up," Adam said and thrust his finger at Garrett, Helen, and Brandy.

"What?" Lloyd asked them.

Brandy said, "Well, it's true. I saw it when I went out to get the blanket from my car. You have a damaged front fender and windshield."

"Is it true?" Adam asked.

"Yeah, my car has damage, but it isn't from hitting your wife. I hit a deer three days ago. That's what caused the wreck," Lloyd said, then sat back down.

"A deer did it? Are you sure?" Adam asked.

"Hell yeah, I'm sure. I pulled the damn thing off the road after I hit it. I killed it outright. There wasn't anything I could have done."

"He's lying. I can always tell when someone is lying," Rebecca King said from Evelyn's side.

"Yeah, I don't think Lloyd's being honest," Rebecca's husband said when he looked from the injured woman to the man at the counter.

Lloyd barked like a cornered animal, "Don't act as if you know anything about me. You don't know me! And don't go flying off the handle and blaming other people for your misfortune. None of this is my fault."

Adam was about to continue the argument when Evelyn drew in a violent breath. All of their heads turned and watched the woman lying on the table. She was shaking. Her head slowly rotated back and forth, and her eyes rapidly opened and closed.

Adam quickly came around the counter and ran to her side. Her eyes briefly focused on him, and her trembling hand reached for him.

As Adam took her blood-splattered hand, he said, "Evelyn, I'm here. Everything is going to be all right. Can you hear me? Everything is going to be just fine. We're going to get you to the hospital as soon as possible."

They could all see her blue-tinted lips working, but only Adam could hear her. He leaned in, his ear close to her mouth.

"What was that?" Adam asked.

Adam's face went pallid and slack as he listened to his wife whisper in his ear. His eyes slowly rotated to Lloyd, who was still at the counter with a compassionless expression as he watched the group around the woman.

Evelyn's mouth moved as the group watched, and then her jaw quit working. Her eyes went soft, and the rest of her went slack. Her head rotated to the left by the simple lack of muscle restraint.

Adam's eyes quickly spilled tears as his hand gripped his wife's lifeless hand.

"Eve, don't leave me. Eve, can you hear me?" Adam pleaded.

In a strange sense of astonishment, Brandy thought, *Adam and Eve, the same names as the first man and woman. What are the odds?*

Adam shifted his sight to Lloyd and said, "Are you happy now? Do you see what you've done? Do you feel anything?"

"It's a shame, sure enough," Lloyd said with little emotion.

Without fully knowing what she was doing, Brandy briskly walked to Lloyd and slapped him hard across the cheek. Her entire body was shaking from a fit of anger that surfaced without warning.

"How can you be so cold?" Brandy spat.

"Don't touch me again. If any of you even think about laying a hand on me, I won't be responsible for the action I take," Lloyd said to the group.

In the cold, flickering candlelight, they watched him.

"What are you going to do, Lloyd? Are you going to plow us down as you did to this poor woman? Are you going to murder all of us in cold blood?" Helen said as she stepped to Brandy's side.

"A damn deer is what I hit on the road. I'm not a murderer. Just back up now!" Lloyd warned.

As Garrett joined the other two, Lloyd quickly backed up.

"I'm not staying for this mad show anymore. I'm not staying, and you can't stop me."

Garrett grabbed the collar of Lloyd's jacket and harshly pulled him to the floor.

"You're not running off just yet. I think the police are going to have a few questions for you. No one is leaving until the authorities get here," Garrett said.

Lloyd thrashed. His arms and legs became working pistons that desperately tried to propel the man off of him.

"Someone help me, dammit!" Garrett shouted.

Lloyd had caught Garrett's forehead with a random kick and sent the large cook falling backward against a table that toppled and crashed to the floor.

Lloyd was immediately on his feet and backed against the counter with his fists raised and ready for a fight. In seconds, his eyes wildly searched the entire diner. He saw the dead woman on the table and the enraged husband. He also saw the diner patrons watching him with fierce eyes. He also saw the steak knife on the counter to his left.

As Lloyd gripped the steak knife, Helen moved forward. Lloyd's arm reflexively swung, and the blade came across the uniform and skin of Helen's chest. Helen released a terrifying scream that halted the crowd's forward movement. She collapsed on the tiles, gently placed her hand on her chest, and then pulled her blood-soaked hand away.

"He cut me, Garrett. Look what he's done," she said.

"This is madness! I've done nothing wrong. Don't move any closer. Look what you've made me do," Lloyd shouted in confusion.

In the dim candlelight, the crowd moved in like a pack of blood-hungry wolves. They quickly surrounded Lloyd, and all at once, they were on him. Their hands became raging claws and fierce vices as they seized him. Their feet became malicious, bludgeoning rams as Lloyd spun, fell, and rose as he tried to break free.

"Madness!" he screamed.

Helen had found the will to lift herself from the diner floor and moved into the crowd. The group then slammed Lloyd against the wall. The diners and staff embraced the animal instincts of survival, and there, they took Lloyd's life from him, one brutal strike after another.

As Lloyd's lifeless body sank to the floor, the crowd eased. With their clothes splattered in blood and their bodies exhausted, they turned in unison to the man clapping behind them.

Strangely enough, Adam was smiling brightly. His hands came together in applause. They thought it was an odd sight to see a man thrilled with a brutal murder, especially when his wife had just lost her life.

Adam stopped clapping, pulled back the sleeve of his jacket, and looked at his watch.

"I'll mark that as time. It's been fifty-eight minutes since we entered the diner. I'd say that I won the bet, dear," Adam said.

"I don't understand. What the hell are you talking about?" Garrett asked.

Then all of them took a massive step backward as the dead woman on the table slowly sat up. Her head rotated as if slow-turning gears operated it until her sight found the group.

"Damn, two more minutes, and you would have lost the bet," Eve said.

"It can't be. You died," Brandy dreamily said.

Eve slid off the table and stepped to her husband's side. Her exposed skin was a pale blue, as only her undergarments remained. Before their unblinking stares, her complexion returned as if poured back into her. The three wounds she had sustained from whatever ungodly incident had occurred pulled closed, and the spilled blood on her skin retracted into those closing lacerations.

Adam and Eve stepped forward.

The small crowd took another step back.

"Now, just hold it right there," Garrett said as he held out his hand.

"Fifty-eight minutes means I won," Adam said.

"What the hell does that mean?" Helen screeched and looked around at all the faces as if her diner companions knew the answer.

"We must collect payment of life and soul for your sins," Adam said, then grinned in such a terrible way that the entire group shuddered.

"I thought for sure this group would be mine," Eve said, then curled out her lower lip in a silent pout.

"They're not yours this time, my dear. Besides, you got the last bunch. It's only fair. The bet was for one hour or less. Fifty-eight minutes, so I won this round," Adam said and held out his arms to the group as if expecting an embrace.

In a quaking voice, Brandy asked, "What did you win, mister?"

Eve said, "My, my, you must be the obtuse one of the group. He's won your souls, of course. We can't touch the innocent. You could say that it's a sort of divine law. But the sinners are all fair game."

"Hold on, none of us are sinners, not in any kind of way you may mean. You must be insane," Helen said.

"Oh, that's where you're wrong. The higher power above agrees that murder is one of the worst sins on the market," Eve said.

"This man was a murderer, not us," Garrett said while pointing to the dead man slumped against the wall.

"Do I look dead? That's what I love the most about your kind. Humans are so easily deceived. You all follow a predictable pattern. Haven't you noticed that the eight of you are always here on Tuesday nights? Repetition is your greatest fault. We've been watching you for some time. We anticipated what each of you would do if you were in a dire situation with someone who you believed to be a killer. The man you beat to death was no murderer. He killed a deer a few days ago, just as he claimed. After seeing his damaged vehicle, we put the plan together and turned each of you into sinners," Eve said.

"Sinners of the worst kind," Adam agreed, then opened his mouth with an endless yawn. He drew in a long, steady breath. His chest expanded like an overfilled balloon. His arms rose and fell at his sides as if he were trying to take flight.

"Don't you see? They're demons, and they feed on us. They need hate and violence to survive," Brandy screamed.

Any other time, Garrett and Helen would have attributed Brandy's statement to an overreaction caused by her ongoing obsession with horror films, but not today they wouldn't, not today of all days.

Adam's mouth stretched wider than humanly possible. His eyes were impossibly wide as well. His stare held their unwavering sight and seemed to reach deep down to their very souls.

The group buckled down to their knees as their breath, and whatever mystical soul-like thing lay hidden inside the human body, pulled free from its anchors and raced into the vortex of a whirlwind Adam created with a strange, everlasting deep breath.

As Brandy felt the light of life dim, she thought, *Adam and Eve, how can you pretend such innocence? It was the both of you in the beginning. You're the original sinners.*

Fate Always Knocks Twice

One.
Two.
"Someone's at the front door, Ann," Hal Sanders yelled.

Ann Sanders wiped her hands on a dishtowel and said, "Who in the world would be knocking at this time of night?"

Although it was just after nine o'clock, they weren't used to and didn't desire unexpected guests. The majority of unexpected house calls were the obnoxious door-to-door salesmen who tried to sell a truckload of junk for an outrageous price and simply wouldn't take no for an answer.

"I don't know why these damn people can't read the sign. It's posted right there on the screen door. No soliciting. Doesn't anyone give a damn about privacy anymore?" Hal hollered and hoped the person at the front door had heard and was already slinking down the front porch and heading for the next house.

"Just calm down. You're going to get your blood pressure back up again. I'll see who it is."

Ann went to the kitchen door, pulled aside the curtain, and turned on the porch light. In the soft glow, she saw something that made her feel uneasy.

"Hal, can you come here a minute?"

"Christ Almighty, just tell them to go away. There's no reason for both of us to do it."

"I'm not sure I want to open the door to do that."

"Then yell it through the glass," Hal said irritably.

"Would you please just come here?"

Reluctantly, Hal grabbed the handle of the recliner and retracted the footrest. His large body came out of the chair with great effort, and he went to the kitchen while cursing the intrusion.

"What's the problem?" he asked as he entered the kitchen and stopped at the door beside Ann.

"It's a woman. I don't like the sight of her. I think it's a homeless woman."

Hal said, "You've got to be kidding me? Now they have the gall to come to someone's door and beg for food? I told you to send her away."

"You do it. That woman scares me some."

"For crying out loud," Hal said. He disengaged the deadbolt and opened the door.

The woman was small, appearing contorted by years of endless arthritic suffering. She was wearing garments that looked as if she had found them at the bottom of a trash bin. Her dirty gray hair framed her face, and her skin was like battered leather, cracked and darkly tanned by a hard life. Her nose was long and hooked. Her chin pointed and covered in fine white hair, but none of that bothered Hal much. What he found most disturbing was a yellow eye staring back at him. A milky cataract covered her other eye, but that yellow eye reminded him of a snake's eye.

"Whatever it is you want, you've got the wrong house," Hal said and began closing the door.

"Mr. and Mrs. Sanders?" the old woman said in a frail voice.

Hal paused and pulled the door open again.

"Yes, that's right. Who are you?"

"Who I am isn't important, Mr. Sanders, but what I want is," the woman said.

"Whoever sent you this way must have made a mistake. Now, if you'll please leave."

Before Hal could close the door, the woman said, "You're the one who sent for me, Mr. Sanders."

"I'm afraid I don't follow. I've never met you before. I'm pretty sure my wife hasn't met you either. Neither of us wants you here. You'll need to leave before I call the police," Hal said.

"No, we've never met. If you wish to call the police, then very well, but I suggest you don't do that just yet since I'm here to discuss the young boy you ran down four years ago. Of course, you remember him, don't you?" the old woman asked.

Hal felt the blood flush from his face. He felt his knees willing to give out. He also felt the world dramatically take a horrifying spin.

"My God," Ann said as her hand went to her mouth. "I knew it would all come back to haunt us. I knew we could never escape the consequences of what happened."

"Hush up now, Ann. You just keep it zipped, and I'll handle this. Look, as I said before, you've come to the wrong house. We don't know what in the hell you're talking about, and we'd like you to leave."

"I'm here to offer you a choice. I suggest you let me inside so that we may discuss what's going to take place in a moment."

Hal desperately wanted to close the door in the woman's face. He needed to shut out the woman's crude appearance and never know why someone suddenly came knocking after the incident four years ago. But despite all of his mental urging, Hal couldn't get his body to act.

The old woman stepped inside, removed Hal's hand from the knob, and closed the door.

"Well, should we find a more comfortable spot before we get down to the bare bones of the matter?" she said.

Hal and Ann followed the old woman from the kitchen to the living room. She found a seat on the couch and placed her battered handbag on the coffee table.

"How is it after all this time you found us?" Ann asked.

Hal slammed his fist down on the coffee table, which rattled Ann's decorative statues.

"Dammit! Are you trying to cinch the noose tighter around our throats? Why don't you run into the street and flag down the next cop that comes by and confess everything? What are you thinking?"

"Mr. Sanders, you'll need to calm yourself. I want you clearheaded for a little while because you'll need focus before making your choice," the old woman said.

"Can you just tell us who you are and what you want?" Ann nearly screamed.

For a moment, the old woman eyed them, removed a pack of cigarettes from her bag, and lit one.

"You look like one of those…" Hal began saying.

"Go ahead and say it," the woman replied.

"Gypsies. One of those freaks that ride into town with the carnival."

"I am exactly that, Mr. Sanders. Many people call our kind freaks, but we're not. We have special abilities that regular people don't understand. Now, please don't ask me why it took so long to find the people who ran down my grandson. I waited for many years for the vision to come to me in my dreams. I finally received the truth, and that's what brought me here."

"You can't prove anything. What are you trying to do, blackmail us or something?" Hal asked.

The Gypsy pointed a yellowed, crooked finger to the telephone on the living room wall. She pointed through the kitchen archway and to the door where she had arrived with her other hand.

"In fifteen minutes, you're going to have to make a choice. In fifteen minutes, two things will happen. The telephone will ring, and there will also be a knock on your front door. Only one of these you'll need to answer."

"What the hell does that mean?" Ann asked, as her nerves couldn't take much more.

"I know that you didn't intentionally kill my grandson four years ago when you were leaving the carnival grounds in Bixby. But you did leave the area without even bothering to see if he was still alive or getting help for the poor boy. My grandson didn't have a choice. Your son, Thomas, and your daughter, Rebecca, won't have a choice either. At least one of them won't have a choice. I'm going to take one of them because it seems only fair."

"How the hell do you know our children?" Hal furiously asked as he felt this strange woman probing his personal life.

"I know of them and where they are right now. When the telephone rings, and if you decide to answer, your daughter will die. If you decide to answer the door, your son will die." The old woman looked at her antique watch and said, "You have fifteen minutes to make your choice."

"Are you insane? If this is some sort of twisted means of revenge, then I'm not answering either," Hal said.

"Failure to answer one or answer both at the same time will result in two deaths. I recommend you spend your remaining time discussing your decision."

Hal stood from the chair. "Leave my house immediately, or so help me you won't like the actions I take. No one threatens my family, especially my children. They haven't done anything wrong to you."

"My grandson never wronged you, Mr. Sanders. Still, his life is gone all the same. I've given you fifteen minutes to make your decision because that is the amount of time it took the poor boy to die. You can't imagine the pain and suffering he felt before the end. Now pain and suffering have come full circle, and have knocked on your front door. Which child do you believe you can live without? I'm sure it isn't an easy decision, but one you'll have to make."

"Hal, let's talk this over, like she says," Ann said as she nervously rubbed her hands together.

Hal quickly turned and looked at his wife as if she had struck him without provocation.

"My God, have you lost all senses? Did you just say what I think you said? Are you really buying all this crap? How can you seriously justify making a decision that will kill one of our children? How could you even entertain such an evil thought, Ann?"

"I'm not justifying anything! You heard what she said. Rebecca or Thomas will die if we do nothing," Ann screamed.

"No one is going to die. I've had enough of this. I'm calling the police," Hal said and moved toward the phone.

Hal didn't hear a dial tone when he picked up the phone, but someone on the other end was breathing heavily.

A deep-throated voice on the other end said, "Sometimes minutes are fleeting. Sometimes a clock can be deceiving. Soon a precious heart will stop beating. There will come a ring-a-ding and a knock-knock you'll be receiving."

Hal pulled the phone from his ear and stared at the receiver in bewilderment.

"What is it?" Ann asked.

"They're messing with the phone line. We can't call out because they've done something to the line."

"Tick-tock, Mr. Sanders," the Gypsy said.

Hal hung up the phone and returned to the chair.

"Okay, I don't like this sick game you're playing. You're right. I accidentally ran over your grandson at the park grounds. I can't tell you how much I regret leaving and doing nothing for the boy. God, it was dark, and he just ran right in front of my truck. I didn't have time to do anything. Ann wanted to stop. She begged me to stop. I had been drinking most of the day, and I knew I'd go to jail for a long, long time if I stopped. Can you understand that?"

"I understand that my grandson is dead. I understand that it's your fault. I cannot change any of it, but I've taken action so that my grandson's soul is finally at peace. The clock does not stop. You have eight minutes."

The old woman retrieved another cigarette, lit it, and leaned back on the couch.

"Hal, please, I can't lose my sweet daughter. She's getting married soon."

"Sweet Lord, you already made up your mind? Are you really prepared to allow our son to die at the hands of these vulgar people? How can you make a snap decision like that?"

"Okay, okay, so let's discuss this thing," Ann said.

Hal pinched his eyes closed and shook his head. It's an impossible choice to make, and he knew that either answering the phone or the door would forever haunt him, just as the boy's death had all these years.

The old woman said, "I want you to go to the front window. Across the street, you will see a man. That man is patiently waiting to approach your door."

Hal was instantly on his feet and shuffling for the front window, and Ann was a few steps behind. They quickly moved aside the curtain and pulled up the blinds. In the darkness of the neighbor's yard, they saw the dark figure of a man. They saw the faint wink of a cigarette and something else that eerily glowed. Hal thought it was the man's eyes, maybe the horrible, unwavering glare of the Devil's eyes.

"Five minutes, Mr. Sanders."

"I'll kill you. I swear it that I'll kill you and that man outside if you don't stop this," Hal said.

"Oh, prepared to take more lives? Haven't we become quite the soul collector?" the Gypsy said.

"Don't you understand? Don't you see? I can't lose my son. I can't lose the child that will carry on the family legacy!" Hal screamed and collapsed in the chair. He covered his face with his hands and began crying.

"How dare you! How dare you judge me as you did. You made up your mind before I said anything about saving Rebecca. How could you even think about saving Thomas' life over Rebecca's life? He's taken after you, all right. He's become a drunk and spends half of his time in jail. The drinking and driving, the bar fights, the wandering through life with no job, no goal, that's what you call a legacy? I suppose with someone like you as a role model is how he became the way he did. Hell, the only time he even calls is when he needs money. If he's such a wonderful son, then when was the last time he called to wish you a Happy Father's Day or birthday? He never does, and you know it," Ann yelled.

"Oh, and how about your little princess? She's quite the saint, isn't she? Let's see, arrested for shoplifting half a dozen times, knocked up when she was fifteen, and then again at seventeen by two different men. She's been relying on welfare for years and finally hooks up with a man and promises marriage because he's got money. I do love her, but that girl has worn me down like she's a grinding stone."

"Don't you talk about my daughter like that!" Ann said and harshly slapped her husband.

Hal quickly stood and said, "I've never struck you in twenty-six years of marriage, but so help me, if you do that again, I won't hold back."

"Two minutes," the Gypsy said and smiled, showing a row of crooked brown and yellow teeth.

Ann retrieved a cast-iron bookend from the mantel, lifted it above her head, and stepped to the couch. She said, "You've brought this madness to my house! You're destroying my family, and I want you to leave this instant!"

"I will not leave until you make your choice. If you decide to kill me here and now, I promise that your entire family will suffer devastating deaths," the Gypsy said.

"I will not lose my son. I won't. When the phone rings, I'm going to answer. I know that I'll have to forever live with the choice I made, but I will manage," Hal said.

"No, Hal. I'm making the decision. When that person knocks on the front door, I'm going to answer. You know that it's the right choice," Ann pleaded.

Hal looked out the window and saw the dark figure walking across the street. The man moved with a casual stroll, as if he was delivering a pizza instead of death. The man disappeared around the corner of the house, heading for the kitchen door. Hal moved from the window and faced his wife.

"I'm sorry, Ann, I really am, but I've made a choice. Don't even think about going for the door. I'd hate to do it, but I'll knock you to the ground."

"I'll die before I let you take my daughter away," Ann said and moved for the kitchen door.

Hal quickly followed.

When the phone rang and a fist simultaneously pounded twice on the front door, they halted. Ann and Hal looked into each other's horror-struck eyes. The small part of them that believed the Gypsy's story to be nothing more than a method to drive them mad began falling apart, and reality quickly set in.

Ann dashed for the door. Hal instantly lunged for her, caught her around the legs, and they crashed into a heap on the floor. They immediately began clawing at each other. Ann's teeth came down on Hal's forearm, and blood gushed into her mouth. Hal screamed and threw a punch to the side of her head.

The phone rang, and a fist pounded again.

Ann drove her knee up and caught her husband in the groin. He grunted but fought through the pain and wrapped his large hand around her throat.

In a gasp, Ann said, "Stop it, just stop it. I won't let you take away my Rebecca."

Ann's thumbs went for Hal's eyes. In an attempt to avoid losing his sight, he rolled off his wife. She quickly turned over, and in a mad effort, she crawled for the door.

Hal gently rubbed his eyes and pulled his hands away to see if he was bleeding. In a state of grief and exhaustion, he couldn't get his legs to lift him. Hal rolled to the wall, looked up at the ringing phone, swatted at the dangling cord, and tried to knock the receiver free.

Ann scrambled through the kitchen for the door.

As Hal heard the squeak of the doorknob turning, intense pain shot across his chest. With one arm clutched tightly to his chest, he used his free arm and jarred the receiver loose from the cradle.

Hal heard Ann screaming. It wasn't a scream of terror, but one of pain.

Hal brought the receiver to his ear.

The hinges released a rusty bark as the door opened.

In the kitchen, Ann yelled, "Hal, something's wrong with my head. It hurts so badly. Call for an ambulance."

As another shock of pain seized his chest, he croaked into the phone. "My son. I've made a choice. I want to save my son."

There was no response. Only silence filled Hal's ear.

"Hal, it's the Devil here to come to take us away," Ann screamed from the door.

The Gypsy kneeled beside Hal and smiled.

"Mr. Sanders, did you honestly believe that I would punish one of your children for your crime? Oh, I set the curse into place. By answering the phone, Mr. Sanders, you've sacrificed your wife's life. By answering the door, she's sacrificed your life. I told you in the beginning that not answering one or answering both would result in two deaths. I knew the emotional struggle between you and your wife would be spectacular. I was certain your wife couldn't let your daughter go, just as I was certain you couldn't let your son go. It's interesting how both of you were so willing to offer one child to save the other. You and your wife are guilty of the death of my grandson. Neither of you offered yourselves as a sacrifice to save your children. What a shame. You should know that fate comes with many identities, but no one seems to think it will ever come knocking on their front door."

Down the Road

Even after all this time, one year, ten months, and three days, to be exact, I still wasn't used to the bodies in the streets. In fact, there were bodies every which way we looked. My son, Taylor, once told me he tried to think of them as fallen trees, and we should go around them whenever possible. It was difficult not to look. I couldn't think of them as fallen trees. Unlike an eight-year-old child, my mind couldn't erase the facts. They were bodies, and there were lots of them.

"We need to stop and rest awhile. Here, have some water," I said and handed Taylor the plastic bottle.

"I don't want it. It always makes me feel sick."

"I know, me, too. We need to drink, just like we need to eat, or we'll die. You know that. Now take it," I told him.

Taylor reluctantly accepted the bottle and took two long swallows. He grimaced at the taste, but held the water down. He handed the bottle back, and I took a drink of the dirty water. It wasn't dirty in the sense that we had filled the bottle from a muddy stream. The water was saturated with radiation. The water came from the gray snow, and the gray snow came from the scorched sky. The world had forgotten about clean water, clean food, and even clean air. Everything we put in our bodies was slowly killing us.

Death had become a far more powerful and relentless stalker these days.

"Yuck," Taylor said, and wiped his mouth.

I had been pulling Taylor in a red wagon for endless miles. He took ill some time ago, and I couldn't tell if it was a flu virus or if the radiation caused it. I was a plumber once. I didn't think plumbers knew the signs of radiation sickness. At least I didn't. He seemed better today. He seemed livelier than the last few weeks. It all took some adjustment, but just like everything else, humans adapted.

The bombs had fallen. The world had burned. Yet here we were adapting to the aftermath. Even when the scavengers came, I felt myself adapting to them. Some of them we used for food, the smaller ones anyway. The bigger ones we stayed clear of and hid from when possible. The larger scavengers were partly a cause of the bodies after the bombs and the dirty air.

I carried a gun. I'd used all the bullets except for two. Whenever a confrontation arose between other humans or the scavengers, I used the machete for defense. I had to keep the two remaining bullets. There was one for Taylor and one for me. It was the only way I'd let us go out of this dreadful picture together.

I grabbed the handle of the wagon, and we moved down the road. Traveling by the dim sunlight that broke through the endless days of grim cloud cover was the only way to go. It was safer during the day. Nightfall brought out the worst of evils. Sometimes we could see them, but most of the time, we heard them. They scurried down the road or through the trees, always in close quarters to our hiding spots. I couldn't say for sure, but I believed their sense of smell was weak, or maybe they couldn't smell at all. I didn't know. If their smell and sight were more acute, my son and I wouldn't have survived this long. It was a miracle we kept pushing on.

I have something important to say here. Maybe this is my testament to ordinary life and its unfortunate conclusion. These accounts might be the only remaining biography of humanity. The fires took the rest. In any case, I feel the need to boast a little. I always told my friends, the limited few as it was, that John Graver never gives up or gives in. They always laughed at that statement. I suppose I should laugh now since those poor bastards are long dead, and I'm still going. I certainly don't feel like laughing, not for a long time now. I go on because of Taylor. What's a boy without a father to protect him, to guide him along these rough roads of Hell's eternal abyss? If I had done myself in, Taylor would have soon followed.

It was once a sinister world that later became something much worse.

I couldn't say for sure if governments launched the bombs to kill off foreign enemies or if they turned the bombs loose to kill off the species that had now seized control of our planet. I know for sure that nations were conflicting for centuries, and things progressed a step further every so often. I also know that it was only a short while later when I saw the first creature that I now call scavengers. It was over two months later, to be exact. I had seen the small ones tearing apart a man that had long since been dead from one thing or another. That's why I call them scavengers. I've only seen the small ones eat dead people. The smaller scavengers have never attacked us, but that doesn't mean they won't.

I believe, or what I reluctantly tell myself is, that humanity wanted to kill itself off. We've always known war, and war comes in good company with hate and greed. It's an undeniable fact. I expected humankind would walk down this dark road sooner rather than later. I suspected one nation or another turned their bombs loose, and it only made sense to send off ours in retaliation. Rockets passed each other in the sky and brought forth a future no one ever wanted to imagine.

I think the creatures came after the bombs fell. Maybe they were passing by our planet on an intergalactic journey and saw that we had so much to offer because humans decided they didn't want to live anymore. We left so many good things behind just ripe for the picking. I don't know for sure, and I couldn't care less. They are here now, and so are we. We're two species trying to survive, even if it means killing the other.

I've killed some of the smaller ones. I've set traps and snared them with a thin wire, then used the machete to dispatch them and cooked them over a fire. The taste of the meat leaves much to be desired. If I cooked the meat enough, I could almost convince myself that we were dining on blackened chicken. I often wonder if the larger scavengers have a different texture, a distinct flavor. I don't suppose I'll ever know unless I come across one recently dead. I will not try killing one myself. If you saw them, you'd understand. The only way I'll engage one is in a kill-or-be-killed situation, and so far, we've been able to avoid such confrontations.

"Pa, look over there!" Taylor said so loud in the dull silence of the forest road that I jumped.

My hand automatically went to the revolver at my hip. I turned to my son and saw that he was pointing to the left. I followed his finger, and a hundred yards away in the blanket of gray snow stood a white-tailed doe. Her black eyes cautiously watched us. Her ears twitched and rotated to catch all sounds. After a moment of deciding that we were no threat, she craned her head and snatched a low branch, pulling leaves from the tree. The leaves were more dead than alive and probably had little nutritional value. The doe was skinny, starving to death like everything else.

I thought of how much some deer meat could benefit us right now. I also thought that if I dared to take a shot with a handgun at this range and hit and kill the target, it would be a miracle in itself. God knows I wanted to try, but I knew that one less bullet would cost me too much in the end.

"I wish her well," I said and pressed on.

"Where are we going today?" Taylor asked.

"To the same place we go every day, down the road to search for food and to find shelter for the night," I said.

"Do you think there's a heaven?" he asked.

I looked over my shoulder and studied him. It had seemed like one of those questions that popped into a child's mind, and it rolled off their tongue before the sentence was even a complete thought. The question worried me a little. I wondered if Taylor's illness was getting worse. Maybe he knew his time was coming soon, and this was how he clued me in on the fact.

I looked up at the steel-colored clouds and said, "I suppose so. I guess I hope so. I don't think you'll need to worry about something like that for some time, son."

"I hope there's a heaven."

"Are you feeling all right?" I asked.

"I'm tired, is all."

"Yeah, the road just seems to go on and on. Do you want to get out of the wagon and walk a while? You're tired because you're cold. You might need to get the blood flowing."

"I've got these blankets keeping me warm. I'll be all right," Taylor said and watched the bare forest surrounding us.

"I love you, son. Never forget that. No matter what happens today or tomorrow or years from now, I'll always love you."

Taylor was silent. I looked over my shoulder and saw that his eyes were watery, but his face was beaming. I couldn't remember the last time I'd seen him smile. It made me smile, and we moved on down the road.

The fire hadn't completely gone out, but I had drifted off and let the flames die down to red embers. I woke and was throwing some small logs on the fire when I heard it. It was a scurry in the dead, snow-covered leaves in the woods behind us. I tightly gripped the log I was about to set in the fire and seized the machete with the other hand. Several joints popped loudly as I quickly stood, turned, and faced the darkness. Whatever it was, I heard it again.

I looked at Taylor. He was asleep in the wagon with blankets piled around him. All I could see was his face sticking out. I quietly called to him several times before his eyes opened. He became alarmed when he saw my defensive stance and my attention fixed on the woods.

"What is it? What's out there?" he asked in a whisper.

"I don't know. Maybe it's nothing, or maybe it's something."

As I took a step forward with intentions to search the nearby woods, Taylor said, "Pa, don't leave me."

"I won't go far. Keep quiet."

When I took a dozen steps, something heavy leaped from the tree beside the fire, hit my backside, and sent me propelling to the ground. I avoided landing directly in the fire pit and catapulted over the flames, and rolled in a heap on the other side. I quickly shifted onto my knees and prepared for another attack.

Watching me closely on the other side of the fire was a small scavenger. It was four-legged and stone gray, with a long lashing tail, and eyes like oil drops. The lizard-like thing flicked out its tongue, tasting the air. Its attention shifted from Taylor to me and back again. I thought it was deciding which of us were the easiest prey.

"Fight me, you son of a bitch!" I shouted and launched the log at the thing. My aim was high, and the log sailed over its head and landed in a drift of gray snow.

Taylor screamed as the thing charged him. The thing hissed as it darted with the smooth agility of a predator. Its jaws snapped in anticipation of a feast. Taylor protectively threw up his hands as the thing leaped.

I brought the machete down on the back of its neck. The blade cut to the bone on the first strike. I felt vicious and vividly alive with the thrill of the kill. I swung the machete again at the creature, losing all my rational senses, and I didn't stop until I'd detached its head from the body.

Taylor watched me with horror.

I halted my last swing, stood straight, and looked back at him in a silent apology.

"You got it, Pa."

"I couldn't help it. When I saw it coming after you, the rage was just too much."

"It's all right."

I expelled an exhausted breath.

I said, "I can't believe one of the little ones attacked. They're getting desperate because the food supply is so low. They always seem to go after the dead."

"Do you think there are any more of them out there?" he asked.

"I hope not. I've never seen scavengers hunt in packs. I don't think I can sleep anymore tonight after that. Well, on the positive side of things, we have some fresh meat."

Taylor grimaced. "I don't like the taste of the meat."

"I still have a little seasoning left. It'll have to do," I said.

Although the bombs took away most of the things humankind had built and collected, a few rare items remained a particular luxury if we desired to accept them. There were still some vehicles abandoned here and there. Gasoline was hard to find, but attainable if I needed to collect some. I had thought about it long before. I had thought how much nicer it would be to find a decent truck, top off the tank and follow the road that way.

There were several problems with this idea. First, the roads were now a mass of broken concrete. There was also a massive amount of debris scattered across the highways. Maneuvering around these endless obstacles in a large vehicle was more of a headache than I cared to battle. Second, vehicles had a distinctive sound heard from miles around now that the world had gone silent. Rebels moved along these uncertain roads. These were men and women who were trying to survive just like us. However, confronting these rebels was a situation I cared not to consider. They'd strip everything from us and have no problem with leaving two more corpses in their path.

Using our feet was the only way to travel our new world safely. When someone or something came down the road, Taylor and I usually had enough time to hurry into the dead woods, stay low, and wait until the rebels moved on.

Taylor hated this method of travel. He said it took too long to get to where we're going. I didn't have the heart to tell him that there was no destination ahead. I suppose finding tomorrow was the only thing I was searching for, and tomorrow was seemingly hard enough to find.

"Just put it down! I ain't here to hurt you!" the man yelled.

"Stay back, or I swear I'll shoot," I said.

The man was holding up his hands as a gesture of peace. His body was half turned and ready to sprint for the dead woods the second a shot rang out.

I was in a position ready for battle as I held the gun pointed at him, and the machete prepared to swing if he came too close.

"I'm not looking for trouble. I didn't try surprising you or anything. I could have if I wanted to. You saw me coming a long way off, didn't you?"

"I did," I confirmed.

"All right then, would you mind lowering the gun? I've got some things. Maybe we could do some trading."

It had been some time since I had traded with anyone. We had little in the way of valuables, but I was curious about what the man offered.

I lowered the revolver, but I didn't release the hammer. I wanted to keep it at my side and ready. I trusted no one on these dangerous and unpredictable roads. Strangers in passing could be just as deadly as the scavengers or the air we were breathing. Everything was looking to kill us with each passing day.

"What things do you have for trade?" I asked as the man stepped closer.

"Ah, how about this?" he said as his hand slowly withdrew from the large pocket of his filthy overcoat.

He was holding a book. I couldn't remember when I had last seen a book in such good condition. We were once a world filled with books, with stories expanding the imagination, building knowledge and hope inside each of us traveling the pages. There were once billions or even trillions of books. Not long ago, people filled libraries, houses, and offices with these wonderful books. Now they were all blackened by fire and blown away in the gentlest breeze. I had once been an avid reader. My house, before fire consumed it, contained hundreds of books that delighted our family. I had read many of those stories to Taylor. I had wanted to pass down my love of literature to him as he grew older and became a man. Now I owned none.

I returned the machete to the sheath and held out my hand. The man carefully placed the book in my hand as if it were a fragile egg. I turned it over as I inspected it. It was a hardback edition of a classic Ray Bradbury novel, *Fahrenheit 451*. A battered, dirty book with hinges that were near breaking, and yet it was one of the most beautiful things I'd seen in a long time.

"This is a definition of irony if ever there was one," I said as I admiringly turned it over.

When I looked up, the man was staring at Taylor. The look on his face bothered me.

"Hey, what's on your mind?" I asked as my hand tightened on the revolver.

"I wasn't looking at anything, man. So, do you like the offer?"

"Yeah, I like it," I told him.

"What kind of trade do you want to make? Do you have any canned food or bottled water?"

The man looked at us, desperate, tired, and slowly dying.

"If either of those still exists, we certainly don't have them. If I did, I wouldn't give up something that precious for a book. I could trade you this instead," I said.

I reached into the bag that Taylor kept in the wagon. I held out a pair of insulated gloves. The gloves had seen better days, but in the situational world we lived in, no one could afford to complain. It was one item I was reluctant to part with, but I really wanted the book. I could read it to Taylor. I thought the story might help us take our minds off our situation as we bunked down each night.

The man started crying as he fumbled the gloves in his frostbitten hands.

"Yeah, I think this will do nicely. My last pair gave out weeks ago. It's been hard surviving without something so simple," the man said and tried them on.

"I know what you mean. Every little thing matters these days. If I didn't have my son with me now, I don't think I could go on any longer. I wouldn't see the point of going on."

The man looked at Taylor again with disgust. Maybe the idea of having someone with him was a dreadful thought.

"I suspect you should be on your way," I told him.

"I suppose so. Best of luck to you," the man said. He moved down the road, followed the bend, and then disappeared from sight.

"That man scared me," Taylor said.

"Yeah, but I think we probably scared him more."

"Was the trade worth it?"

I rubbed my palm over the book's cover and said, "Yeah, I believe so."

I grabbed the handle of the wagon, and we began down the road again.

A short while later, Taylor said, "What did you mean when you said the book was iron?"

"I said the book was a definition of irony. I meant that the story in the book relates to its survival in our world today. It's a futuristic tale about how humanity can no longer own most kinds of books. Almost all books deemed illegal. When authorities found illegal books, they immediately burned them. Governments also had firefighters going out and searching homes, burning any found books, and arresting the owner."

"Why did they do that?"

"Well, governments believed books were the reason for the downfall of society. The minorities got ideas about something better than their current situation. The authorities thought books opened everyone's minds too much and let them think and act more freely."

"That sounds silly."

"There's one firefighter who learned that literature is a wonderful thing. He rebelled by finding a love for books, turned against his employers, and went on the run."

"Will you read it to me?"

"Of course, I'd love for you to hear it."

I thought of how time had changed everything. Before the end of civilization, I never would have thought of reading this story to a child. By all standards, it was a classic novel, especially in those new times, but people died in the book and people burned. Now Taylor was familiar with such violence. He had seen many people die. He had seen people burn to death. He'd become a boy nearly immune to such traumatic sights. Tragedy happens. We observe, and then we move on. It had become a world where physical and mental survival was the only option.

The following night, I read nearly half of the book before Taylor drifted off. I marked the page, closed the book, and observed him in the firelight. He was so frail, like a glass statue. I knew he was acting braver than he believed he was. He was trying to keep a strong heart for my benefit, knowing I couldn't go on without him. He knew I built my world around him. Without my son, my world would become a house of cards instead of a house of stone.

Lost in thought, I stared into the impenetrable darkness of the night when Taylor's voice startled me.

"It's time for you to let go, Pa," he said.

"You scared me. I thought you were fast asleep."

"I don't sleep anymore. There's no need."

"If you say so. What do you mean by letting go?" I asked.

"You know what I mean."

"No, I don't. Your old man isn't too bright these days. Tell me."

"It's time to let me go. You've held on long enough. It isn't healthy for you to believe in a lie."

I shook my head and leaned closer in the firelight so that I could get a better look at him. I thought he was talking in his sleep. Perhaps verbally including me in his dream, but his eyes were wide open and watching me.

Taylor removed the wrappings of blankets and stepped from the red wagon. He slowly walked around the fire and stopped beside me.

He reached out and said, "Here, take my hand. I want to show you something."

I did as he asked and stood on tired legs. Taylor began leading me up the forest hill. I halted and shook my head.

I said, "No, it's too dangerous right now."

"It's all right. The sun is coming up," he said and began walking.

I wanted to protest again, but I figured this was important to him. I wanted to know what he needed to show me. The crown of the sun broke the horizon as we reached the crest of the hill. Amazingly, I could see the brilliant glow. The clouds had dissipated somewhat in the eastern sky. The sunlight was refreshing as I felt the briefest of warmth touch my skin.

"My God, I've missed this sight," I said.

We watched in silence for a few moments until the gray clouds returned and obscured the majestic view. When the sun disappeared, I felt my sadness return.

"It's not gone forever. Someday, the dark clouds will vanish, and things will return to the way they used to be," Taylor said.

"I hope you're right."

"I am. You'll see."

"How did you get to be so smart?"

"I learned everything from my father," he said and retook my hand.

"Your father sounds like a brilliant man."

"He's the best. Now it's time for me to teach him something. I think it's time for me to show him a new light," Taylor said.

"What are you talking about?"

Taylor gently placed his hand on the revolver in my holster.

"Don't avoid it any longer. When you see it, you'll know. There will be no more need to pretend. It's a new day, Pa. It's time for you to accept the truth."

I looked at my revolver, gripped the butt, and pulled it from the holster. I looked at Taylor, and he nodded. I pushed the latch and flipped open the cylinder. Two bullets were inside.

"Look closer," he said.

"No, I can't."

"You can."

"I don't want to see it."

"You have to accept the truth. Otherwise, you're going to drive yourself crazy. Remember that I love you. I'll always be a part of your life no matter what happens from this day on," he said.

I opened my eyes and looked. I saw everything the way it actually was. I saw the way Taylor always took a drink of water and returned the bottle to me with the same amount. I saw the way the man on the road grimaced with distaste when he looked at my son sitting in his wagon. I saw the way the scavenger attacked us a few nights ago and went directly for Taylor. I saw the depressed primer of one bullet.

When I looked to my right, Taylor had vanished.

I turned around and around as my eyes rapidly switched across the land. The forest was eerily still in the morning hour.

"No, please don't leave me, son. It isn't fair. I can't go on alone."

When I got up off the ground and forced myself to travel back to camp, I removed Taylor's body from the wagon and buried him.

I spent the entire day digging a hole deep enough to keep Taylor's body out of reach of the scavengers. I gathered large stones from the forest and stacked them neatly over his grave. I made a cross out of two thick branches and used a knife to carve *Taylor Graver* into the bark. It was a tribute to a child I couldn't seem to release.

A part of me always knew that Taylor's sickness months ago would eventually overcome him. The other part knew that using the revolver was the most humane, most loving thing a father could do. It wasn't a crude act, not by any means. It was mercy delivered by the hand of his last living family member.

I thought of how bad my delirium must have been during the last month. I had convinced myself that my son was alive, not only that, but also speaking to me, and I was responding without question. A guilty conscience could be a man's greatest turmoil.

I spent the night next to the grave. I talked to him. I finished reading the book to him. I enjoyed it, and I think he would have as well. I kept telling him how different things would be from now on. Although I didn't want to leave his side, I kept my word and left by the morning light.

I have an endless road ahead of me. One mile will stretch into another, just as one day will surely follow another. Life goes on, and survival is the only goal in these uncertain times. A part of Taylor's spirit promised the future would get better. He said that things would one day be just as they once were. I like to believe that. No matter how long it takes, I'll walk until that day comes. There's a curve in the road ahead. I believe a curve in the road holds promise. No one can ever tell what lies beyond it.

The sun broke through the gray clouds again this morning. It was brighter than the day before. It even stayed a while longer.

Hope appears to be a long way from here. It's on another horizon that seems so very hard to reach. I thought that just maybe that was all right. I've got the time, and I've got the road to follow.

The Battle at Dayton Hill

"You're doing it wrong," Don Treager said while thrusting a porky finger at the work in progress.

"I haven't finished. It's the way I always do it. If you don't like it, then do yourself a favor and get us some fresh coffee. I promise it'll be nice and pretty by the time you get back, Don," Clive Strom said while glaring at the pork-bellied man beside him.

"Just do it as I've said. I will not argue with you again. Every day you try to get me worked up over this stupid crap. I'm not doing this again. My father's company is getting top dollar from the city for this Dayton Hill Park project, and I'm not letting you ruin everything because of this piss poor attitude you always have. If you don't like what you do for a living, then move on. I can honestly say that no one will miss you if you leave," Don said.

Donald Treager had finally found his place in the blue-collar society. After fifteen years of being an ungrateful disappointment to his father, Don had gathered enough ambition and invested two years of his life at a community college. There had never been a degree within his reach, certainly not one in civil engineering, and Don had left school with a mild clue on how the world of design and construction worked. Apparently, his father, owner of the largest building contractor in Kansas City, was likely amused with his son's effort. Don had landed a supervisor position on one of the lowest rungs of the company ladder. He was proud of this small feat in life and felt the need to flash his minor accomplishment whenever possible.

Clive glanced at Joseph White, who was busy keeping his eyes on his concrete float and working the area level. Sensing Clive's eyes on him, Joseph shook his head slowly, trying to get the hotheaded young man to cool down and let the argument slide away. Joseph always stayed clear from getting between the two. They fought daily like bloodthirsty pit bulls, tugging and ripping at each other's throats. For three weeks, Joseph had to tolerate the verbal abuse. Ever since Don had joined the team, tempers could get heated first thing in the morning, which made for an incredibly long day.

"Don, I bet you could vanish right off the face of the planet, and not one person would even notice. If it weren't for your father, I'd have no doubt that you'd be pushing bags of burgers out the drive-thru window and wishing people a nice day. That would probably even be pushing the full extent of your given abilities. If you point a finger, I'm not jumping to satisfy you, and your fat ass is going to have to deal with that," Clive spat and drew his focus back to work.

Don stepped behind Clive and delivered two hard, swift kicks to the seat of his pants.

Clive whirled around in surprise, which quickly turned into an uncaged rage.

"Hey, goddamnit! I'll have your ass fired for that!"

"Jump, little froggy. Mr. Treager says to jump!" Don brutally delivered another kick that caught Clive more on the hip than it did on his rump. "Jump. Hoppy-hop little froggy."

"Knock it off. Knock it off, or I swear to Christ I'm gonna have you fired. I'm gonna tell your dad about this! You can sure as hell bet I am!" Clive bellowed.

To Joseph White, the scene seemed fitting in such a place. This public city park would be complete in under a week, and the grounds full of children at play. There would no doubt be scuffles from time to time. Clive looked as if he was getting his ass kicked, literally, by the playground bully.

Violence never intrigued Joseph. He never saw the point in it. No one ever gained anything by beating the crap out of each other. Joseph never bothered wasting precious time watching war movies or even spaghetti westerns where the story's hero almost always won. The bad guy ended up with nothing more than a few extra holes to breathe through.

"I think that will about do it, for now, boys," Joseph said as he laid down his concrete float and approached the two.

Joseph's hulking six foot six inches and a defined two hundred and thirty pounds of muscle had little trouble grabbing Don by the shoulders and pulling him back. Don let out a fury of protests to be released before both of them were standing in the unemployment line.

"I said that's enough. We all know you're the big man on campus, Don. There's no reason to treat everyone as if we're trying to get into your special fraternity," Joseph said.

"He started it. I finished it. That's the way things go around here. You two best remember that fact," Don spat.

Clive immediately dropped all sensibility, sprang to his feet, and thundered forward. His hands were outstretched as he lunged for Don's throat.

"Yeahhhh," Clive yelled to punctuate his attack.

Joseph reached out and stopped Clive with a single hand.

"I said that's enough," Joseph said in a more assertive voice.

"You saw what he did. You saw how he assaulted me. You're my witness. When I file a complaint with his father, I'm putting you down as a witness."

"Sure, I saw it all, but I don't think there will be a need for anyone to lose their job over this. Don will give you a heartfelt apology. You'll both shake hands, and that will be that. We'll all go back to work and be friends again. Does that sound good to you?"

Brushing off his blue jeans, Clive said, "And he just gets away with assaulting someone? Is that how it is?"

"How about if Don buys you a beer after work? I think it will help even things out," Joseph said as he retrieved his concrete float.

With the adrenaline still coursing through his veins, Don had just enough time to see what was coming. He had time to anticipate Clive's next move. Joseph's attention was back on the job, and he never saw his death coming.

With surprising speed, Don dropped his body in a sort of crouch and avoided a direct blast of the flat head shovel.

The shovel narrowly missed Don's head, but perfectly found Joseph's lower skull, and the shovel rang like a church bell. Joseph's body pitched forward, collapsing into the basketball court, and stuck in the wet concrete like a rock in the mud.

"Oh, my God. Look what you did. That could have been me. You tried to kill me, you son of a bitch!" Don bellowed as he stood.

"No, that was an accident. I didn't mean to do that."

"Mean it or not, you damn near crushed in his entire head."

Clive dropped the shovel, kneeled beside Joseph, and dug his hand in the wet concrete until he found Joseph's throat. His fingers searched for a pulse as his mind prayed that there was one.

"He's dead, Don. I can't find a pulse. What are we going to do?"

"What are we going to do? Hey, you're the one that just murdered someone. I'm going to get on the truck radio and call the office. You're going to jail. That's what we're going to do."

As Don began moving his enormous body toward the cement mixer's cab, Clive said, "I'll say you did it. I'll tell everyone that you were the one that got angry and killed Joseph. Everyone knows what kind of temper you have. They'll believe me. If they don't, then it's your word against mine. You started this whole thing by kicking me around. If you hadn't done that, this would have never happened," Clive said.

"You're going to try blaming this all on me? I'd like to see that stick."

Clive came at him with the shovel. His arms were rearing back for a death blow.

"I could finish you off now. I could do it. Or I could wipe clean the handle of the shovel, and no one could prove which one of us did it. I point my finger at you, and you point your finger at me. In the end, we both go to jail. You might have a rich father and all, but even murderers with money pay the price. A jury doesn't care if you have money. Joseph has a wife and a baby girl. A jury will see sympathy on his behalf. Both of us might just get a place on death row."

"There's no way that could happen," Don said, but there was serious doubt in his voice.

He wondered what would happen if one person blamed the other, and lawyers couldn't prove which one committed the murder. Sure, he had heard many times over the years of people claiming their innocence and being sent off to prison for life anyhow. It was possible that in an imperfect world like this one, some of those people were probably telling the truth. Maybe some of them had spent time on death row and were later executed before the proof of their innocence saw the light of day. It seemed possible, after all.

Reluctantly, Don said, "What can we do about this?"

Clive lowered the shovel as he understood Don had given in. They could work together by solving the dilemma or take a death row needle and die together.

"Okay. First, we have to get rid of Joseph's body. We have little time. I figure the next cement truck should roll up this way in about fifteen minutes. If you want to stay out of jail, then do what I say," Clive said.

The police reports and questions concerning Joseph White's disappearance and the frantic pleas from his wife to the public for assisting with information leading to his whereabouts resulted in a stalled investigation.

Clive smiled at his cleverness. He had done it. He had unintentionally murdered a man, unfortunately, the wrong man, and walked away from the experience, free from the chances of prison life.

Clive believed that if anyone deserved a concrete burial, Don Treager was that person and not Joseph White. Circumstances, or maybe fate, had played its nasty hand at the heat of the moment and done something Clive hadn't anticipated. Joseph White was now a month into an eternity sentence of death.

Clive casually watched the four boys playing two-on-two basketball. The park turned out far better than he expected. Clive enjoyed coming here on his days off. He enjoyed watching others play among something he helped create. He had worked hard, left behind sweat and someone else's blood in his backbreaking efforts to make this place what it was today.

Clive thought, *It's a good thing Don has kept his fat mouth shut during all this. Surprisingly, something as gruesome as murder in this place has yet to be solved. I seriously doubt the police will start turning over every rock in order to —* Clive's thoughts came to a screeching halt when his eyes fell on the area where Joseph's body lay encased in concrete. He wiped the sweat from his eyes and focused on the finger resting on the surface of the basketball court.

"No, that's impossible," he whispered.

"I've got some moves here, fellas. Check this out," a boy said as he dribbled the ball quickly between his legs to show off his skill.

Clive couldn't blink as the kid's left sneaker skidded across the knuckle of Joseph's index finger, which left a small black scuff.

"I've got moves that aren't even in the book," he said.

The basketball came down on the finger with an echoing wonk-wonk-wonk. The skin of Joseph's finger was decayed, blue and wrinkled after four weeks since death had come.

Clive's eyes switched to the boy dribbling. The kid watched the ball pass between his legs, looking right down at the finger, yet the kid showed no signs of even seeing it.

Clive thought, *How could no one notice a finger partially sticking out of the basketball court for weeks? How could this have happened? It must have been a pocket of air trapped under Joseph's hand. Sure, yeah, that makes sense. When the concrete was setting, the trapped air pushed his hand up just enough that a single finger broke the surface. Sweet Jesus. What the hell am I going to do? I can't move the body, for crying out loud. Shit, shit, shit! They're going to see it. How can they miss it? It's right there under the kid's goddamn foot. Come on, guys, finish the game and go home.*

Clive paced the court for nearly half an hour before the kids quit for the evening, gathered their gear, and headed down the hill. When the kids left for the evening, and Clive was sure no one else was hanging around the park, he ran across the court and kneeled beside the finger.

With hesitation, Clive held out his forefinger and slowly touched it. The skin was cold and spongy. For a moment, Clive actually thought the fucking thing would twitch.

"Just sit tight. I'll be back in a little while. I'm going to take care of you," Clive said. He then stood and ran back to his car.

Gray clouds hung heavy in the sky when Clive kneeled and placed the chisel, hammer, and mortar patch tube beside him.

"All right, I'm back, you little bugger."

Clive leaned close to the surface of the court and searched. In the growing dark, he had a hell of a time finding Joseph's finger. He was on his hands and knees for nearly ten minutes before discovering the pale finger lying flush with the concrete.

Clive retrieved his tools, placed the chisel's blade against the second knuckle of Joseph's index finger, and raised the hammer over his head. As the hammer was about to begin its descent, a voice broke through the night.

"I hope, for your sake, you're not tearing up my brand new, beautiful basketball court. That would be a shame and would entitle you to serious consequences of possible bodily injury."

Clive lowered the hammer and studied the three figures in the night.

"Who's that?" he asked as he felt his body involuntarily turn and prepare to run.

"I'm the man who pays your bills, my friend. I suggest you place the hammer in a safe position before my boys figure that you're not messing around."

Clive knew the voice all too well. It was a thick New York accent that didn't quite fit right in the Midwest. It was Donald Treager Sr. and a couple of his bone-breaking personal assistants that never left his side.

"Sir?"

"You know, I designed and constructed this city park for the mayor at a substantial discount as a personal favor. One hand always washes the other, if you know what I mean?"

"Ah, yes, sir. Of course, I do."

"Then tell me exactly why it is you're out here in near darkness with a chisel and a hammer and prepared to break up this wonderful thing I've created?"

"I don't think it's exactly what you think it is."

"Enlighten me, Mr. Strom. I'm a reasonable man. I'm usually good-natured and understanding. Tell me exactly what it is you're up to?"

The three hulking figures stood at the edge of the court and watched Clive with interest.

"Yeah, boss, sure looks like he has intentions of doing some destruction," the man on Mr. Treager's left said dumbly.

"I…" Clive started, but then clamped his mouth shut.

"That's it? That's all you can think to tell me? Okay, so I'm going to take a wild guess and say that you've got it in your mind to somehow break up that concrete with that little chisel and hammer, remove all the dirt, and then move Joseph White's body, right?"

Clive felt his face flush.

"If that's the case, then you're a bigger fool than I thought."

"How would you know something like that?" Clive asked.

"Kid, my son can't blow his nose without telling me first and receiving my permission to do so. He told me the minute he got back to the office. He knew he was up shit creek and needed my advice. So I gave it to him. I told him that if the body is that well hidden, he was clear until doomsday. However, I warned him that he should keep a strong eye on you. I told him that if anything was going to blow this thing up, it was a man with a guilty conscience. Now it appears to me that your guilt finally found the surface, and you're about to do something incredibly ignorant," Mr. Treager said and crossed his arms over his thick chest.

"No, no, sir, I wasn't. I was here earlier in the day when some kids were playing. I saw something I couldn't believe. One of Joseph's fingers was partially sticking out of the concrete. I couldn't believe it at first. I thought I was hallucinating. But as soon as the kids left, I came in closer and saw this," Clive said and pointed to where the chisel's blade rested.

A flashlight came on, and the beam moved to where Clive pointed.

"I'm afraid I don't understand what it is you're trying to tell me," Mr. Treager said.

Clive looked down. The chisel's edge pressed firmly to the concrete. Clive quickly shifted his eyes and scanned the area where he had earlier seen Joseph's finger.

"Somewhere here," Clive whispered.

"Still sounds like a guilty conscience to me. But that matter isn't so important right now. I've been following you for another reason."

"Following me, sir?"

"Right. For several days now, I've had you watched."

"Why would you do that?"

"Where's my son, Mr. Strom? Tell me where he is right now, and I promise things tonight will go a lot smoother for you."

"What are you talking about? I have no idea where Don is at. I haven't seen him since Friday afternoon."

"I'd like to believe that, but I'm not the trusting sort. No one has seen my son since after work on Friday. He doesn't call, and he doesn't come by the house. Things like this worry me. I told you before if I snap my fingers, my son knows to come running. But now he's nowhere to be found."

"I honestly don't know. I'm not Don's babysitter. Maybe he took a vacation. Maybe he met some girl and hooked up for the weekend," Clive said, but seriously doubted his last guess.

Mr. Treager stepped closer, directed the beam in Clive's face, and said, "I told you not to make things harder on yourself. The next lie you tell me, I'm going to have Vinnie here break all the bones in your right hand, for starters, that is."

"I swear I don't know. I just came here to cut off the damn finger, filled the hole with a patch, and go home."

"Here's what I think. You're a decent man, and you've made a bad mistake. You accidentally killed Joseph when you were really aiming to kill my son. But in all the chaos, you decide the best thing to do was hide the body where no one will ever find it and teamed up with my son to create some story everyone will believe. A little time passes, and those dreams that have probably been keeping you up at night have got the better of you. So you decided to kill off the only other person who knows what happened and where Joseph's body is stashed. Okay, I understand. You're looking out for number one. But what I don't like is that it was my son who knew this information and the trouble he could be in. I think you wanted to silence my son because you were afraid he'd squeal to the authorities. My son is no squealer because I ain't no squealer. The Treager's are strong to their word. Don agreed to help you out of that mess, and you pay him back by killing my only son, my successor?"

Clive held up his hands. "No, Mr. Treager, that isn't right. I would have never done anything like that. I swear it. Yeah, I made a big mistake, and Don was noble enough to help me out of it. I promise you that I haven't seen him in days."

"I'd like to believe that, but I think the truth will come out in a few moments. Anthony, hold his right hand down on the ground. Vinnie, use your boot. Make it hurt because I ain't got all night to stand around here and have you lie to me. Sorry, kid, I tried to be reasonable."

Anthony stepped behind Clive, laced one of his thick arms around Clive's throat, pressed him to the ground with ease, gripped his right forearm, and forced Clive's right hand flat on the basketball court. Vinnie moved beside the two, raised his massive leg, and let it hang briefly until Mr. Treager gave the nod.

The four of them held steady for a long minute. Clive kept waiting for that boulder of a foot to come crashing down and splinter every bone in his hand. Clive waited for the primary tool of his trade to be broken to fine bits. He was sure that if he lives through this evening, doctors would recommend amputation because the bones were now a fine powder. All possibilities of reconstruction of his hand would be nothing more than a highly laughable fairy tale.

"I swear..." he managed to cough out as Anthony had nearly crushed his throat in the embrace.

Clive thought, *You did do something to Don, didn't you? No. I blacked out for a while earlier because I had too much to drink. I was nearly drunk, just as I am every Sunday, and I slept it off. I couldn't have done something to that fat bastard. I would have certainly known the consequences of trying anything, even after drinking too much. I would have known that if I did something violent to Don, I would be in the exact position I'm in now.*

"In another second, I'm going to give Vinnie the go-ahead. It's your last chance, Mr. Strom. Tell me where my son is."

Anthony's grip loosened a little to allow Clive to speak.

"It was all Joseph. It had to be."

"I think I'm a little confused. Are you telling me the dead guy beneath you, the guy who's been dead for nearly a month, is responsible for my son's disappearance?"

"Yeah. Yeah, man. Joseph was into some weird shit. Voodoo and shit like that. He was always reading books about voodoo and the afterlife. He was kind of bat-shit crazy obsessed with the whole thing. Just maybe he's somehow getting his revenge in the afterlife. I know, it sounds crazy as hell. Trust me. I saw his goddamn finger partially sticking out of the concrete earlier. He's trying to drive me bug-shit crazy to get back at me for what I did."

Mr. Treager rocked back on his heels and delivered a long, bellowing laugh that echoed across the deserted Dayton Hill playgrounds.

"Don't that beat all? The man is so desperate to work himself out of this situation that he's blaming voodoo on my son's disappearance. I've heard a lot of bullshit excuses in my time, but that one definitely tops the chart."

Clive's mind was cranking. He was trying to put some sort of plan into overdrive to get himself out of —

Something rubbed against Clive's right knee. No, that wasn't right. Something scratched his right knee.

As difficult as it was with the gorilla on his back and having his neck in a vise hold, Clive was able to shift his sight just enough to see something he didn't like.

Although the sun rays barely touched the horizon, Clive saw something moving beside his knee. He painfully craned his neck to fix both eyes on the thing.

Joseph's finger, which had gone missing earlier as he tried to show Mr. Treager, was now back. Not only that, but the goddamned thing was alive. The finger bent and extended at the middle knuckle. The yellowed and chipped fingernail scratched desperately on the denim of Clive's pants.

Scratch, scratch, scratch.

Clive's eyes went wide. His mouth opened in a silent scream. His whole body tensed and then violently went into action. With enough force, Clive propelled backward hard enough to off-center the gorilla. They both landed hard on the concrete, but Clive had broken free from Anthony's grip and was quickly on his feet.

His eyes searched the area where his tools were. He wanted to see it. With his head unrestrained, he tried to look directly at it and know, and believe, that it was actually a moving finger that shouldn't be doing anything except decaying in the ground.

With the slickness of a gunslinger, Mr. Treager removed a gun from his inside jacket pocket and pointed it between Clive's eyes.

"Don't even think about running, kid," Mr. Treager said.

Clive saw it. Joseph's grotesque finger was thrusting from the basketball court like a thick worm breaking the surface. It moved in a strange, almost seductive dance. It was nearly hypnotizing.

"You heard him. Don't even think about running," the angry gorilla said as he got back on his feet.

But Clive did run. He was on the move before it was even a thought in his mind. Clive's whole body had turned, faced a darkened area of the park, and he was on the move. He didn't care if a bullet tore half of his head away. He didn't care if a bullet punched through his back like a freight train and splattered the green grass in red. All he cared about was getting the hell away from the damn finger that seemed to taunt, to beckon him to come down into the darkness with it.

"That's impossible!" Clive screamed as the blackness of the park surrounded him.

"Don't just stand there looking stupid. He's getting away," Mr. Treager bellowed.

Both gorillas were on the move.

As Clive headed into the thick night, he struck a tree head-on and fell backward. As dizziness washed over him, he understood that it wasn't a tree at all, but the towering figure of Joseph White and Joseph was reaching for him.

"No! Christ, no! You're dead, man!"

Clive frantically crawled until he could get his feet under him and then bound away like a chased rabbit. He tried to cut a path through a row of hedges, but the branches transformed before his eyes and became groping, clawing hands that desperately tried to hold him. The roots snaked from the ground and tried to trip him up, make him lose balance, and end his flight.

"It's all impossible. Impossible!" Clive screamed as he thrashed and broke the hold the hands had on him.

"What the hell is with this guy?" Mr. Treager asked, confused as the three of them closed ground on Clive's lead.

"You got me, boss," one of the gorillas said.

Clive was running like a madman. He was screaming, and he was waving his arms at trees and bushes as he passed. Clive yelled at them, warning them to stay back or he would burn them to the ground. He swore it to Christ he would.

Don Treager Sr. had enough running, as his lungs simply couldn't suck in enough air. He raised his arm, took aim, and fired off a single round.

An angry wasp came across Clive's right temple and thunked into a tree.

Clive heard and felt the near touch of death. Unable to control the reflex, Clive spun, tripped, and rolled down the hill through a tangle of fallen branches and into the creek. Water went over his head and into his mouth. He came up spluttering and reached for the shore.

Something unseen in the water grabbed him. Something seized his clothes, his arms, and kicking feet and pulled him toward a terrible darkness deep in the water.

"Please, let me go. You know I didn't mean it. I'm sorry, man!" Clive pleaded.

Clive was quickly pulled under water, fought his way to the surface, but instantly something dragged him back down. His body became a fiercely working piston as his arms and legs hammered. He felt the breath leaving him, but desperately tried to hold on to life. His lungs hitched, and a force of bubbles ruptured from his mouth as he tried to scream one last time.

Don Treager Sr. and his associates watched the thrashing man for a long while. They watched the man desperately trying to throw off the branches he had become entangled in when he had rolled down the hill and into the water. He was screaming for them to release him as if the branches had purposely taken hold of him.

When Clive's movement ceased, Mr. Treager ordered his men to pull the body from the water. In the flashlight beam, Don Treager Sr. would swear it before Mother Mary that the ligature marks on Clive's arms and throat didn't look at all like something made by branches but by someone's gripping hands.

Sacred

Hey, over here, fella. Yes, yes, come a little closer to me. Ah, there we go. Now don't tell me a finely dressed specimen like you is this far out into nowhere by accident? No, I thought not. Are you just passing through the desert land, or have you come to visit someone? Ah, I see. Well, I have to tell you the truth, it's good to see someone who, well, looks halfway normal. I like your tie. You must have picked it up at Ron's in Gradyville. No? Is it Italian? I don't suppose it really matters, does it?

Come on and sit down on the bench and relax a spell. You look a little queasy from the heat. Just sit down and let the wind wisp away your worries. Would you like a beer? I've got some in the cooler here. Nah, I didn't take you as a beer drinker.

Ah, that damn well hits the spot. What's that? Oh, you mean that place over there? Well, that's Georgie's Meat Packing. Yep, you guessed right. They closed it up a few weeks ago. I don't figure it will open back up until they work the bad stuff out of that place. Yeah, bad stuff, all right. No, I shouldn't share the stories. I don't think it's up to me to open the box of demons and give this poor town an image worse than it already has.

Wait! Don't go! All right, I've enjoyed your company, and I'd like you to stay just a little longer. Sit back down, and I'll tell you a tale.

It all started when George bought that piece of land rumored to be an old Indian burial ground. It took a little while, but the trouble, maybe even evil spirits, eventually came around.

The thing is that Gerda Evans was a hard lookin' woman. She had the face of an old catcher's mitt, leathery, cracked, and worn out. I suppose the years of alcohol and drug abuse were partly to blame. Of course, her husband worked her over from time to time. Her husband abused her, you see. Well, she took it for years, and then one day, Gerda decides she's topped out. She loads up his shotgun, walks onto the front porch, and blows him right out of his rocking chair. Hell, he didn't even let go of his beer bottle as he lay dying on the porch. Sure, she got a hell of a sympathy vote from the jury. She only did five years in Jasper Penitentiary for the crime. I've seen armed robbers do more time than that.

Well, anyway, I suppose it's the packing plant you're asking about and not Gerda. In a way, Gerda was the beginning of everything that went badly in that place.

Gerda was the only night shift janitor working at the plant. Even though she killed her husband, the owner, George, couldn't fault her for what she'd done and hired her once she got out of prison. Of course, she took the job and was pretty good at it, from what I hear. I don't figure it would be something that would interest either you or me, but some people are happy doing just about anything. Part of her job was cleaning up after the second shift ended. The building always had one hell of a mess left behind. Besides emptying trash cans and whatnot, Gerda had to spray down the conveyor belts and the floor and clean up all those discarded cow parts. If someone didn't clean the facility right, well, you'd have yourself a packing plant filled with more rats and mice than butchered cows. You understand.

On the night Gerda died, there was one hell of a storm that people around here still talk about to this day. The damn sky was like a continuous display of fireworks going off way up there in the black clouds. The thunder just about rocked the houses down to the foundations. Even a tornado wiped out a big part of Cauldor County just to the south of us. It was a terrible storm, all right.

So Gerda turned up for work as usual. The crew said goodbye to her and made off for home. Some of those men didn't like Gerda so much. Some of those men do the same thing to their wives that Gerda's husband did to her. Maybe what happened to Gerda's husband scared some of those guys straight. Who knows? Anyhow, Gerda loaded up her cart and got to work. I can't imagine what that place is like at night, but I'll tell you the truth that I'd never spend a night alone in there. I'm sure she kept herself busy enough that she didn't think about it too much to bother her.

It started as Gerda was hosing down the belts and getting that raw meat off there. It started with a thump. It was like a simple knock. In a place as big as that and having all the machines quiet, it must have echoed like hellfire. Gerda dropped the hose as if it became a serpent. She whirled around and studied the area before finding the nerve to call out.

"Who's there?"

No one responded. At first, Gerda probably figured one guy was still in the locker room, taking off his gear and getting cleaned up. Of course, the locker room was nearly on the other side of the building, but as I've said, the slightest sound in that place could echo like a son of a bitch.

She picked up the hose and started cleaning again. Well, I suppose a few minutes went by before that thumping sound came again. Only this time, it wasn't a single thump, but a hell of a series of them. The noises were rapid and almost desperate, you could say.

Now Gerda thinks that someone has definitely stayed behind and was having a little fun with her. She figured someone wasn't so eager to get home, decided to stick around and create trouble for her. Well, Gerda isn't the sort of woman any man in that place should play practical jokes on. She snatched up a cleaver from the rack and went to investigate the sounds.

Gerda went through the facility. She searched every corner and studied the areas around every piece of machinery. I suspect Gerda screamed out when frantic thumps started coming from the meat lockers. She must have thought some poor worker trapped himself inside the cooler and probably near frozen to death as he desperately tried to break out of there.

Gerda reached the meat locker, pulled the lever, and opened the steel door. She probably thought she'd find someone lying on the ground, shivering, but still able to thank her for saving his life in the nick of time. Only that wasn't what she received. Gerda couldn't see anyone. Cattle were hanging from hooks on the ceiling, and she found little else inside. Gerda wasn't a vegetarian or anything like that, but seeing those headless and hideless cattle was almost enough to drive her to the point of swearing off red meat for good.

"Hello? Is someone in here?"

She didn't get an answer. What she got was a movement where there shouldn't have been any kind of movement. The damn cattle were coming to life like some sort of sickening animatronics. They were thrashing their legs around, swinging on the hooks that ran right through their backs, but yet the damn things were alive.

As you can expect, Gerda did scream, and she screamed loudly. But, hell, with the storm raging outside and that building being as big as it is, there was no one to hear her or to come running. Those cattle thrashed around so much that the hooks ripped right out of their backs. Now Gerda is standing there, staring at a couple of dozen cattle that should very well be dead. Sometimes things don't like to stay dead, I guess.

Well, a good long moment went by as Gerda watched and considered all of her options. What limited few there were when those things worked themselves around so much that they somehow got up onto their legs. Even though they were headless, I'd be damned if they didn't know Gerda was right there watching this whole terrible show. They knew all right. I don't know if that made them angry. I don't know if it was about revenge, but those things came after her. I believe to this day that those things meant to trample her to death.

Now you might wonder why I said that maybe they wanted revenge. I honestly don't know why. Gerda was never part of the slaughtering crew. Never once in that building did she take a blade to the meat. Maybe this strange sacred burial ground they built the business on had a small window of time to get even for disturbing those trying to rest. Perhaps the storm, and it was a hell of a storm, awoke the land. Maybe the thunder was strong enough even to wake those old buried Indian bones. I couldn't say for sure. All I know is that those cattle were mean, and I'd be lying if I said that I didn't believe they wanted blood and lots of it.

Well, the nearest cow to Gerda received a shoulder full of cleaver when it knocked into her and nearly pinned her against the machinery. I can't imagine Gerda's slashing did much good, seeing that the things were already long since dead. You can't fight evil forces like that, you just can't. The best thing to do in a situation like that is to turn tail and run as if Satan himself were after you.

That's just what Gerda decided to do. She ran. I figured she could have easily outrun them. With their hoofs cut off and not having heads and all, it would be impossible for them to catch her. But remember, the floor was wet from Gerda hosing it down. She took a couple of nasty tumbles. A few cattle caught up and brought those stumpy legs down on her and probably caused more pain than I care to imagine. She avoided most of the stampede, but not before being nearly crushed to death against the machinery. Those big things worked her over. They stomped, and they rammed.

By the time Gerda could pick herself off the floor, she didn't have a stitch on her. Those cattle had somehow battered her around so much that her clothing completely shredded off her.

I don't figure she had much left in her, but she used what little strength she had and pulled herself onto the conveyor belt to get out of reach of those things. That was all a good idea, but evil always has a second plan.

The goddamn conveyor belt started up! You're damn straight that it did.

So there's Gerda, stark naked, lying on a conveyor belt that's rolling her right toward the grinders. She's got dozens of cattle carcasses surrounding the beltline on both sides. Every time she makes a move to jump off the line, a cow comes forward and gets her right back on that line to stay put.

She screamed for help. She begged for anyone listening to come to her aid. Hell, she must have gone stark raving mad just before those grinders first touched her skin. I know I would have.

Well, there you have it. That's how it all began there at Georgie's.

Gerda? No, they never found her. The truth is, when the crew came in the following day, none of them even knew anything was wrong. The machines weren't running. The cattle still hung up on hooks, just as they had been the day before. Hell, even Gerda's torn clothes had disappeared. No one even missed Gerda until she didn't show up for work that evening. Most people figured she ran off. Maybe she'd found herself a new man, a good man, and decided this little town wasn't much for her anymore and took her life down the road. It happens from time to time. Most of us think little of it when someone around here who just doesn't seem to fit in moves on somewhere else. That's life.

So here's the best part. I heard this from old Fred, but he's dead now. God bless him. Fred said that his great-granddaughter attended the birthday party of Davey Simmons. Well, the party was going fine, fun and games, but when his father flipped those burgers off the grill and served them to everyone, his son took a big old bite and immediately complained that he had a hair in his burger!

Doesn't that beat all? You see that they never found Gerda. Do you understand what I'm telling you?

Wait, you don't have to go! I'm just passing along the story as someone told me. I wasn't there, of course. None of us were. We can only guess what happened. I know that land has a curse, and I'm sure that Gerda was the first of the mysterious disappearances after they built the packing plant.

Are you going? I wasn't trying to scare you off or anything. Say, how about I make it up to you for getting you all worked up over a silly story? How about we head on down to Isaac's, and I'll buy you a milkshake and a cheeseburger? What do you say?

Perfect Circles

October 14th, 2015

Okay, this is how it's gonna go. I'm going to have to write everything down in a journal. I'm afraid that if I record everything on my phone's voice recorder, I'm going to do some stupid shit thing and delete everything by accident when I really meant to change my voice mail message or something. This discovery is too important not to have written down on paper.

For the written record, I unintentionally opened a dimensional doorway to a parallel universe. At least, I think. This phenomenon all happened just yesterday, so I haven't had much time to study the damn thing. I feel stupid for saying this, but it opened from one of my notebook doodles.

I'm sorry. I should probably introduce myself first and give you a super quick background if you don't already know me. My name is Charlie Evans. I'm 22 and a student at Georgia State University. I'm studying engineering. I don't live on campus. My parents have rented me a three-bedroom house for the duration of my enrollment. My parents are rich, like stupid rich. Neither of them worked a day in their lives. They got the money from their folks. My grandparents were snobby assholes. My parents are snobby assholes. I decided not to be an asshole. So here I am, trying to learn and make something of myself. I can't imagine being an asshole is an astounding path in life. Was that a quick enough background update for you?

So anyway, I was sitting at my desk staring at my laptop for something like five hours straight. My left hand tends to doodle nothing in particular on a notepad as the rest of my thoughts focus on the mind-numbing crap I need to memorize.

Then it happened! I opened a fucking portal! I'm sorry if you have sensitive eyes, but I'm gonna cuss a lot on these pages, so deal with it.

It scared the shit out of me. It was like someone flipped on a vacuum that had something wedged in the tube that caused an annoying whistle along with all that sucking. I quickly rolled away from the desk because I didn't exactly know what had just happened. I saw the pages of the notebook fluttering as if a window were open. Where the pencil circle on the white sheet had been was now a black dot about the size of a dime. I could actually see dust get sucked into the hole and probably vanish forever.

I freaked the fuck out! My brain immediately told me to plug the hole. So what does someone plug a hole with when you have nothing around to grab in a hurry? Right, you use a finger. When the pad of my thumb slid over the hole, and the sucking momentarily paused is about the moment when I realized I'd made the biggest dumbass move in the history of dumbass moves. I had just plugged a vacuum of space with my own flesh. Now I instantly knew I wouldn't be able to pull my thumb straight off. I had to slide my thumb to open an edge and break the seal. The suction was starting to hurt. It wasn't easy, but my thumb found the edge, and my hand quickly pulled away.

I looked at my skin and saw a purple hickey formed into a perfect circle. I massaged it, trying to get the feeling to come back. After a few minutes, the hard numbness went away, and my sense of touch returned. Thank Christ.

After that, I didn't really know what to do. I stared at that unusual hole for a very long time. Then, very carefully, I grabbed the edges of the notebook and lifted it. Now here was a feat of magic. The hole didn't go through the entire notebook. I put it down again. I then took the edge of the top sheet, being very aware of keeping away from the hole. I opened to the next page. I take back what I said before. The real surprise came when I found the paper lacked a black sucking vortex on the other side. It was nothing more than plain white paper—a possibly endless hole on one side and memo paper on the other side. I felt like I should madly laugh because I believed I was losing my shit.

There was only one thing to do in this situation to prove it wasn't a delusion created by a sleep-deprived mind. I had to experiment with this strange discovery. I opened my desk drawer, grabbed a paper clip, and tossed it onto the paper. It fell an inch short of the hole, but it didn't matter because the sucking vacuum had a hold on it. The paper clip slid to the hole and just vanished from existence. I pulled up on the sheet again. A small part of me expected to find the paper clip neatly tucked between those two pages, transported from a black hole on one side and appearing on the other. But instead, I got what most people would have figured. The paper clip had blinked away from my house.

Next, I dropped in a pencil, and the hole gobbled it up to nothingness. A small wad of paper, four more pencils, and a dozen more paper clips followed each other. I had to experiment further. I wondered if what went into it could come back out. I unhooked the USB end of my mouse from the computer. It was the only thing close at hand that would fit, and I could hold onto it. When the vortex pulled the cord from my grip, the mouse would stop the cable from completely disappearing. I fed the cable in all the way and then slowly pulled it back out. The cable was still there, not hot or cold, not destroyed in any way. I plugged it back into my computer and found that everything worked perfectly fine.

For the next three hours, I vanished every tiny object that would fit until many rooms of the house were void of anything smaller than a dime. It was getting late, and I had class in the morning. I couldn't leave a dimensional portal or black hole or whatever the hell it was open to continue sucking away the Earth's oxygen. So I plugged the hole with something I knew would never get through. I dropped my bowling ball on it. I hadn't sealed the hole entirely because I heard the slightest whistle of air. It would have to do for now.

October 15th, 2015

The fucking portal ate my bowling ball! Well, I wouldn't say it's completely gone. The odd-shaped steel center that gives, or gave, the ball its spin is still here, as well as hundreds of tiny pieces of the bowling ball material. The rest of it is now floating around in dead space somewhere with a bunch of my other former possessions. If I wasn't already wise enough to the situation, I'd be that kind of dumbass who stuck his eye up to that spy hole to see if I could spot any of my discarded items flying around in there. Being quickly minus an eyeball, I would praise myself for my complete shit-for-brains mindedness. I could see several of my friends doing that very thing before I could get out a warning.

I had a few thoughts just before I drifted off last night. I wondered if I should call someone. Maybe the NSA, NASA, Homeland Security, or the FBI. First, I thought it was a horrible idea. They wouldn't take me seriously. They'd probably figure I was just another crackpot college student who smoked too much, well, crack or pot, and I was seeing shit not really there. Then I thought I should contact a theoretical physicist. If I wasn't laughed at and hung up on, I could get a professional to come to my house to study the hole and precisely explain what the hell was going on. I could take it to someone because it was a portable portal. That was also a dumbshit idea. Whatever this is shouldn't be carried around as if it were a regular notebook.

October 16th, 2015

After class today, I went to an electronics store. I had an idea that was very much like the mouse cord experiment. Only now I needed a line with a camera on it. I've seen them in movies where a SWAT team used one to snake through the air ducts so they could see what the hostage situation inside was like.

The salesman said the only kind they had available came with an eight-foot line. He said if I needed more reach, I'd have to order one online. Apparently, no one had ever come in before looking for a camera to feed deep into the depths of a black hole to answer the questions that have baffled scientists since forever. I said that was fine. It was stupid expensive, but as I said, I have stupid rich parents who give me a hefty monthly allowance.

After charging the battery and reading the instructions, I was ready to investigate. I'm not gonna lie here, but I was fucking nervous about what I might see. Have you ever seen one of those sci-fi movies where there's an army of monsters waiting for a dimensional portal to open so they can move in and invade the dominating species? Well, that's the film reel that played in my head. What good would come of this if I did see something like that? If the portal was slightly open, couldn't the monsters open it more? A planet Earth invasion from light-years away that all began from Charlie Evans' notebook doodle. What a way to end the world.

I turned on the instrument and the screen blinked to life. I could see my desk where the camera pointed. The thing came with a bright light on the camera end that fried my eyeballs because I stupidly switched the light on as I pointed the camera at my face. When the glowing sun left my eyes, I began feeding the camera into Satan's Butthole. Yeah, that's what I've been calling it, Satan's Butthole. It seems like an appropriate title because this might very well be an opening to Hell through the butthole. It almost sounded like it could be a tourist cavern in Colorado.

And now, ladies and gentlemen, we bravely probe the dark reaches of Satan's Butthole. Follow me on this incredible journey as we track the elusive Floringarang. Never before has this rare creature been caught on film. It has four sets of eyes, six legs, and three giant cocks. He is a territorial creature that will eat the ass end of any animal daring to approach his domain.

It was somewhere between a wildlife announcer and a sad B-rated sci-fi movie voice intro playing in my head.

Even in that dark abyss, the small light was pretty powerful, if there was anything to see at all. When an area lacks all color, you get a nonreflective blackness. I used the control to redirect the camera and slowly rotated it to catch a view of every angle. There was nothing, nothing at all. I was surprised when I captured a sight I wasn't expecting. I was looking at the backside of the small hole. The camera light showed blackness flowing to heavier light that was coming from the room. The camera line looked cleanly severed, having grown from nothingness. It was bizarre to have the camera pointed right where I should be standing, but finding only blackness. I was here, but also not here. A fucking freak-out experience to the highest degree.

I thought that even if I had a thousand-foot line, I'd still find nothing. I started pulling the line back in when I saw something flitter by the camera. I held position and watched the video screen. I figured it was just one of a hundred things I fed into the butthole days ago. After several minutes, I thought my eyes were simply fatigued from staring at a black screen.

When I pulled the line, something pulled back. It wasn't my imagination. It was a gentle tug, like a fish testing the bait. I began pulling slowly, and that's when something ripped the entire unit out of my hands. The line ran into the hole until the main unit prevented it from going any farther. I reached out, and the screen fell into my hands. The eight-foot camera line was now less than one foot. Something mangled the flexible rubber and fiber optics line.

Satan's Butthole had just eaten the critical end of my stupid expensive camera system. But the good thing was that the video recording was still there and intact.

I moved away from the butthole. I pushed buttons on the unit to start playing the video. The footage began with my face, looking surprised at the bright light shining into it. The footage then rolled to a thick blackness as I fed the line inside. Small particles passed by the lens, almost like tiny bugs attracted to the light. I figured it was only small debris the butthole had sucked out of my house.

Something gray and slightly reflective flittered by the lens. It was fast and large. I stopped the video, and frame by frame, rolled back the recording. Do you remember the opening scene in the first Star Wars when the star destroyer slowly passed overhead? It was kind of like that, only in reverse and not made of metal. The thing was agile and moved like a squid in water. It was so close to the camera that all I could see was dark, scaled skin. When I got to the beginning of when it first appeared, I caught an eye on the screen.

I paused the video and stared back at that jelly orb just as it stared at me. I was sure it was an eye, the eye of a creature living in the butthole. Inside that strange phenomenon of a portal were living things, at least one. But where there's one thing inside, there's gonna be more.

October 17th, 2015

This next bit has nothing to do with the portal. I just got the shit kicked out of me by a punk-ass thug who stole my wallet, laptop, and smart watch. I was coming home from class when this shit clown lowlife punched me in the back of the head, nearly knocking me out. I couldn't even fight back because my head was spinning, and I needed to throw up because of the dizziness. What's worse, after he took my things, he kicked me twice in the ribs and once in the face, splitting my lower lip. After he left, I just laid there in someone's yard until the old bastard came out and started yelling at me to get off his lawn or he was gonna call the police. I told him I needed the police. He only slammed the door to my pleading.

In what year was it that humanity became so self-focused? When did we stop caring about each other? A man beaten to a pulp lying in the grass deserves compassion, and he deserves help. I didn't get an act of human decency because the old man never came back out. He didn't even call the police. Before I could push myself off the ground, five cars had passed by without braking and offering help. It's quickly becoming a sad state of the world when people have lost all heart.

I didn't call the police and file a report. I didn't call my parents either. Their solution would be to replace my stolen items, sending them by mail. They would never show concern for my well-being. So I didn't bother with a call.

I sat in the room for many hours and stared at the hole. The noise of the sucking hole had become so common that I barely even noticed it anymore. Actually, it became a soothing white noise, like the static hum of a television station off the air or how they used to sound before the digital age.

I'm going to have to be honest here. My thoughts were very dark at the moment. I suppose anyone violated in any way would be on the same trail of thoughts as I was. It's human nature to want revenge, to want justice when the law would most likely fail in doing so.

I thought of the first day when the portal opened. I had panicked and tried to plug it with my finger. The pressure of that vacuum was incredible. If I had left my thumb there, I'd be minus a digit now. I thought of the bowling ball and the significant damage the void did to it over a short time. My thoughts were now getting darker. If I ever found the thug who robbed and beat me, I could feed him into the void piece by tiny piece until nothing was left. Sure I could. It would be a lot of hard work and cleanup, but it's something I could do. But do I believe I could ever go to that extreme for revenge?

I shook my head, trying to force out those vicious thoughts. Rotating my eyes up from the carpet to the dime-sized hole, I saw something poking out of it. Reflexively, I pushed my chair back and away from whatever it was. My heart hammered at the thought of something tearing through into our world. It would begin its world destruction with the slaughter of the person who opened the doorway.

What had come out of the black void was a nail, actually more like a talon. It wasn't long and sharp-pointed like an eagle talon, but shorter and blunted. It was dark gray with a bit of green on it, like mold. It circled around and around as it probed this side of the strange wormhole. I fully expected some monstrous arm to come tearing through the notebook paper, and that arm taking a firm grip on this side as the creature pulled itself into my world. It didn't happen. Even though the thing tried to break through, the dime-sized dimensional ring could not be torn or stretched. The creature could never slip through to my side. At least, I was pretty sure it had no hope of getting through.

Right now, I was thanking Christ my doodle was small enough. Otherwise, the creature would come through and splatter the room with my blood as it gobbled down my remains. I wondered if my parents would find it inconvenient to call in a maid to scrub down the walls and floor that I so rudely bloodied while being torn to pieces. They probably wouldn't get the security deposit back from the rental company, and I laughed at the thought.

My laughter seemed like a strange thing at that moment. It even alarmed that probing talon because it pulled back inside the hole.

So now I know that not only can I send stuff into the hole, but whatever is born on the other side can also come through into my world. A doorway between dimensions can be the only logical answer.

I needed more information on what I was facing. I needed to get more video recording on that side. I figured buying a replacement camera would waste money and time because the creature, or creatures, would rip it apart again. I needed a small, durable camera able to livestream what it saw. Either that or I needed a larger hole. Maybe both.

October 27th, 2015

It's been ten days since my last entry. I've been a little more focused on another matter. I don't have much more to report on the butthole. The claw has come back many times over, trying to force its way through that universal anomaly. I'm pretty sure those probing digits aren't from the same creature every time. There could very well be an army just on the other side, desperately trying to figure out a way through.

I have to be honest here. I've been spending a lot of time doing research. Not any kind of scientific research about dimensional holes, but research about human nature. Was there ever a time during the rise of humankind where there was total peace? Have we always been consumed by hate and greed and the need to self-destruct? The statistics I've found are alarming. The more we advance as a species, the more we lose control. We believe we're brilliant when we're the dumbest and most barbaric species, forgetting the roots of our existence.

I'm not a preacher, so I'll step off my pulpit now.

The other thing consuming my time is watching. I've been spending a tremendous amount of time searching for the brute bastard who mugged me. I found him. I spent evenings doing surveillance. During this time, I witnessed him beat and rob six other people. I could have filmed it and turned it over to the police. What good would that do? He'd probably be back on the street in a month and continue his crime spree, never worrying about an extended stay in prison. People like this are the reason for the downfall of society.

There's an answer. There's always an answer. It might not be an answer most people would decide on, but I've never been one to be like most people. Tonight I'm going to take vigilante justice.

October 27th, 2015

It seems stupid to write my confession in a journal, but I have to put it down because the experience was overwhelmingly satisfying! I feel righteous about what I've done.

I followed the man for a long while. He mugged two more people before we reached his slum house. The second man he had severely beaten, as he had done to me. I almost stepped in to help, but it would have destroyed my plans. In my thoughts, I told that poor, beaten man I would exact justice many times over for him, for us. This thug would never rob and beat another person again. I vowed to set things right.

The thug wasn't a large man. His only upper hand is the element of surprise. Does anyone honestly believe they're about to be mugged and are they ever fully prepared for it? I didn't doubt that I could best this man in a fair fight.

It wasn't a shock when we reached his home. It seemed a fitting place for the slime of society to live. It was the sort of place where the building siding was falling off, with the roofs near collapse, and the grass areas were covered in garbage and discarded cigarette butts. People in these parts mostly kept to themselves. If they were one of those unfortunate people having no choice but to live here, they didn't go looking for trouble.

No one even really looked me in the eye as I passed. I kept my sight low, but I also had a hoodie pulled up to help conceal my features. I didn't want my face remembered. I stayed back far enough that the man wouldn't notice me as he went to his apartment door at the end of the building. He flicked a cigarette into the parking lot. The butt bounced off someone's windshield, and he slammed the door.

He had one neighbor to the right and one neighbor above his apartment. As I passed the window of the adjacent apartment, I could see it was vacant. Only a heap of garbage covered the floor.

My heart was hammering so fucking hard when I went up to the door. I had to act fast before I lost my nerve.

If he answered the door with a gun, I had a notebook.

If he answered the door with a knife, I had a notebook.

It was absurd. It was insane. It was the dumbest thing in the history of my life I'd ever done, and I've done some dumb-shit things in my time.

When I heard him coming to the door, I thought in a spaghetti western voice, *never bring a gun to a notebook fight, amigo!*

When the guy opened the door, he only managed to say, "What the fuck do you want, shitheel?"

It was a microsecond later when I threw myself at him. I crashed into him, and with all of my buck fifty weight, I off-centered him. We went down to the disgusting stained floor with arms and legs flailing. I didn't like the idea of an unfair attack, but I pulled a trick from this guy's autobiography of chicken shit fighting techniques to receive an upper hand. I rammed my knee into his crotch before he had a chance to fight back. Rolling around, the man groaned and called me vulgar names through clenched teeth.

I used my right hand and pinned the notebook to his chest. I heard the vacuum muffle as his shirt sucked up into the hole, and then he started to scream. It was a scream of pain. I knew the hole had already eaten through the fabric and was now attached to his skin.

His right fist landed a hard kidney blow. I tried to hold him down, but the hit had racked my body with incredible pain. He pushed me off and immediately began fighting the notebook suction. Paper ripped away as he pulled, and as I had done with my thumb, he slid the notebook off the side of his body.

He wobbled his way up to a stance and inspected his wound. A perfect circle of missing skin and some flesh stared at us. The injury freely pumped blood down his shirt. With a look of total confusion, he studied the notebook and the black hole that had just plucked a dime-sized plug from his body. He then looked at me, to the notebook, and again at the flowing wound on his chest. The man's mouth started to work, but he was too confused about what he needed to say.

At that moment, I kicked his right knee. It was a hard blow that folded his knee in the opposite direction with a horrifying crack of bone and cartilage.

A more violent scream rolled out of him as he went down to the ground again. He tried cradling his injured knee but couldn't because of the odd direction of his bending leg.

I wondered if someone had already called the police. Then again, I remembered where I was, and the police weren't a trusted source in this community.

I grabbed the dropped notebook. I threw myself on the thug again. With both hands, I pressed the notebook to his forehead. It took him a moment to pull himself away from the pain of his knee to realize there was a more significant pain viciously pulling away tiny pieces of his head.

He fought me. His strength was fading, but he got in a couple of good shots. The worst one was his fist instantly breaking my nose. The pain didn't matter as I held on. I wanted to get the hell out of here. I needed this moment of insanity to be over.

There was a pop, loud like a champagne cork releasing, followed by a wet sucking sound. I immediately knew what it was. His skull gave out, and his brains were now floating off into the void. His eyeballs vibrated from the suction. Sections of his sinus cavities ruptured and air pulled in through his nose and mouth with an ungodly wheeze.

I took only a moment to take in what I had done. It was a sickening sight, but I felt justified in my actions.

I pulled the notebook free. There was a small amount of blood and brain matter around the hole in the notebook. The blood from my broken nose had spilled all over him as we fought. There was physical evidence of me at this crime scene. My DNA and fingerprints weren't in any databases. Any concerns I had fled with me out the door.

It wasn't until now, as I write this entry with shaking hands, that I realized one crucial mistake was made. Maybe it was because of the intensity of the situation. My mind screamed at me to fly like a fucking bat out of hell before the police arrived. I forgot to search his apartment for my stolen wallet, smart watch, and laptop. The police could easily trace the three items back to me. The thief most likely sold my laptop and watch at a pawn shop, but the wallet could be another matter. If he hadn't discarded the ID or credit cards, I worry that the police might come knocking on my door. The detectives would say they discovered my wallet at a crime scene where a man had been murdered by having his brains sucked out. They would ask why I never filed a police report about being mugged. I'm a terrible liar. I can't do anything about it now except to wait and see what happens next.

Additional note: There was a quick story about it on the news. The details were vague, only saying the death was suspicious and to contact the police if you had any information.

A suspicious death? Are they saying human brains don't usually vacate the skull when someone drops dead of natural causes?

November 20th, 2015

I apologize for taking so long to write again. I'm going to catch you up on a few details. No police ever came knocking on my front door. The blurb on the news on the night of the mugger's death was the only thing ever said about the man. I'm sure the investigation continues because the circumstances in which he died were too strange to file away and forget. It wouldn't surprise me at all if the FBI investigated the bizarre murder. Maybe the case was handed over to an oddball agent working the so-called X-Files in the basement of the J. Edgar Hoover Building.

I've closely watched the news on television and online, searching for any new leads in the case. What I've learned is that with every passing day, our world becomes more of a cesspool. People have lost their minds in every logical way. Yeah, I know, I'm one to talk. Society sees mass murders, rapes, robberies, human trafficking, endless wars, and a thousand other things humans do out of greed, hate, or morbid pleasure as a common occurrence. It isn't getting any better. As the world population grows, it's become a volatile way of life.

What drives us to this method of self-destruction? How do we stand against it?

I'm going to experiment with an idea. It could be the cure-all for this human madness. So I have to see this plan through.

July 19th, 2016

I see from the last entry I told you I had a plan. I'm very pleased to share with you that the first hole wasn't a fluke. The dime-sized doorway to God knows where isn't the only opening I can create.

I decided to see if I could recreate Satan's Butthole on a larger scale. It wasn't easy at all. In fact, I had more than fourteen thousand failed attempts. For the longest time, I believed the pencil was the key to opening the doorway. I was near giving up when I finally achieved a manhole lid-sized opening—another perfect circle. The sudden opening scared the absolute holy fuck out of me.

I would have been sucked up and gone for good if I hadn't the forethought to use heavy-duty rope and tether myself to brackets bolted to the concrete floor in the basement—score one for common sense.

It wasn't a perfect freehand circle. On a larger scale, it became far more complicated to recreate. Just the slightest wobble of the pencil and the attempt was a failure. I used many tools along the way to assist in my trials.

The only thought about how something becomes this I followed with the only logical answer. It wasn't the pencil, paper, concrete floor, or anything else where I created circles. I am the key to the doorways. I don't know how or why, but I'm positive the opening of these dimensional thresholds can only be done by my hand alone.

To my knowledge, in the history of the world, these circles have never been done before. At least not known to the public. There could be some government facility somewhere riddled with large and small buttholes created by people just like me. I won't ever know for sure.

Terrorists shot down a civilian plane carrying 343 people. Sixty-four of them were children.

A mall shooting happened in Sacramento. Twenty-seven people died, and forty-four others were wounded. The shooter killed himself before capture.

The Middle East is raging in endless war.

Those are only three of the major headlines this week.

There is no end in sight to the madness.

Whatever is on the other side of the portal wants to come through. It has tried. The concrete is scored with nail marks as it has clawed at the hole. No person or creature can increase the portal except for me.

I'm having wicked thoughts again. I keep trying to talk myself out of it, but the world won't let me. It convinces me more and more with the daily newspaper, newscasts, and online reports. I keep praying for humans to extinguish hatred, greed, and pure insanity.

July 31st, 2016

Another school shooting happened. A recently expelled student killed four teachers and twenty-one students.

August 7th, 2016

A semitruck driver intentionally drove through a crowd of concertgoers outside an arena. Seventy-one died, and 102 were injured.

September 2nd, 2016

A U.S. embassy bombing in some shithole third world country. The blast killed nineteen and wounded thirty-one.

June 23rd, 2017

My parents died in a drunken automobile accident while heading home from a snobby uptown party. If that wasn't bad enough, they took a family of four with them. Two of them were children under the age of nine.

This world needs a serious reality check.

I've become the sole beneficiary of their companies and fortune. I don't want it because that isn't my idea of a good life. Their lives were a masquerade, and their hearts were empty. I don't think I'll miss them.

August 11th, 2020

I could have gone on day after day by stating the tragedy of everyday life in this world. Reading and writing about it puts me in a severe depression. Instead, I placed my focus elsewhere. The portal is the answer. What is through that dark hole holds the only solution. I was very serious when I spoke about the human race self-destructing. As the world population continues to increase, violence will steadily grow with it. It's simple math. Although the majority of the people in this world are good-hearted, bad seeds rapidly spread in our field of wonder. It will consume like an unchecked cancer and destroy everything good surrounding it.

Why delay the inevitable future?

As you can see, it's been some time since my last journal entry. Over three years blinked away since I last wrote. I have remained productive during this time. I've used a sum of my family inheritance and bought a large facility twenty miles outside of Atlanta. A company that once built commercial airplanes had owned the facility. It's an area large enough to house four jumbo airliners. It's perfect for my intentions.

Much of the design process was of my creation. I am an electrical engineer, of course. There were many parts of the process that were either beyond my capabilities or beyond my knowledge. So I had to hire subcontractors to help get the machine functional. I didn't inform the hired hands of what the machine would ultimately do. I'm sure finding such people to help with the project would have been impossible had they known my true intentions.

It's hard to imagine at this point that one man, one mugging, brought me to this frame of mind. Of course, as I've added in my journal over the years, you can see that many things contributed to the cause.

I've named my machine. It's called: The After Party. I've even gone so far as to paint in ten-foot-high lettering around the soon to be perfect circle. Across the top curve reads: "The," and at the bottom half reads: "After Party."

I chose this because it's much like a teenage drinking party while the parents are away, and the cops roll up because of noise complaints. Everyone scatters like roaches. We are the roaches. What's on the other side of the portal is the police. Instead of being arrested, there will only be annihilation.

It's a long process for one man to start the machine. I'm going to stop writing in my journal now. I will continue through a headset recording once the machine begins.

Check, check, is this thing recording? Okay, it's been nearly two hours now to set this thing up and get things rolling. The machine's arm has rotated almost halfway through the perfect circle's three-hundred-foot circumference. The laser is working perfectly. The beam is cutting straight through the concrete flooring. I know the cut didn't need to be so deep because even the first portal started from a pencil on paper. I only wanted to make sure something happens here, or I've completely wasted a lot of effort and money. So I've amped up the laser cutting to go all the way through the concrete.

I hope this audio is coming through because the machine is deafening in here.

I'm currently on one of the platforms beneath the machine and inside the laser's circumference. I wanted to make sure I had a prime viewing position for everything that comes next.

For those of you who survive and search out the origin of where these things come from, I want you to know you can find my journal and an additional copy of this recording in a personally designed vault on the south side of the premises. I've embedded the vault in an underground chamber specifically constructed to withstand the massive girth of these creatures coming through the portal. I want those who may survive to know exactly why I've taken such drastic action against the human race.

We're now three-quarters of the way through. Everything is working exactly as intended.

I want to say I'm sorry for those good people in the world whose lives will be extinguished because of my actions. I'm also sorry for those who may survive the aftermath. I'm sorry it has come to this, but the hate of the world won. I know you tried to live your lives honestly, being good and kind, but we all lost in the end. To those of you who were nothing more than the black sludge found in sewer drains, I say fuck you. The end of our time and the beginning of another is all your fault.

I welcome what comes next with open arms. It's time for the depravity of the world to end. It's time for something else to emerge from our ruins. Scientists consistently predicted a sixth mass extinction on our planet. I had no idea it would be by my hands when I opened the first perfect circle. I have no regrets. Whoever is listening to this in the future, I want you to know and understand that statement.

Okay, here we go, folks. The laser is reaching the endpoint. The circumference cut is nearly complete.

That's it! The concrete just fell away into another beautiful black void. It fucking worked! It's so wonderful, like looking into a starless night sky. Oh, I wish you could all see it. The sight is truly remarkable.

As I suspected, when I opened the void in the basement of my old house, the suction decreases when the diameter of the circle is greater. It only feels like a mild draft inside the building.

Something just went by the hole. It almost seemed like it was swimming more than flying in that oily darkness. It was like a squid in water. I didn't get a good look because it was too fast. But it was big, like Godzilla big.

There's a hand, or maybe a claw, now breaking through the dimensional fold. It's dark gray, kind of scaly, with curved nails. Oh my God, you wouldn't believe me unless you got a chance to see one.

The eyes are in the black distance, reflectively glowing like a cat's eyes in low light. The thing is squinting at me, studying me, I think.

It's coming through now. This is it, ladies and gentlemen. This moment is one I've waited years to see! There's another monster directly behind the first one. They're eagerly coming through the portal now! My God, they're so heartbreakingly perfect. You have no idea the incredible beauty the end of our world offers to all those who accept what comes next.

Nightline

When the answering machine beeped, the man said, "Mrs. Sarah Jacobs of 415 Newberry Way, I think I have to kill you tonight."

Then the line went dead.

Sarah Jacobs stepped from the shower and wrapped the bath towel around her. She stepped on the scale, frowned, and then went to the mirror and wiped her hand across the steamed glass. As she checked her appearance, she pulled her tangled, wet black hair straight and then stepped from the bathroom.

Sarah moved into the bedroom and sat at the vanity. She used a towel to blot her hair and then used the hairdryer. As Sarah flipped her hair back, the mirror reflected a red flashing light on the answering machine beside the bed. She swiveled in the chair, stood, and walked to the bedside table. She pressed the PLAY button and listened.

"What the hell?" she said when the message finished.

She picked up the phone to call Neal. Of course, she knew he was still in Cincinnati at the conference until tomorrow, but he would answer his cell at this time of night.

"Hello?" Neal asked in a tired voice.

"Neal, hey, it's me."

"I know I saw the caller ID. How are things?"

"Neal, I was just in the shower and—"

"Oh, I like this phone call already."

"Just stop it and listen," she said in a voice near panic.

"Hey, what's going on? You sound all worked up."

"Someone left a message while I was in the shower. It was a man, and he said, 'Mrs. Sarah Jacobs of 415 Newberry Way, I think I have to kill you tonight.' I don't know what to do."

"Are you being serious?"

"Hell, yeah, I'm serious. I'm not going to joke about something like that. I'm freaking out here."

"Okay, okay, just try to calm down. It's probably some kids messing around. They're probably calling a bunch of people and saying the same thing. They're just trying to get people into a frenzy for no reason. Did you make sure the doors and windows are locked? Is the house alarm set?"

"Hell, I don't know. I just got the message a minute ago and immediately called you. I don't think kids were messing around because it sounded like a man's voice but distorted somehow. You should have heard the way he spoke. It sounded, I don't know, deranged."

"Okay, put the phone down, go check the locks and alarm and come back to the phone, and we'll figure this out."

"Okay, all right, don't hang up. I'll be right back," Sarah said, and placed the phone on the table.

To avoid causing the stairs to squeak, she took each step carefully to the main level. She looked in all directions as she moved toward the front door. She had nearly reached the door when she quickly stopped.

She wasn't quite sure what it was she was seeing. It was raining inside the house. Several wet shoe prints marked the hardwood floor. The footprints were simply there in the middle of the family room.

Slowly, her sight rotated to the skylight high on the vaulted ceiling. It was propped open, and a gentle rain came in.

When Sarah Jacobs heard movement behind her, she tried to scream, and she tried to run, but the forceful thin cord wrapped around her throat prevented her from doing either.

"So he came in through the skylight?" Detective Angela Halloran said as she leaned over the body of Sarah Jacobs.

"Yeah, it's a hell of a jump, if you ask me," Detective Brian Anderson said as he studied the open skylight.

"I'll say. The guy should have broken his legs when he came down, unless he used something to propel himself down here. How did he leave?"

"All the windows and doors were locked when units arrived after the husband called the local police from Cincinnati. The responding officers had to bust the front door down, which set off the house alarm. I've got a guy on the roof checking for any device the perpetrator might have used to lower himself through the window. If he came down through the window, then maybe he went back up that way. Who knows for sure right now?"

"But you can say for sure that it's our guy?" Halloran asked.

"Oh, yeah. As you can see, our perp strangled Mrs. Jacobs with a fine cord."

"Yeah, I happened to notice that, but it could have been a copycat."

"I don't think so. The guy left his calling card on the answering machine. I don't need an analyst to confirm that it's his digitally altered voice he leaves at each crime scene," Anderson said and kneeled beside the body.

Halloran thrust her hands in her pockets and watched Anderson study the woman and said, "This guy sure knows how to pick them. Every one of the victims was very beautiful. I still find it unlikely that each one is random. What does this one make, number twelve?"

"Yeah, twelve in all. We know the unidentified subject plucked each victim's name from phone books out of the rare phone booths still found in the city. All phone booths contained hundreds of fingerprints, but none of them matched any of the prints recovered from all the phone booths. He selects a name living in the area, makes the call, rips the page from the phone book, and then makes the kill."

"What little we do know about this guy isn't getting us any closer to catching him," Halloran said.

"I know. The guy is a seriously twisted piece of work."

"Tell me about it. If this guy doesn't make a mistake soon, we don't have a chance in hell at catching him."

As Detective Halloran sat at her office desk and stared at the board covered with pictures of each victim, she found her mind going down the same path it had gone down a thousand times before.

"You're going to burn yourself out. Why don't you take a break," Anderson said as he sat in his desk chair and took a long pull of his coffee.

"It seems unlikely that the killer randomly selects his victims. I've tackled more cases than I could count, and there's always some sort of connection. The trick is always finding it. One thing that stands out about each of these cases is that the husbands all have rock solid alibis," Halloran said as she studied the Jacobs file.

"Huh?"

"It just hit me a moment ago like a ton of bricks. I was looking over the current case file and realized something. Mrs. Jacobs' husband was in Cincinnati during the murder."

"So? That's the reason we're not looking at him. The guy was in another state."

"Exactly. Every murder committed by the guy called Nightline happened when all the husbands were away. How could it be possible that each husband has a job that requires him to go on out-of-town business trips? Each husband is away when the murder takes place. Doesn't that seem way too coincidental to you?" Halloran asked.

"Do you think there's a method to this guy's madness? You think he's watching the household and knows exactly when each husband goes away on business?"

"Actually, I was thinking something entirely different. There's something that's connecting all of these men. I'm sure of it. Do you remember the Hitchcock movie *Strangers on a Train*?" Halloran asked.

"It's been a while since I've seen it, but I kind of remember it. Why?"

"One man agrees to kill the other's wife as the other agrees to kill the man's father. In turn, each man is supposed to have a solid alibi and can in no way whatsoever fall under suspicion for the murder."

"Whoa, let me get this straight. You're saying that all the husbands are behind the Nightline killings? You're saying that it isn't the work of one guy killing those women, but a group of men in some twisted murder pact?" Anderson asked as he sat at his desk with an amused grin.

"Why not? Each wife had a substantial life insurance policy. Maybe each husband grew tired of being married and didn't want to go through a long, agonizing divorce.

Maybe the men formed a pact to help each other out of a crumbling marriage."

Anderson finished off his coffee, shook his head, and said, "I wish you the best at trying to get the District Attorney to prosecute twelve men for twelve murders. I'm sure it will be as fun as hitting your head against a brick wall, especially since you don't have any evidence to support your theory. I think you're getting desperate to solve this thing."

"You're damn right that I'm getting desperate. Aren't you? If we don't give the public an arrest soon, they'll hang us up in shackles, pile up the wood, and then burn us at the stake. They believe that we're sitting on our ass while this guy terrorizes the city, making everyone feel unsafe. We know he electronically alters the messages he leaves on each answering machine. Our techs still can't filter out the digital alteration and uncover the man's real voice."

"We've been down this road. It's because Nightline doesn't want us to hear his real voice. If we had his actual voice, we might have a better shot at catching him and throwing him to the modern-day gallows. That's why he disguises his voice. Any evidence collected at the crime scenes is so far circumstantial at best," Anderson said.

"Or because it's twelve different voices, and we'd automatically know what the hell was going on. It's a lot smarter to make the police believe that it's one psychopath randomly targeting beautiful young women. Who would ever suspect all the husbands had a part in it?"

"You would, I guess. Like I said, good luck proving that suspicion," Anderson said.

"Thank you for coming in, Mr. Jacobs," Halloran said as they shook hands.

"Of course. I'll do whatever it takes to help with the investigation. Are there any new developments?"

Halloran motioned to the chair beside Anderson and closed her office door.

"Please have a seat. Would you like some coffee or water?"

"No, I'm fine."

"Would you mind if I recorded our conversation?"

"Why?"

"So that I can refer to the answers later on if I need to."

Mr. Jacobs shrugged and said, "I suppose it's all right with me."

Halloran removed a recorder from the top drawer of her desk and began.

"This is Detective Angela Halloran and Detective Brian Anderson interviewing Neal Jacobs on September $25^{th,}$ 2021 at 2:48 p.m. Mr. Jacobs, can you refresh our memories and tell us again where you work?"

Neal Jacobs' eyebrows narrowed as the question seemed out of place.

"Sure. I work for Garrett and Howe Architectural Services."

Halloran and Anderson knew the answer was correct, but they closely watched for any signs of nervousness. Neal Jacobs calmly watched the detectives.

"We think we have a solid lead," Halloran said.

"Really? You have a lead already? That's great news."

"Have you ever heard of a man named Greg Prescott?"

Mr. Jacobs's eyes went left, and his hand began massaging his neck.

"No, not that I remember."

"But you have heard of Nightline, right?"

"Of course. He's the psycho blamed for the recent murder spree. He killed my wife."

"Do you know how he got the name Nightline?" Anderson asked.

"I don't know for sure. I think after the police discovered the second victim, the newspapers started calling him that because he always attacks women alone at night and strangles them with a wire."

"Actually, it isn't a wire, but braided cord like one would use for a clothesline. The man attacks at night and his only method of killing is by strangulation with a length of clothesline. Hence the name Nightline."

"Okay, so you think this Prescott guy is Nightline?"

"Greg Prescott is the husband of the eleventh victim. I was only trying to see if you've been following the case at all," Halloran said.

"No. I'm too busy with work projects. I don't have time to follow the news about current events," Mr. Jacobs said, and scratched his nose.

"Have you ever met any of the other husbands of the victims?" Anderson asked.

Neal Jacobs's eyes went left again. Anderson detected several more facial micro-expressions as he answered the question.

"No."

"Never?"

"No. Look, I had a very long flight early this morning. I had to go to the county morgue and identify my wife. I spent the last two hours calling relatives and informing them of the recent tragedy. So you could say that right now, I'm an emotional wreck. Then I willingly come down here, and suddenly it feels like you're playing games with me. I've got to tell you that I'm not in the mood for this harassment bullshit. I've just lost my wife to a maniac. I feel like I'm under interrogation here."

Halloran held up her hands.

"No, I'm sorry if we made you feel that way. We're just trying to find out if there's a connection between the wives or the husbands. We're not so sure the murders are random like everyone else has believed. We're trying to establish some sort of link between the victims."

"To my knowledge, my wife and I have never met any of the other victims or their husbands."

More facial expressions made Anderson believe it was another lie rolled out.

"Okay. That's good to know. We're trying to go down every road possible until we catch this guy."

"So tell me about this lead you think you've got."

"We can't discuss an open case. Sorry," Halloran said flatly.

Neal Jacobs's anger finally found the surface.

"Then why the hell did I come down here if you can't tell me anything new?"

"Please calm down. We just had a few questions for you."

Neal Jacobs stormed out of the police precinct, swearing he'd file a lawsuit for harassment by the end of the day.

Anderson said, "Congrats. You've managed to piss off a grieving husband and put our ass in a sling in record time."

"It's just the beginning. I've still got eleven more grieving husbands to piss off before quitting time," Halloran said.

"I hope you're joking."

"Not in the least. I need you to contact the husbands of the first six victims, and I'll contact the remaining five. Let's see if we can get them all here around the same time. I want them to see me questioning the other husbands. One of them is bound to break down when he has a lifetime of prison staring right at him."

"Okay, I'm going to roll with this only because I can't wait until the chief finds out and personally hands you a termination notice. It sounds like fun," Anderson said, grabbing a stack of files, and reaching for his desk phone.

By the time Halloran finished with the final interview, she was exhausted, sore from being stuck in her chair for over two hours, but smiling all the same.

"I'm not sure why I couldn't be part of the interview process with the other eleven husbands," Anderson said as he entered the office.

"You saw how Mr. Jacobs got all worked up, almost like we were teaming up against him. I wanted a more one-on-one with the other husbands so they wouldn't feel like a cornered rat," Halloran said.

"Okay, so I made sure each one saw the others when I brought them to your office. What's the verdict?" Anderson said as he took a seat.

"It's speculation, not fact, but I believe they're all lying. Each husband gave certain tells of a lie when I asked a question they didn't like."

"As you said, it's speculation. Where's the proof to move forward? If none of them rolled over on another, then we're still stuck in the same position we were before."

"On the contrary, dear Watson, the fun is just beginning. I have one of my crazy gut feelings that we've rattled them enough that they're going to want to meet each other and discuss the interviews and what move they can make next. Tonight we're going to follow one of the men I believe was ready to buckle during the interview," Halloran said and smiled.

"I hate your gut feelings. Usually, it results in me having to shoot someone."

Angela Halloran and Brian Anderson followed Greg Prescott along the dark country roads. Halloran had to hold back nearly a mile to avoid Prescott from seeing the headlights cut through the night.

"Where the fuck is this guy going?" Halloran asked.

"Hey, it's your show. I figured you knew. I'm just along for the ride."

"I haven't seen any other cars since we left the highway."

"Maybe he's running early or late for the get-together."

"Maybe they knew we would follow someone, and they're setting us up for a major ass-kicking," Halloran said.

"Great. I always figured I'd die while running through the woods and screaming like a little girl," Anderson said as he pulled his service weapon and flipped off the safety.

"Christ. Just relax. I was only kidding. Didn't you know these are all sophisticated and upstanding men with reputable careers? I'm sure I've just been full of shit the whole time and creating a big mess all for nothing," Halloran said and winked.

"I know you don't believe that. You believe that all of these men are guilty. When we reach the end of this road and find them all together, then I'll be a believer in your theory."

"Damn right you will."

Halloran killed the headlights when she saw the glow of brake lights. Prescott was parking beside a row of cars in front of a house tucked away in the woods. The house appeared abandoned.

Halloran quickly parked and cut the engine.

"Why are we stopping here?" Anderson asked.

"I think this is as close as we can get without alerting someone that we're out here. We'll walk from here," Halloran said and stepped from the vehicle.

"I'm starting to think that not bringing backup was a bad idea."

"We'll have a look, and if the situation appears beyond our control, then we'll come back to the car and call in for assistance. Sound good?" Halloran asked.

Anderson chewed thoughtfully on his thumbnail and said, "I guess. Let's get this over with."

They moved down the gravel road. While avoiding fallen branches and piles of autumn leaves, they moved up the drive to the front porch.

"Take the front door, and I'll cover the back. We'll have a look around, and then we'll decide what to do," Halloran said and moved toward the back before Anderson approved of splitting up.

When Halloran disappeared under the cover of night, Anderson went slowly up the front porch to keep the boards from squawking. When he reached the front door and peered through the oval pane of glass, he saw something he didn't like.

All twelve men were standing in a large circle. None of them spoke, and each man stared at the floor as if meditating or waiting for something to happen.

Anderson went to the corner of the house and whispered for Halloran. When he didn't hear a response, he decided to do something that went against his better judgment.

Anderson tried the doorknob, found it unlocked, and moved inside. He wanted to finish this sickening game. He wanted the truth, and he wanted justice for the wives that lost their lives for whatever disturbing reason these men created. Anderson made no effort to hide his advancements. He wanted the men to know they were no longer alone. He removed his sidearm and held it in front of him.

"Sorry for the disturbance, gentlemen, and please don't think about running. My partner is here as well, and I'd sure hate to shoot any of you in the back," Anderson said.

As Anderson moved into the room, he heard the distinctive squeak of a floorboard. When he turned to face the person behind him, something hard came across the side of his head. His gun spilled from his grip, and his sight ran toward blackness.

Someone was slapping his cheek. Anderson blinked and felt the haze of his mind begin to lift. He raised his head and studied the twelve men watching him. He tried to touch the area of his head that pulsed with a blinding agony but couldn't move his arms. He saw that his arms and legs were bound to the chair with a white cord.

"What the hell do you think you're doing? Do you know who I am? You're restraining an officer of the law. All of you are committing a serious crime, and you better thoroughly think things through before you take drastic measures. If you untie me now, I promise that I won't put this in my report, but you will answer for your other actions.

"No one is going to answer for anything, except maybe you, of course," Anderson heard Halloran say from the back of the crowd.

When Halloran broke through the group of men and stepped in front of him, Anderson said, "I'm glad you're here. Get me the hell out of this chair."

"Hmm, no, I don't think I can do that. I put this situation together for a reason. You see that I've known for some time. I'm a good detective. I'm smart in the way of picking out the smallest details," Halloran said.

Anderson struggled to break the cord.

"What the hell is with you? How could you assault me and place me in this chair in front of these murderers?"

"Them? Oh, they aren't murderers. I only wanted you to believe that I believed they were killers. No, I've suspected since the sixth murder that you're Nightline."

"Me? Have you lost your mind?"

"No, I have all my wits. It was you who removed possible evidence from several of the crime scenes, as you were always the first detective on the scene. You also snuck into the evidence room and stole incriminating evidence before I got a more thorough look at everything. All of that is the reason you've been able to avoid detection and been able to keep killing. Justice comes full circle. Now it's time to finish your madness. I'm going to let these men have peace of mind by giving them revenge for the killing of their innocent wives."

Anderson looked at all the men and said, "Listen to me, all of you, I'm not a murderer. I'm a detective that's been trying to solve the murders. This woman, this detective, before us is the real murderer. I've been onto her for several weeks. She's Nightline, not me!"

"It's too late to trick your way out of this situation. They know the full story because I told it to them in the interrogation room when you thought I was trying to uncover some deal they had with each other. These men never met each other before today. I told them to meet us out here, and I'd give them the man that took away their wives. You are Nightline."

"Christ, listen to what she's saying. Everything she said is a lie. I did take evidence from lockup, but only because I wanted to get it before she could destroy it. Don't you understand? I had finally pieced it all together that Angela Halloran is the real Nightline. That's why she brought me here. She wants you to kill me because I'm the only person who has ever suspected that she's the killer of innocent women. You can't do this. If you kill me, then you've killed the only person who can stop this woman from taking another life," Anderson said with pleading eyes.

Halloran clapped and said, "Very clever, partner. That's pretty smart to make these men question that I might be Nightline. Honestly, how many women in history have been serial killers? Not only that, but a woman serial killer who has targeted other women? It's absurd to believe. I'm sure that for years you've wondered what it would be like on the other side of the law. I'm sure you've probably questioned the unending battle you face every day. I'm sure it's worn you down after all this time. Face it that you don't like being a cop anymore because being a cop is far too difficult, but being a man rebelling against the law and doing as he pleases is much easier. I assure you these twelve men know the truth."

"Only a truth conceived by you. Just because it's what you told these men doesn't mean it's the truth. I've only killed one person in my entire life, and that was in the line of duty."

"Bravo. Quite the performance," Halloran said.

"So, if you think I'm Nightline, then why haven't you arrested me? Why haven't I been booked on the charges of twelve counts of murder? Because you know that it's a lie and nothing will stick."

"I've brought you here because you've already destroyed all the evidence that would put you on death row. I know all that I need to know. Right now, these men deserve justice and closure."

"You're damn right they do, and that's why they should untie me so that I can take you in. During this entire investigation, you've been purposely running down bad leads to keep the focus off what you've been doing. Justice will only come when you're under arrest, and no more innocent women die by the hand of Nightline," Anderson said.

"Unfortunately, justice will be served, but it will have to be in this abandoned house instead of an execution chamber. Don't worry, because I promise that no one will ever know you were Nightline. As I said, the evidence is gone. So you will receive an admirable funeral," Halloran said.

"What are you getting out of this?"

"Oh, I'm getting a reward all right. I've promised these men revenge for what was done to their wives, for a small finder's fee, of course."

"Finder's fee?"

"Sure. You know that a cop's retirement isn't what it used to be, what with constant budget cuts and all. So I've made this investment to retire a few years early. These twelve gentlemen have graciously donated fifteen percent of the life insurance policy each of them received."

"Donated to your front pocket."

"Well, yes, for services rendered. I wish I could stick around for the finale of your life, but I have some paperwork to finish up. It's been a pleasure to work with you. I'm sure my new partner won't be as outgoing as you, but I'll have to make do. At least I know retirement is just around the next corner."

When Halloran exited the front door and walked toward her car, she could hear Anderson yelling for her to come back, to admit guilt.

Angela Halloran returned to the office and searched through current cases files on her desk. After leafing through each, she stacked them and frowned. It was a disappointment. There was nothing in all the open cases that could compare to the work of Nightline.

What the hell? It's a good thing I'm heading for early retirement anyhow, she thought.

Halloran could see Captain Cross on the telephone. He was evidently upset about the phone call. When he hung up, Joseph Cross looked through the office glass and saw Halloran watching him.

Captain Cross left his office, slowly approached Halloran's desk, and said, "Hey, I just got a disturbing call. I'm sorry to say that a motorist discovered Brian Anderson's body alongside Highway 21. You better come with me."

What a hell of a day, Angela Halloran thought as she peeled off her clothes and threw them in the hamper. *Brian's dead. Now Nightline will die with him. Nightline will become a classic serial killer like Jack the Ripper. A series of murders, and then they just suddenly stop. No one will ever know why or the true identity of the killer. I guess sometimes it's better if people never know the whole truth. I can't believe that clever son of a bitch tried to point his finger at me and get everyone guessing what the truth really is.*

Halloran threw several logs into the fireplace. She walked to the nightstand, and from the drawer, she removed twelve phone book pages and a lighter, lit one end, and placed them on top of the logs.

When Halloran stepped into the bathroom, closed the door, and turned on the shower, the phone rang.

When the answering machine clicked on, a man said, "Ms. Angela Halloran of 72 Jasper Street, I think I have to kill you tonight."

Then the line went dead.

A Devil of a Deal

"Come on in, everyone. It's easy as pie. It's a piece of cake. Just one quarter could win you one of these," the carny said and grabbed the paw of a purple, giant-sized teddy bear.

A man in black had his hands in his trouser pockets and watched the people move in and try their luck. Quarters bounced off the colored plastic plates, fell onto the plywood board, and slid into the man's daily collection bin.

"Easy as pie, I tell you," he claimed.

The man in black stepped forward, removed two quarters from his pocket, determined a quick judgment of velocity and angle, and flipped the quarters toward the plates centered in the carnival booth. Both quarters caught the plate with a dull *tink*, slid off, and rolled into the collection bin.

"Oh, so close, mister. Try your luck again. Better luck will find you the next time around, guaranteed! Just one quarter wins you one of these," he said and grabbed the bear's paw again.

Men and women around the carnival booth tossed their coins. All the coins were close, but no winners.

The man in black removed two more quarters from his trouser pocket, fixed his aim, and flipped the coins toward the plates. One quarter caught the plate again, slid, and toppled off the edge. The second quarter, on edge, bounced off the plate and immediately fell onto the painted plywood and slid from sight.

The man in black searched his pockets and found them empty. He removed his wallet, placed a dollar bill on the counter, and received four quarters. One by one, four quarters took flight and briefly found the plate and disappeared.

"Next time around will win you one of these," the man said and touched the hanging bear again.

People tossed coins, all missing. They shrugged and moved on to other carnival games.

"It's a cheat. The plates are all slanted. A quarter can't stick fast on a plate," an agitated customer claimed.

"No, sir, I'm no cheat. The games and parks commission oversees every entertainment booth here. My games have a great chance of anyone winning. I've given away more bears this season than you could fit in your house. All my games are fair and legal. Step right up and win your girl a prize she'll never forget," he called to a passing couple.

Tempted by the offered prize, the boy stepped up to the booth, went through two dozen quarters before giving the man a dirty look, and ushered his girl down the walkway empty-handed.

The man in black produced another dollar and tossed his four quarters.

"You almost landed those, sir. Your luck is going to turn around. I can feel it," the carny said.

The man in black retrieved five dollars and received his exchange in quarters. He methodically flipped one quarter after another. None of the quarters stuck.

The carny smiled. It had been quite some time since he'd reeled in a suckerfish like this one. He thought the man would play the game until his pockets were bare.

"Your luck is turning around, mister. You almost had two of those babies. So, so close. Try again and walk home with one of these," he said and pointed to a blue bear with a crooked smile.

An elderly man who had been watching the man in black leaned in.

"Hey, save your money. You can buy one of these cheap bears down the street for less than you've handed over to this guy," he said.

The man in black paid no attention to the advice. He removed another five dollars and received change.

"My bears aren't cheap, buddy. These prizes here are the highest quality you can get for your money. I only give away the best," the carny said.

"I've been standing here for fifteen minutes. I haven't seen you give away anything," the old man replied.

The carny waved his hand at the man as a way of dismissing his claim.

"Step right up, folks. Win here and win big. All it takes is one quarter to land on a plate and bring one of these fantastic bears home to your wife or kids. Anyone can be a winner."

The man in black removed ten more dollars from his wallet. Quarters took flight, struck the plate, and slid into the collection bin.

By now, a small crowd had gathered to watch and cheer on the man in black. Although the group knew the carnival ran fixed games, they wanted to see the man receive something for his efforts.

They encouraged him to press forward every time one of his quarters hit the plate and fell.

When the last quarter left his fingers and failed to win a prize, the man in black finally spoke.

"I'd like to make a wager, sir."

"You bet. One quarter wins one of these wonderful bears. Take one home to your wife and children, and they'll love it!"

The man in black slowly shook his head and said, "No, a different kind of wager."

The carny stopped pacing around and looked for a long time at the man in black.

"What are you talking about, sir?"

"I want to wager everything in my wallet."

"Sure, mister, it's your money. You can do that if you like. You keep playing, and you'll win for sure."

"I don't want a bear."

"Well, that's all I've got for prizes, mister. If you're looking for some other kind of prize, the carnival has lots of games. You could try your luck somewhere else, but I can see how close you are to winning this game. You've got your rhythm down. I know you're close. It's your choice to stay and play or try elsewhere."

"No, I like it here. But I don't want a bear. I want to make a man-to-man wager. I'll bet what you want, and that means you bet something I want," the man in black said.

The crowd watched with intensity. A large wager greatly interested the group.

"Well, I can't say that I'm sure of what it is you want. Hey, I'm not allowed to alter the rules. A quarter on the plate wins you a bear," the carny said.

There was a strange twinkle in the man in black's eyes that the carny didn't like. The night was growing late, and part of him wanted to close up shop for the evening and call it a night. He was sure the collection bins held over five hundred dollars for the day's take. He could close up and be happy with a profitable day, but something about the stranger intrigued him.

"I could lose my booth if I did that, mister. If there were any illegal betting going on around here, it would have to benefit me more than you're willing to wager," the carny said.

"I don't think anyone around here is going to speak to your fellow employees about this, especially when you lose the wager," the man in black said.

He retrieved his wallet again and removed the remaining cash. Slowly, he fanned the bills out on the counter. Thirty-two one-hundred dollar bills lay before the carny.

The carny stared at the crisp bills and ran his pink tongue across his crooked, yellow teeth. His eyes switched from the money to the man and back again.

"That sure is a lot of money, mister. What kind of wager are you talking about?"

Now the crowd was restless as voices rose and fell while being told to be quiet so they could hear the man in black.

"I'll wager this money here that I can land four quarters in a row on one plate. I'll only need four quarters. If I miss a single quarter out of four, you win the bet."

The carny thought of how many quarters the man had already gone through this evening. There was no chance the man could even land a single quarter, let alone four in a row.

"Sounds like a rich bet. And just what is it I'm putting into the pot for this wager?"

"I don't want a bear, that's for sure, but I sure would like your car if I win."

The faces in the crowd turned to each other and whispered.

The carny released a bellowing laugh that sounded eerily like the hee-haw of a burro.

"That's a strange bet, mister. You don't even know what kind of car I drive. What made you want to bet that money against my car, of all things?"

The man in black shrugged. "Are we making a wager or not?"

The carny looked at the row of bills again. He thought of his beat-down, rusted sedan that was more reasonably ready for the scrap heap than to change hands for a hefty payday like this.

"Why the heck not make the deal? It sounds like you sure need a car. I suppose I could wager my car against your cash. So you know, my car is about one hundred miles north of here, in the town of Gilda. That's where I live, you see? Depending on how things go, you'll have to go about collecting it yourself. I'm sure not going to deliver it to you."

"Fine," the man in black said and held out his hand.

The carny looked at that pale hand for a long, uncomfortable moment.

"I wager this money. You wager your car. Just so we're clear on this bet, I want everything currently in your car as well. It's the bet between us, and it's a fair bet," the man in black said.

The carny thought of the rusted tools in the trunk, the ashtray filled with cigarette butts, and the floorboards littered with fast-food wrappers.

Still holding out his hand, the man in black said, "When you make a wager with a man, you shake his hand."

The carny stepped forward and took the man's hand. The handshake was brief as the carny quickly pulled away.

He thought for sure the man was secretly concealing embers of a fire in his palm.

"Quite a shake you've got there. All right, so let's play, and no tricks. You've got to stand right there and make your throws. There's no hopping over the counter and dropping the quarters on the plate," the carny said. He placed four quarters beside the row of bills.

The man in black slowly picked up the quarters, studied them with an amusing wonder, selected the first one, and tossed it. The quarter landed, briefly slid, and remained on the red plastic plate.

The crowd roared and clapped the man in black on the shoulders.

He selected the second quarter, made his throw, and landed the quarter beside the first.

The crowd came alive again.

That's impossible, the carny thought. *This man's luck sure turned around. There's no way he'll land three of them. I've never seen a person land three.*

The man in black threw another quarter, which hit the other quarters and held in place.

The crowd hollered and clapped, but they quickly fell silent with anticipation at the throw of the last quarter.

The man in black offered a smile that disgusted the carny. The carny was sure the man had played him from the beginning. He was sure the man in black had purposely missed the quarters earlier to raise the wager.

The carny thought, *Even if the damn quarter sticks, he's going to be disappointed with what he receives for his efforts. He thought he could con me, well, maybe he did, but he can have the piece of crap car. Let him go up there and collect it. He'll be kicking himself once he gets a look at it.*

The last quarter flew, hit the plate, and in a strange sense of slow-motion, it landed on top of another quarter.

The crowd went wild. Cheers ran across the darkening carnival.

The carny held up his hands in an easy surrender to the man in black.

"That was a hell of a show, buddy. I suppose fair is fair. As I've said, you'll have to collect the car yourself." The carny shuffled under the counter and removed a pencil and paper. He jotted down his home address and held it out to the man.

The man in black waved away the offered address.

"There's no need for that. Unfortunately, your car lost control a moment ago. It crashed into a building and then caught fire. I don't have use for it anymore."

"What the hell are you talking about, mister?"

"A bet is a bet. I told you I wanted your car and everything in it. Your wife, Melinda, was on her way to her sister's house to watch their favorite television show. However, vehicles sometimes get a mind all their own. I'm sorry to tell you she didn't survive," the man in black said, collecting his money and placing his wallet back in his pocket.

"How the hell did you know my wife's name? Saying something like that isn't funny, mister," the carny said.

"I never tell jokes. I only make wagers. I've been doing it for a long, long time. I suggest next time you fully understand all that's at stake before shaking someone's hand."

Dread

Nick Andrews lives with dread. It's a simple thing to understand. Every human has, at one time, suffered the emotional touch of dread. Although each of us feels it briefly come and go, the sensation never left Nick's heart or mind in the past twelve years. With a certain absent-mindedness, Nick learned to live with the overwhelming condition. The overpaid doctors and psychiatrists over the years claimed nothing was mentally wrong with him. They said they could not cure what was undamaged. They lied with a straight face, and he knew it. Something was wrong, and the deep seed of dread starting in the core of his brain had grown over time and was now running wildly through his veins and now consumed him completely.

For Nick, dread was a difficult thing to cope with these days. But murder, well, murder was easy. Nick had lived and breathed murder since he first realized what lay beneath the skin of human beings. There was much more than flesh, muscle, and bone. There was evil within, lying in wait, uniting, and destroying the very fabric of civilization. Long ago, humankind was a creation of perfection. The world was once a place of perfect harmony. Now love had corrupted and torn apart at the seams. The thing living inside humans was at fault. It was to blame for the hate, greed, and terror they invoked. Nick was finding them, and he was taking back what was rightfully his—to live without dread.

Nick Andrews stood before the study's large picture window and watched the night. There was a serenity about the night, a reflection of calm, of being born to a world alone. There was no fear, no dread, about the night, but what lingered *in* the night was an entirely different matter.

He sipped a snifter of brandy as he watched the headlights of the limo cut through the blackness and pull into the driveway. The car parked under the portico, and two men emerged. The driver rounded the vehicle and removed the luggage from the trunk. Both men then entered the estate's front door. Nick could hear them walking across the marble floor of the entrance and moved up the staircase.

Nick glanced over his shoulder. A light flickered on in one bedroom down the hall. A moment later, Henry stepped into the dark study and stood obediently in the doorway.

"I trust everything went well? Have you accommodated Malcolm's needs?" Nick asked.

"Yes, sir, I arrived at the university on schedule. The drive home was without problems. I tended to his things and placed him in the guest room you recommended. He is washing up at this moment," Henry said.

"Well done. When Malcolm finishes, please show him to the study."

"As you wish, sir." Henry quickly slipped out of the room.

For Nick, a long, grueling spring semester had finally passed. Nearly five months had gone by since he had seen Malcolm. Five months seemed like an eternity to be apart from the only person in the world who could understand him. Now Malcolm was here for the summer before returning to school in the fall. They would have nearly three months to rebuild the friendship that Malcolm's quest for higher education interrupted.

"They say that when you stare into the night like that, the night stares right back at you," Malcolm Reynolds said as he walked into the study and searched for the light switch.

"I see the malevolent capabilities of the night, and in return, it sees mine as well. Maybe we feed off each other, nursing on the other's strengths and canceling out the flaws."

"Or maybe you're full of crap, and you've been giving yourself too much time to read between the lines that don't exist," Malcolm said and laughed.

Nick cracked a smile and nodded in agreement. They approached each other and embraced. As Nick drew back, he regarded the mildly changed appearance of his longtime friend.

"You look well. I hope you've been eating right and getting proper exercise. I trust you're not keeping your nose buried in those books all day long."

Malcolm studied his friend and grinned. "You should really worry about yourself. I know I do. When was the last time you broke down these walls of yours and stepped outside in the sunlight? You're going to drive yourself mad if you continue down this wicked path you're on. Has Henry tried to convince you to get out and breathe some fresh air?"

"Henry knows better than to broach a subject like that. I pay him to take care of the estate and my requirements, not to befriend me and convince me to do things I don't wish to do."

"Besides me, Henry is the only other person on the

planet who cares about your well-being. He's taken care of you since you were a kid, especially during the time since your parents passed away. With me away at school all the time, he's the only one who can watch over you," Malcolm said as he walked to the bar and poured himself a scotch.

"For your information, I do leave the estate from time to time."

"Ah, I have an overwhelming notion telling me that the only other place you retreat to is the cabin. Tell me that I'm wrong."

"There's a certain tranquility about the cabin. It helps me collect my thoughts and be at peace. What's so wrong about that?" Nick asked.

Malcolm sipped his scotch and casually watched his friend over the rim of the glass. The complexity of Nicholas Andrews was great, and Malcolm didn't have the mental strength to delve into the matter at hand. So he offered a gentle smile and shook his head.

"I suppose nothing at all. I just want you to see the horizon of possibilities. Each day is a gift. Just don't live your life with regrets of lost time. I'm going to change the subject because I can see your face is contorting in that certain way when you get irritated. How about we go down to the kitchen and cook something spectacular? We have a lot to catch up on," Malcolm said.

As the summer days came and went, Nick found himself in a perpetual state of enlightenment. Malcolm's return was the remedy Nick required for some time.

They first met in the early years of childhood at the Woodbridge Academy. The private school was only open to gifted youngsters from wealthy and socially elevated backgrounds. Less than two thousand students were allowed to attend each year.

Nick and Malcolm discovered they had a lot in common. They had both been born and raised in Massachusetts. They each had an IQ testing off the charts. They were the top students at the academy, and with that honor, they received special privileges. To a certain degree, they had become untouchable by the faculty. There were frequent days that the teenage boys needed to unwind and release any burdening frustration. It had begun with mild destruction of school windows, the unexplained injuries of the adjacent neighborhood dogs, and eventually escalated to fights with other students on the school premises. The teachers, mostly, looked the other way about their destructive behaviors.

Malcolm had learned to let go of his hate over time and remained one of the most remarkable students the academy ever produced. Nick had pushed beyond the limits the school delegates would allow. His senior year, Nick went on a tangential rage near the end and viciously assaulted a teacher for reasons unknown, and was immediately expelled.

Malcolm graduated and continued his education at the Massachusetts Institute of Technology, focused on political science. His overall plan was to follow his father's footsteps into the U.S. Senate.

Nick withdrew from the world at an alarming rate. His social curiosity wilted, and he quickly built an impenetrable wall around himself, and only a select few could reach him through this barricade. Henry could only breach the structure so far, but Malcolm was sure that he was the only person not knocked back by Nick's emotional defenses.

"So tell me, is there a certain female someone I should know about?" Nick asked as they wandered the garden in early July afternoon.

Malcolm paused, inspected a tulip, and slowly breathed in the scent. A sly smile played across his lips, and he shifted his sight to Nick.

"Actually, I have a certain female someone. Even during my overabundant class schedule, I've attracted a beautiful young classmate. Her name is Victoria Bell. She's something else. I hope you understand that you've ruined the surprise. She is coming here next week, and I want you to meet."

A brief show of dread raced across Nick's face. "She's coming here?"

"I thought it was time for you to make another friend. I promise that you'll adore her. Her personality is something to admire. I've never met someone so free-flowing, so unbound by the worries of the world."

"But you didn't even ask for permission to bring someone to the estate. Don't start getting yourself an enormous head. Remember that this is my home, and you're my guest. Frankly, I find it rude of you to presume that something this dramatic would be just fine with me."

"Dramatic? Nick, I think you're getting a little worked up. I only wanted her to stay for a day or two. That's all. She's important to me. You're my best friend, and I hoped that you'd be happy for me."

Nick turned and observed the grounds. The dread was there, but it was brief during the day. They couldn't get to him during the day, only at night. If he were inside at night, then he'd be safe. They couldn't penetrate the house walls. They could never take his life as he had taken theirs.

Nick forced a smile and gently touched Malcolm's shoulder. "I'm happy that you're happy. I was just a little surprised. Forgive me. You know how I am around new acquaintances. It would delight me for her to come. I'd love to meet the woman who stole your heart, Malcolm."

The day Victoria Bell arrived was when Nick felt the hatred within flare more intense than Hell's fires.

Malcolm was jittery all day with anticipation of her arrival. He strode the front grounds of the estate, his eyes continually switching to the long drive in expectation of seeing her vehicle approaching. The sun raced across the sky, and Victoria had still not come. Nick felt a specific relief at this. Even a single day with an unwanted stranger in his home was one day too much.

Nick spent that afternoon and evening mimicking Malcolm with an opposite expectation of the events to come. Nick stood at his usual place at the study window and casually watched Malcolm's pacing, then briefly found a seat on the cobblestone stairs and then continued his pacing. Suddenly Malcolm's attention fixed on something in the distance.

Nick felt his heart drop. He spotted a red sports car cresting the estate entrance as twilight found the land. The car parked in the front drive, and a slim blonde girl, maybe just past her twentieth birthday, stepped out. Malcolm quickly stepped to her, and they embraced. Their faces were bright and overwhelmed with love. Malcolm retrieved her suitcase, and they walked to the edge of the garden. Victoria took in the majestic view of the estate.

The sun disappeared beyond the horizon, and beautiful orange and yellow light cast across the sky. The shadows were growing long on the estate grounds.

Nick's eyes shifted from the reunited couple to the yard. The ground began moving. At first, an untrained eye wouldn't be able to witness this, but Nick had become accustomed to the unnatural movement to the slightest degree. Things were coming alive under the cover of the stretching night.

The things that came alive under Nick's observation were the things he dreaded the most. It began with a minor tremble of the earth, shifting flecks and clumps of dirt that pushed toward the sky as if something massive and sinister were breaking free from a tomb beneath. But there was nothing beneath the shifting ground. Whatever forces in the universe that controlled the category of revenge definitely had a wicked and creative mind.

The ground drew together as two columns morbidly formed arms and hands. The groups of dirt pushed higher, and as it did this, the transformation became more defined as heads, arms, torsos, and legs appeared. As each section of the yard solidified enough to become stable, the figures stood.

There was nothing human about the figures in the yard. They were soldiers brought forth to exact revenge long since deserved. They stepped closer to the house. There were thirty-two bodies, and they filled the front grounds. Some of them had grass-covering parts of their structure, others had flowers jutting from various places on their bodies, and some even had small stones and twigs that had become part of their structural makeup.

They stood in the vanishing twilight and rotated their heads to gaze up at him. They wanted him to come outside. They desired to extinguish his life. As much as they longed for these things, he would not let them take his life. Not tonight or ever would they get what they wanted most.

Of course, Malcolm and Victoria couldn't see them or even hear them. They only showed themselves to Nick. He believed that even though the two were standing among the hoard of dirt figures, those ungodly creatures wouldn't harm them. Victoria was pointing directly at one of them, but of course, it wasn't the freakish creation she was directing Malcolm's attention to, but something lovely in the distance.

"I dare you to take her. Seize her and tear her apart by the limbs," Nick whispered to them.

They continued to stand in place and watch Nick, showing no interest in Malcolm and Victoria.

He knew all the strangely distorted faces. In the last dozen years, he had taken each of their lives. The dirt had not been perfectly molded, but well enough that the features were recognizable. His sight shifted to the two figures standing before all the rest. Oddly, they were holding hands. The creations bore the faces of his parents, now ten years dead.

Malcolm and Victoria moved across the grounds and came inside.

Nick stepped away from the window and the sight that had become a regular nighttime scene. Even though he no longer stood at the window, Nick knew they would not leave. They would stare at that empty window until daylight broke. The estate grounds would then appear as lustrous and perfect as it did each day, as though the earth was undisturbed.

Nick was so unimpressed with Victoria that he distastefully shook her hand, offered a half-hearted smile and a curt remark. He then excused himself, claiming he had taken ill, which was true. The thought of this woman in his house made him nauseous. She intruded by coming between two best friends, and would consume Malcolm's time during her brief stay.

As he lay in bed that first night, he heard them making love. They weren't secretive about their passion. Honestly, Nick knew Victoria had purposely made such a ruckus in the bedroom to torment him by feeding his jealousy. She was claiming through her moans that she was the center of Malcolm's attention. She showed dominance in the household, and she dared Nick to take action against her. Nick was sure that even Henry could hear them from the servant's quarters behind the main house.

As Nick quietly listened, he realized something. For the first time in years, he wasn't feeling the never-ending daily cycle of dread. Nick was feeling something much different. He was experiencing rage, and the emotion tasted like a fine wine. An idea was consuming his mind. He closed his eyes and let that single thought flourish.

Victoria's moans and cries for God faded as Nick's mind played games. He decided he was going to do something despicable. The idea could destroy his friendship with Malcolm. For the first time, Nick decided he didn't care anymore. Malcolm became someone entirely different from their school days. Their once closeness seemed to be on the fast track out the door anyhow.

A curious thought circled through Nick's mind as he drifted off to sleep.

I wonder what Victoria dreads?

The brief stay had automatically extended from two days to four and then five. As a week came and went, Nick decided he'd had just about enough of Victoria Bell.

Nick quietly observed as Victoria and Malcolm roamed the estate grounds. They constantly held hands and kissed while strolling the elegance that the estate offered. As the days moved on, Nick could feel the rage grow more intense.

On Tuesday night, Malcolm said that he was going to town to get champagne to celebrate. What he planned on celebrating was unknown to Nick, and he didn't care. Nick lost interest in Malcolm and everything that made him happy.

Victoria remained at the estate. It was the moment Nick saw a perfect opportunity and took it.

Nick became the gracious host and offered Victoria a drink and a relaxed conversation in the study. When Victoria's head swam and felt strangely abnormal, Nick started asking more personal questions. There were certain things about Victoria he wanted to know. She was reluctant at first to disclose these private things, but the drug Nick had mixed with her brandy had lowered her guard and loosened her tongue.

What Victoria dreaded most was a simple thing that consumed millions of people around the world. Victoria had an overwhelming phobia of heights. She felt a vicious phase of vertigo when she traveled higher than two stories.

Happily, the highest point of Nick's mansion reached over four stories.

Nick was sitting in a leather wingback chair reading in the library when Malcolm returned to the estate.

"Hey, I bought the most expensive champagne they had. I'm not sure if it's any good, but I figured we could give it a shot."

"I'm curious about the occasion," Nick said impassively.

Malcolm offered his prize-winning smile. It was a smile that had won over the hearts of many young women along the way. Only this smile was a little different. It wasn't the typical smile Malcolm used to get what he wanted. It was a smile that said he already had what he wanted. Nick thought that this was the look of a fortunate man and one satisfied with his current life position. It was a shame that Nick had to ruin Malcolm's moment in the blissful sun.

Nick took the bottle of champagne to the bar. He removed the foil from the bottle, unscrewed the fastening wire, and popped the cork free. The cork shot across the room and caught the edge of a painting, knocking it askew. Foam erupted from the bottle, and Nick quickly placed a glass beneath the bubbling stream.

Malcolm appeared nervous as he checked himself in the mirror and tried collecting his thoughts.

"What we're celebrating is my engagement to Victoria. I proposed earlier today, and she said yes! Can you believe that I'm getting married?" Malcolm asked and then laughed with delight.

Nick's lower lip curled down, and his head nodded solemnly. Nick turned from Malcolm as he poured the drinks. He reached over the bar and retrieved a small glass vial. He spilled the contents into one drink.

"That sure is something else. I must admit that you've caught me by surprise." Nick smiled as if he had sampled rotten fish. In fact, Nick was nowhere near that strange turn in the road that some called "surprised." During Nick and Victoria's intriguing drug-induced conversation, he had learned all he wished about the marriage proposal and much more.

Nick handed Malcolm a glass and said, "To a prosperous future for the both of you. May your days be grand, your nights even grander, and I wish you wonderful children along the way."

As they clinked glasses and drank, Malcolm's eyes switched around. "Wait, I think we should have Victoria here for this. I think she's also becoming a big part of your life. Our friendship now includes Victoria as well."

"This moment is just for the two of us, a moment between close friends. She'll be here in a little while. Just drink up and enjoy. I'll make sure we save her some," Nick said and drank the pleasant tasting champagne.

"I didn't see Victoria on the front grounds or in our bedroom as I came in. Do you know where she's gone off?"

"Henry took her out dove hunting."

Malcolm nearly spat out the mouthful of champagne as he said, "Dove hunting? Victoria wouldn't shoot a harmless dove."

Nick returned to the wingback chair. "I'm only kidding. I spoke with her earlier and I learned she was incapable of hurting animals."

"Don't you mean she *is* incapable of hurting animals? You said she *was*."

"Yes, I said what I meant. Victoria told me about her beliefs that all things deserve life and that even in extreme cases, she couldn't force herself to harm another person or creature. I took that statement into account, which made it so much easier for me to do what I did."

Malcolm was suddenly alarmed. He was well aware of Nick's darker alter ego. He was never aware of Nick's killing rampage over the years, but he knew Nick could quickly lash out in unspeakable violence without warning.

Nick dropped the champagne glass, and it shattered with a concussion in the awkward stillness of the study.

"What the hell did you do, Nick?" he said as he moved forward, his fists clenching.

"Relax. There's no need to come undone. Instead of telling you, I believe showing you would be a little more interesting," Nick said.

By the time Malcolm hit the bottom of the staircase, his head had gone from a feeling of glorifying high spirits to a brutal crashing tidal wave. Something was very wrong with how he was feeling. Malcolm enjoyed champagne many times before, but never felt intoxicated after a single glass. Champagne usually made his sight and thoughts loopy after too many drinks, but this was something entirely different.

Malcolm kept a firm grasp on the railing as he made his way down to the front door. He was feeling a definite uneasiness and a little worried about Nick's erratic mood change. Malcolm hadn't seen Victoria since his return from town. Whatever Nick wanted to show him, he was sure that it wasn't necessarily something he wanted to see.

As they made their way outside, Malcolm felt his nerves dramatically calm. He held his hand in front of his face and inspected it. He wasn't sure why he had done this, but it confirmed something he had earlier suspected. His hand blurred, and there were too many fingers dancing around. Malcolm was sure that Nick had put something a little more than champagne in his glass.

Nick comically watched Malcolm's strange performance. A wicked smile curved his lips.

"As you must be well aware, I've introduced you to a super cocktail of my creation. It won't harm you in any physical way. It will only make you more compliant than usual. There are questions I'm going to ask, and I desire the truth."

"What have you done with Victoria?"

"Follow me. Victoria's in the garden waiting for us."

Malcolm stumbled across the cobblestone walk as they moved toward the garden. He turned his attention to the sky and observed the aura surrounding the sun—a multitude of colors pulsing from the giant yellow orb. The sky seemed to be alive with a playful radiance. The clouds jumped about as if they were children playing in a field of sunshine. The beautiful blue sky was calling out to him, calling for him to fly upward and play in the endless fields of wonder. He thought that if maybe he could reach out a little farther, he could touch —

Nick was snapping his fingers in Malcolm's face. His attention drew back. He was desperately trying to find some level of focus.

"Are you back with me now?" Nick asked.

"Where's Victoria?"

"I always thought that you were a man with a one-track mind. I apologize. It seems I gave you a stronger dose than I gave Victoria. Before I show you where she is, there is only one thing I wish to know."

"Where is she, Nick?" Malcolm was trying to build the rage within, but the drug counteracted his attempt.

"In due time you will see her again, old friend. First, answer this one simple question: what do you dread?"

"Are you serious? Dread? What do I dread?"

"That's the question on the table. Let's see if you're brave enough to answer it," Nick said.

The dizziness overwhelmed Malcolm, and he took a seat on the garden bench and held his head in his hands. His mind wouldn't quit goddamn swimming. Dread? Was that an honest question? If he answered the question, would Nick take him to Victoria? If it was that easy to satisfy Nick, then Malcolm was going to give him the answer.

"Victoria is waiting for you."

"Why is it you don't already know the answer to that question?"

Nick gave him a puzzled look.

"You know how my parents died. You know. So that means you also know what I dread. I don't know why you're doing this, but as soon as you take me to Victoria, we're leaving the estate. I'm afraid you've gone too far this time. I can tell you with all sincerity that I won't ever return."

Nick hadn't even heard the last part of Malcolm's statement; he could only focus on a time long lost. Nick thought about Malcolm's parents, which he'd only seen half a dozen times before their death. They seemed like nice enough people, a little dull for Nick's taste. It was a shame that they had to die so horribly.

A light brilliantly flickered in Nick's mind.

"Yes, they died in a train wreck. I remember now. Your father had been drunk as they drove home from a charity auction. He tried to race the car across the tracks before the train got there. A simple lapse of judgment had cost them their lives. A massive impact like that had probably blinked out their existence before the gas tank ruptured like it did, burning them to a blackened crisp."

Malcolm stood and hurled himself toward Nick. His balance and aim were wrong, and he went crashing painfully to the ground.

"How could you say something so awful? My parents were decent people. Please tell me what the hell you did with Victoria. Where is she?" Malcolm screamed.

"I gave you my word that I would take you to her. She's right there," Nick said and pointed idly to the garden.

Still lying on the ground, Malcolm shifted his head and, through blurred vision, searched the area Nick directed.

"I don't see her, Nick. I can't see her!"

"No, I can't imagine that you'd be able to. I'm not suffering the drug effects as you are, so not even I can see Victoria beneath several feet of dirt."

"What do you mean beneath the dirt? What did you do, Nick?" Malcolm yelled as he tried to find the strength to push himself from the ground. He wrapped his arms around his face, mumbling something incoherent.

"There was a slight accident while you were in town. With only a moderate dose Victoria had ingested, she freely spoke of her fear of heights. I took it upon myself to show her the wonderful view of the estate grounds from the north gable. Unfortunately, the drugs made her balance a little out of whack, and she tumbled right out the window to the patio below. The sound of the impact her body made was horrifying, as you can imagine. I took it upon myself to tend to her remains. I buried her in the garden, right beneath the tulips I often watched her admire. I'm truly sorry for your loss, my friend."

"No, Nick, that isn't true. Not even you could be stupid enough to do something that cruel."

"I speak only the truth. If it's stupidity you wish to call it, then very well. Since we're speaking on the matter, I believe that I'm going to do something else foolish," Nick said, and quickly stepped forward and jabbed a syringe in the crook of Malcolm's neck.

Malcolm's hand went to his throat. "You bastard! I don't understand why you're doing this. We're friends, good friends."

"I know. It was a wonderful friendship while it lasted. Unfortunately, you just had to bring an outsider into it. You've changed a great deal. You've become someone I no longer trust or respect. I'm afraid I have no choice but to dissolve this relationship. I'm going to miss you, Malcolm. You're the only one I've ever cared about in my life. Godspeed, old friend."

Someone was whistling from miles away, whistling that same steady rhythm. Whatever the tune was, it was vaguely familiar to Malcolm.
Whaaan. Whaaan. Whaaaaaan!

The haze was slowly lifting from his mind like a retreating shadow. His arms and legs moved as if lead weights were binding him down. After a few moments, the invisible restraints released.

The darkness of the area was nearly complete, except for a pinhole of light at his feet. He tried to get closer to the light, but he couldn't maneuver in the confined space.

Malcolm felt around in the darkness, finding nothing more than a steel surrounding and carpet and not much else. He placed his hands on the coffin lid and pushed. The thing wouldn't budge. After another moment of investigation, he understood the horror of the situation. He realized it wasn't a steel coffin, but the trunk of a car.

By closer inspection of prodding the hole with his foot in which the light shone through, Malcolm figured out that it was a rust hole in the car's rear panel. Whatever kind of car it was, it had to be small because he was having a tough time getting himself situated enough by rotating his body. After an agonizing minute of his spine crying out while he flipped the position of his head and feet, he could get his eye close to the hole. The rusted hole was low on the panel, but if he pressed his cheek to the carpet, he could get a much better view of the light shining through the opening.

Whaaaan! Whaaaan!

It was now that Malcolm realized how much he misunderstood the situation. It was a far stretch from a whistling tune. It was actually the thundering blare of a horn. Somehow in the night, the engineer spotted the car resting on the tracks.

"Oh, sweet Jesus," Malcolm whispered.

The train barreled down the tracks like a relentless force.

Malcolm took only another moment to study that glaring yellow eye before sheer panic fully gripped him. He turned onto his back and frantically searched the trunk latch. Malcolm's fingers worked in blind desperation as he tried to pop the latch free. He gave up the attempt a moment later and delivered blows with his knees to the trunk lid. He couldn't get enough force behind each strike in the restrained area of the car's trunk.

Malcolm fixed his attention on the rear seats. Although he didn't know what type of vehicle he was in, he knew some models came equipped with folding rear seats. He couldn't find release levers in the darkness to open the back.

The rumble of the tracks was nearly deafening as he struggled to grab the next brilliant idea. The horn came again. He thought his ears were going to rupture if that damn piercing blast got any closer. He kicked at the trunk lid, and for a moment, he could have sworn that the latch had given a little.

It was a sound that was unmistakable. The engineer, now realizing that the car on the tracks had no intention of moving out of the way, initiated the emergency braking system. The train kept a steady course as the tracks ran right beneath the car.

Malcolm gave in one last time. He wanted to get an idea of the train's distance. He needed some idea of exactly how much more time he had to work with before the clock stopped.

He cocked his head and pressed his left cheek to the carpet again. He heard the screeching sounds of metal on metal and the intense scream of the horn. What he saw was a bright yellow unblinking eye looking right into his soul.

Nick took another long swallow of the scotch as he looked at the clock on the wall. He had finished the task. The train's schedule was nearly as reliable as the clock.

There was no turning back because, according to the clock, Malcolm had found death moments ago. Nick felt an odd mixture of sadness and relief. The sadness was only because Malcolm had once understood the strange workings of Nick's mind. He had once been the only one that cared. Even those days had seemed to change lately. Malcolm had betrayed him. Malcolm had emotionally pulled himself away from Nick. Malcolm had fallen in love and focused his life on another road that didn't include Nick.

In Nick's opinion, something like that was torture he simply couldn't bear. So, like cancer, Nick figured the best way to cope with such a thing was simply to cut it away.

The authorities wouldn't be able to trace the beat-up old car back to him. He had purchased it years ago, and it had sat in the garage since. He had never registered the vehicle, and the seller hadn't even bothered to take down his personal information.

He never understood the impulse to purchase the vehicle so many years ago. He now figured that just maybe he had a premonition that such an opportunity like this would present itself. He was sure that the police would never find the link to their friendship. He was also positive that they would never come to the estate asking questions about the accident.

After he downed his third scotch on the rocks, Nick felt dizzy from the excessive alcohol intake this evening. He decided it was time to call it a night. When Nick reached out for the phone to call Henry to help him get to bed, he noticed that his hand stretched as if it was no longer skin, flesh, and bone, but elastic rubber. After a moment of studying this strange unknown phenomenon, he understood it wasn't a transformation of his human abilities but the warping of his mind.

He snatched up the phone and told Henry to come to

the library immediately. By the time Henry left his quarters behind the main house, Nick had slipped into a semi-catatonic state.

Henry entered the library with a casual stroll. He approached the wingback chair and smiled gently.

"Sir, I can tell by your expression that it's time we move you out of here," Henry said.

"Yeah, get me to my bedroom," Nick mumbled.

"Oh, no, I don't think that's where you'll be spending the night. I've prepared something exceptional tonight. I can see that the effects of the drugs I placed in your scotch have taken a firm hold on you," Henry said as the smile never left his face.

"Drugs? You, you drugged me?" Nick stammered.

"Of course. You must have realized that the scotch wasn't going to make you feel that way. You've just ingested twice the amount of drugs that you injected into Malcolm. I always told myself that if you did it one more time, I would see an end to everything."

"I don't understand. What have you done?" Nick said as he tried to stand, but the power of the drug was too great, and he collapsed in the chair again.

"For many years, I've looked after you as if you were my son. I knew what you had done to your parents. I knew you had killed them all those years ago. I also knew about the many others you destroyed before working up the courage to do away with your parents. Truthfully, I never cared much for your parents. I know I was their servant, but they still showed me a proper amount of respect and appreciation. However, I wasn't sad to see them go. As for the others, I looked away because I thought that killing them was one of the few things that made you happy. It was ignorance on my behalf. You weren't even happy when you did kill someone. You were simply distancing yourself from an entire world that wanted to get close to you. Then when you killed Malcolm tonight, your best friend, I knew that it was only a matter of time before you came after me. I suppose that it's in your nature. Nevertheless, it all stops tonight."

Nick tried to raise his hand to ward off Henry's advancements, but the strength simply wasn't there.

"I know what you see, Nicolas. Somehow I see them, too. Maybe they've allowed me to see them because they're relying on me to do what's necessary. When the darkness comes, I know they come out. I know they watch the house. They watch you. I think that it's a matter of them not being able to enter the light. Maybe that's what stops them from getting to you. All those people you've killed over the years want you very much, Nicolas. I think tonight I'll give them exactly what they've been longing for because it's only fair. You took everything from them. Now everything will come full circle. Have you ever found it strange that they appear the way they do? I mean, they're dirt, right? Why do they appear as dirt figures?"

"Please, Henry, please don't do this."

"I'm going to take you to the cabin. I think out there you won't be able to flee in the night. There's nothing but darkness out there. The cabin is miles from any sort of safety."

"Please."

"Full circle," Henry said again.

Henry picked up a pewter bookend from one of the shelves and hefted it to check the weight while determining exactly how hard the blow should be.

"Please," Nick murmured once more before the pewter statue clubbed the left side of his head.

Through the haze of his mind, Nick could feel the

night closing in around him. It was almost suffocating, the way it enveloped his entire body. He could even feel the black probes of the night worm into his ears and twirl around in his mind, taunting him.

Nick's eyes fluttered open, closed, and opened again. His skull was throbbing with short bursts of lightning strikes. Even in the darkness, he could tell his vision was far from normal. The cruel effectiveness of the drug Henry had given him, and the fierce blow to the head had done something wicked to his vision. The objects he was able to see in the darkness appeared in ghostlike doubles.

Nick was astonished to realize he wasn't bound. Before Henry struck him unconscious, he thought that he would awake tied down and left with nothing to do except wait for a predictable death.

Nick wearily pushed himself from the cabin floor. His legs felt incredibly wobbly, but they were able to hold him up. He took one unsteady step after another. Nick reached the front door and flipped the light switch. There was a dull click, but the lights failed to come on. He tried several more times before giving up. It was apparent that Henry had killed the main power.

As Nick started for the fuse box in the rear bedroom, he caught a movement from the corner of his eye. He pressed his face to the windowpane and glared out. At first, he thought someone was outside but only saw the night looking back at him.

Just before being bashed in the skull, Nick remembered Henry speaking of them. He remembered Henry confirming that they were real because he had also seen them lurking on the estate grounds.

They were the faces of the dead that had somehow, for some reason, come back to life to torment him, to drive him mad. It was common to see them at the estate because they had known where he lived. But out here, none of them had ever been guests at the cabin his parents had built a year before their tragic deaths. Malcolm was aware of the country cabin, but Nick had never brought him here.

So, with this sort of logic, it stands to reason that none of them would be in the night outside the window. It would be impossible, he thought.

He laughed as he pulled away from the window. Henry was a fool to believe that his plan would indeed come full circle, as he'd stated. When morning came, Nick would somehow find his way back to the estate and take care of Henry for good.

Pretty soon, old friend, you'll be one of those dirt figures staring up at me. You won't be able to enter the estate and seek revenge as much as you may desire. Like all the others, you'll have to wait for the opportunity. Someday I might get ignorant and make a mistake, but I'm sure that will be a long time from now, he thought as he carefully made his way to the fuse box.

Something thudded against the window. Nick felt an icy hand briefly seize his body as he whirled around and studied the window and the blackness beyond. His heart began to beat again with a rapid and almost painful thump.

"Who's that?" he shouted, much louder than intended.

An empty silence spoke back.

After a moment of carefully watching the window, he decided that it was nothing more than a tree branch tapping against the window from a gentle breeze.

When he turned around again to resume his heading for the fuse box, something slammed hard into the front door. The hit was hard enough to form a long, jagged crack in the wood that Nick stared at with confused horror.

"Stop it!" he shouted in a terrified voice, making it evident to the intended intruder that his fear found the surface.

Something hit the window beside the front door again, just as a forceful tap hit the window above the kitchen sink. Someone tapped with eagerness at the window in the back bedroom.

"This isn't funny, Henry. If you stop this now, I promise I won't fire you."

I'll just send you to your grave twenty fucking years early, he thought.

Something struck the front door again with more determination. The wood splintered more but held. Something was thrown or swung against the siding to his left. He spun, and half expected to see the wall collapsed from the blow.

"Stop it right now. I know there's more than one of you. None of you know what I'm capable of doing. If you stop now, I'll let it all go. If you don't stop, I promise all of you that I'm going to get my revenge in the worst possible way," Nick shouted.

Something stepped up to the window beside the front door. It was a large, almost inconceivably huge, man. No, that wasn't right. As Nick focused more, he realized that it wasn't a man at all, at least not anymore.

Malcolm, who once stood at five feet nine inches tall, was at least a foot taller. The facial structure was the same, but the body was much different, as it was now a physically intimidating creation. The Malcolm-like figure was now composed entirely of dirt, small branches, leaves, and gravel. The Malcolm-like thing smiled at him, grotesquely brown lips pulling back in what could be mistaken as a sneer.

"No, no, that's impossible. You aren't real. It's just my mind. It's my confused, drug-induced mind projecting the image," Nick whispered more to himself than to the creature outside the window.

Then Nick saw more of them. They were rising from the ground. They formed like some strange amoebas that were small granules of dirt moments ago and now stood as human imposters.

Nick snatched up a small dolphin statue from the coffee table that had been his mother's and hurled it at the window. The figure crashed through the window to the right of the Malcolm-like thing and disappeared into the night.

The Malcolm-like thing rotated its head and studied the hole. Its arm slowly came through the new opening. To Nick's amazement, the arm fell away at the elbow to the cabin floor. It fell into a powdery mess and began moving. The rest of the Malcolm-like thing started shifting through the hole until enough dirt had transferred through to reform the entire structure.

Nick watched with familiar dread as the thing completed its formation. Something else then hit the front door again, except the door no longer held as it violently broke inward. Four similar figures stood before him. They were well-known faces.

A jarring sound of breaking glass came from the bedrooms and was then followed by movement inside the cabin. The window above the kitchen sink shattered in a shower of razor-sharp fragments. Nick could hear things shuffling in the back rooms.

Nick bolted for one of the bedrooms. Large clumps of dirt were pouring in through the window. He ran to the closet, ripped open the door, found the fuse box, and flipped the main breaker.

The house remained in heavy blackness. It took a moment for Nick to understand the reason for the absence of power. Henry had already removed the fuses, and the lights would never come on.

Panicked, Nick tried to get his mind to process faster beyond its ability. Only a few ideas came to mind, but all results would reach the same conclusion: death.

Out of options, Nick barreled back through the bedroom door and into the living room with no clear idea of what he was going to do next. The place was alive with faces from the past.

Over twenty humanlike figures crowded in the living room and kitchen, and others appeared from the bedrooms and bathroom.

"It's impossible! You aren't real. It's impossible!" Nick trembled as the monstrous figures moved ever so closer. As they reached for him, Nick opened his mouth and screamed.

"All right, all right, I'm here," Detective Joe Sanders said as he entered the county morgue.

"About time. You know that you were the one hounding me about this. I can't be playing favorites by moving one case ahead of another. You know that. But I finally got around to your boy here. I guess that even when someone has more money than the vaults at Fort Knox, it doesn't stop death from eventually knocking on your door," County Coroner Michael Riven said.

"No, I don't suppose it does. This man took over his parent's pharmaceutical company when their car brakes failed and they crashed into a tree. So what did you figure out?"

"I have to say that when I began the autopsy on this man, I excitedly got into my work. It became a fascinating study right off the bat. I've read the report of the crime scene, and I have to say that the case enthralls me," Michael said.

"Great, thanks. I put a lot of hard work into the details of my reports."

"No, that isn't what I meant. Of course, your report was well done. I'll give you that. I was referring to the conditions in which you discovered the body."

"How so?"

"Well, according to your report and the photographs of the scene, you determined that Mr. Andrews died in the very same spot in which you found him."

"Do you find something to contradict that?" Joe asked.

"Well, yes, and no. Lividity suggests that the body never moved from the position on the cabin floor. Look here," Michael said as he rolled the naked corpse on the examination table.

There were dark purple splotches along the backside of the body.

"You can see that blood pooled in the lowest parts of his body. It's a clear indication that he died exactly in the position you found him," Michael said.

"All right. So I got it right, and Mr. Andrews died by the front door in the cabin."

"However, when I opened him up, I began to question your findings."

"Why?"

Michael Riven walked to a table, picked up a steel pan, and handed it to Joe.

"Okay, what's this all about?"

"What does it look like to you?" Michael asked.

"Dirt, grass, and maybe some gravel," Joe said.

"Right. Actually, it's just over six pounds of the earth I collected. I removed all of that from Mr. Andrews' lungs. He died of asphyxiation."

"You've got to be kidding me? How could someone inhale all of this? Are you saying that he was buried alive and then dug up and placed in the cabin?"

"Unlikely. I didn't find any dirt on Mr. Andrews' clothing or skin. Besides, it would be impossible for someone to inhale this amount of dirt. Even a tiny amount of this would be enough to suffocate someone. All I'm saying is that this material was in his lungs, which I found expanded nearly three times the average size. I didn't find any traces of dirt in his mouth or trachea. It's like the earth had a mind of its own and crawled down his throat, into his lungs, and refused to come out."

I Am Dimension

Endsbrook, Maryland
1938

The perplexity of my sight derived the admittance that such an astonishing vision was surely to be delusional. The vastness of the creation drew upon me something of an unimaginable fright that led me to believe that the sight before me was merely an amalgam of past and present tales collated into a single haunting vision.

I felt the rough surface of the wrought-iron gate of the estate. My hand recoiled with such terror that I nearly turned abruptly on my heels and fled for the sake of sanity.

In large cast-iron letters centered above the gate read:

Usherland

"Usherland," I said hollowly under my breath. My heart stuttered in disbelief at the name that I could only conceive in a fictitious sense.

I felt compelled to reach out once again and assure my mental state that it was a reality. As if on cue, the giant gates parted before me. I searched about but discovered no wandering eyes preying upon my arrival. It did not seem feasible that the iron gates had awakened at my touch and parted ways to my welcome.

I returned to my vehicle and shifted into gear. Hesitation overwhelmed me. I felt reluctant to break the barrier into the unknown. It would take little effort on my part to shift back gears and return down the long path I had already traveled.

I needed a bit of reassurance to convince myself that this excursion was well worth my while. I reached over to the passenger seat, retrieved my satchel, and withdrew from it the brief letter which persuaded me to journey twelve hundred miles as my response. I read the letter for perhaps the fifteenth time since its delivery. I read with a watchful eye, willing to decipher the slightest clue within the single paragraphed letter. However, I now believe that the single word printed above the gate revealed more than the mysterious letter.

The name Usher was the fictional character derived from the alcohol-induced creative nature of my great-great-grandfather.

Now you know the truth of the matter. These days I go by the name William Connelly, but my real name is William Riley Poe. My father was Jonah Clark Poe. My grandfather was Jonathan Richard Poe. My great-grandfather was Victor Garrett Poe, and my great-great-grandfather was the infamous Edgar Allen Poe. I am perhaps the last descendant of the Poe legacy. You will soon know the reason I have come to such an unraveling conclusion.

The single paragraphed letter reads:

Dearest Mr. Connelly,
I bring a most pressing matter of importance to you. Forgive the letter's briefness, but I strongly believe that we should have our conversation in person. I can only say this: our future depends upon your quest to my estate. I have enclosed a business card to which you may locate

me, as well as a generous amount of money to assist in your travels. Your promptness will be greatly appreciated.
Ratigan Usher

I knew not of the person's name or the small town of the estate's location.

It was so odd that my curiosity had overruled my decision. My first instinct was to discard the strange letter and contribute no more thought to such an outlandish request. I found it odd that someone I'd never met would believe I'd be willing to partake in such a long journey. Yet here I am. My vehicle was now idling in front of the strange estate that bore the equally strange name.

It was mystifying as to how the invisible hand of curiosity guided me here. Now I've concluded that the unanswered questions finally end and place a description to the name that coaxed me to this eerie and desolate country acreage estate.

The courage held me, and I traveled across the threshold of the entrance. I drove with a snail-like crawl down the winding gravel road to the mansion that escaped view from the perimeter.

The grounds were breathtaking. A vast collection of maple trees covered as far as the eye could see. The mountain range in the distance also added much to the scenic beauty. The solitude of the property was almost overwhelming.

I was curious whether this Ratigan fellow lived alone or with family members or even in servants' quarters. Indeed, owning such land drew me to the conclusion that Mr. Usher was financially stable and family and servants seemed to fit perfectly within the picture.

Approaching the crest of the hill, I could barely make out the roofline of the house, and just from that sight alone,

I could conceive that the house was massive. As the whole picture came into view, I witnessed not only the full scope of a mansion, but something of a living entity in itself.

"Good Lord!" I expelled.

I have never seen nor heard of anything that held such splendor. It held superiority over every great thing experienced in my lifetime. It was a mansion ten times my expectations.

I pulled forth and circled the large marble fountain. I came to a halt in the portico. As I exited the vehicle, a cordial-looking individual who offered an overwhelming sense of appeal greeted me. He was in his late fifties, with silver hair and a brilliant glow about his face. He wore the attire that perhaps only a butler of the old code would be required to wear.

"Welcome to the Usher estates, Mr. Connelly," he said as he took my hand and delivered a firm handshake. "I'm Mr. Newstead, Mr. Usher's associate."

Usher. The name stung like a wasp.

"Are you telling me that there is such a person as Ratigan Usher?"

He offered a gentle smiled and nodded. "Mr. Ratigan Usher is the sole owner of the estate. We weren't certain if you would entertain the invitation to the estate."

I couldn't bring myself to accept the coincidence of the surname that came calling from past generations. Ratigan Usher, sole owner of the estate. Incredible.

So the name on the gate was genuine. I had known such a name existed. I never expected an introduction to someone bearing the name.

Mr. Newstead retrieved my single suitcase from the trunk and gestured for me to follow his lead. We entered through the giant solid mahogany doors and into a vast entryway with marble flooring and a breathtaking crystal chandelier. Multiple hallways lead to the mansion's various wings and a spiral staircase ascending to the upper floors.

Mr. Newstead placed my suitcase at the foot of the stairs and motioned for me to follow. We walked down a brightly lit hallway lined with beautiful statues and an impressive framed collection of artwork. Some of the artists were well known to me. I ascertained that I must have passed nearly a million dollars' worth of artistic mastery in fifty feet of space.

I found myself more impressed as our journey continued. I have never been in the presence of such art and décor. I believed that even the most notorious museums around the world would be envious.

I felt that I was getting slightly winded, but thankfully we entered a sitting room. Covering the house's dark wood flooring were beautiful oriental rugs, with leather wingback chairs sitting beside the massive stone fireplace. A large roll-top mahogany desk cluttered with paperwork sat by the floor-to-ceiling windows at the north wall. Oak bookshelves with elegant leather-bound volumes lined three of the long walls.

The crackling fire was the only source of light.

Mr. Newstead led me to one of the chairs facing the hearth. Sitting before the fire was whom I presumed to be Mr. Ratigan Usher.

"Sir, I am greatly honored to introduce Mr. William Connelly," Mr. Newstead said.

Mr. Usher did not attempt to rise but only extended his hand. His fingers were long, pale, and almost ghostlike. When I shook his hand, the coldness of his touch made me quiver. He motioned for me to take one of the adjacent chairs, and wordlessly, I sat.

"Would you care for something to drink, sir?" Mr. Newstead asked.

"Cognac, please," I replied.

"Very good, sir." Mr. Newstead quietly left the room and in his wake was an awkward silence between Mr. Usher and me.

For several minutes, neither of us spoke. Only the random snaps of the fire awakened the silence. We gazed intently at one another, deciphering each other with an absence of words.

Mr. Newstead returned. He passed me a snifter of cognac, gave a short bow, and left the room once again.

As I raised the glass to my lips, I noticed that Mr. Usher had retrieved his glass from the table and mimicked my motion. His drink was also a rich shade of amber, and I thought perhaps we shared the same taste in alcohol. The cognac was smooth and greatly assisted in settling my nerves.

"Why Connelly?"

Mr. Usher's words startled me and nearly caused me to spill my drink.

"I beg your pardon?"

"Connelly isn't your real surname."

"It was my mother's maiden name," I said.

"Yes, yes, I know that. Why have you decided to change your name? Why did you not keep your original surname?" Mr. Usher said irritably.

"You mean Poe?"

"Yes." I detected the slightest hiss in his word, almost snakelike. He seemed pleased with the validation of my heritage.

I didn't understand how Mr. Usher had obtained his knowledge. I also didn't know why such a conversation should find the light of day. I honestly had nothing to hide.

So I decided to play his game unless he wanted to dig deeper into information that was not his concern.

"Well, at one point around six years ago, I believe it was, the Poe name was revived by the tale my great-great-grandfather wrote. A movie studio turned 'The Fall of the House of Usher' into a feature film with my permission. Since I'm the sole living descendant of Edgar Allen Poe, naturally, the papers and magazines wanted to interview me. Unfortunately, the movie turned out to be a sinking ship, and the studio lost money on the production. Everything was swept under the rug and forgotten."

"Yes, I've seen the movie. It was a dreadful piece, to say the very least. You still haven't answered my question. Why did you change your name?"

I shrugged and said, "I never cherished my family name. We've grown famous simply because of the strange visions of a drunk. I don't know how it is that you've uncovered my altered identity."

"I have money and connections, nothing more."

I glared at him for a long, uncomfortable moment.

"Why Usher?" I countered.

A smile danced across his lips, and he said, "It's my name, of course. I believe you know of it from the tale, but not the personal side of the matter."

"So you mean to tell me that Ratigan Usher is your real name?"

"That's exactly right," he said, as he steepled his fingers and placed them at his lips.

"So are you telling me Edgar based the characters of the short tale on actual people and events?"

"People, yes, events…" he trailed off with a slight humming sound. I thought he would leave the question unanswered when he continued. "The events that took place in 'The Fall of the House of Usher' were fictional, well, most of them anyway."

Usher quickly removed the wool blanket from his legs and stood. I hadn't suspected how tall the man was, but now realized that he towered over me by several inches.

"If you would be so good as to join me."

Without waiting for my response, Usher moved to the door. As we walked down the brick corridors, Usher began to tell his tale.

"It was in early 1840 when a mutual friend introduced our great-great-grandfathers. Edgar worked as a journalist, a literary critic, wrote essays, poems, and short fiction as a part-time career. It was early in his writing career, and already he had taken to the drink. I always believed that alcohol was the lifeblood of his creative nature. I think without the drink to fuel his imagination, Edgar would have passed through history unnoticed. Anyway, my great-great-grandfather, Darius, was a young twenty-eight at the time, and he intrigued Edgar very much. Darius was influential, wealthy, and mysterious. No one knew how he achieved his fortune or why he became obsessed with spending so much money on building such a large estate so far from any signs of civilization. Edgar had achieved some success, enough to gather Darius's attention, and he invited Edgar to the estate. Darius explained his hidden motives on the second night of Edgar's stay. Darius said he quite admired Edgar's writing. He said that he very much desired Edgar to write a tale involving the Usher family. The writing should delve into certain strange activities that would be greatly enthralling in a fictitious sense, of course. Darius wished to read and enter a world in which no other literature could compare."

"Interesting. I've never heard this story before," I told Ratigan.

"All of this information was brought to me by the documents kept in the upstairs study. Anyway, the next full day, Edgar created parts of the tale within his drunken state of mind as he snuck drinks from the bar. The rest of the story haphazardly derived from observing my relatives. The night before his departure, he finished the tale and brought it before Darius to read. The tale shocked Darius so much he forbade Edgar to speak of such doings once he left the estate grounds. Edgar gave his promise, asked for the tale back, and claimed he would be gone by the morning. Darius denied returning the work, but promised Edgar that he would be paid handsomely for it. Edgar accepted the offer and returned to his room for the final night. Mysteriously, Edgar and the work of fiction vanished sometime during the night."

I thought I knew where Ratigan was going on his indirect quest.

"I assure you that I don't know this story or the current location of this stolen work that he took. I never received any of Edgar's original tales."

Ratigan waved his hand and said, "No, no, that's not the direction in which I was heading. I'm quite sure Darius destroyed the original Usher tale. Mr. Poe, if you don't mind me calling you that, the original tale contained devastating secrets of the Usher name. My family omitted such information from the tale everyone knows of today."

"So you're telling me that Darius located Edgar and convinced him to alter the story before any publications could come to terms?"

"No, Darius and Edgar never saw each other again. Fortunately, Edgar had decided to do a series of revisions of the work. Perhaps Edgar feared extreme legal disputes if he published the story as it was. For the most part, the Usher name was one of the few things remaining within the work. Darius was distraught that the public might research personal information into the Usher family business. Darius sought the matter no further, and the rest is history."

I shook my head in disbelief. I said, "Then why exactly did you persuade me to come to your estate?"

We had reached the staircase located by the front entrance. I noticed my suitcase was missing.

"I will tell you what you wish to know tomorrow. As for now, I know you've had a long journey, and the day is late. I bid you goodnight, and I will see you in the morning for breakfast at 7:30 sharp in the dining room," Ratigan said and pointed to one of the back rooms that I assumed was the dining area.

Ratigan traveled back down the corridor and soon vanished around the corner.

Mr. Newstead cleared his throat and shook me from my trance. I quickly turned about to face the caretaker.

"I've taken the liberty of placing your things in your quarters for the night. If you will follow me, please."

We ascended the staircase to the second level. My room was extravagantly decorated. I felt like a street person taken in by wealthy relatives and told to enjoy the luxuries they offered. Ratigan, raised in such wealthy surroundings, undoubtedly found all the furnishings common, but I found everything astonishing.

There was a four-poster, king-sized bed curtained in white silk. Only skilled craftsmen with decades of experience could create the intricate carvings on the surface of the furniture's woodwork. Although I wasn't the best at identifying different species of trees, I was pretty sure I had never before seen the type of wood that covered the floor, as it was nearly black and shined like marble in the glow of the firelight.

Mr. Newstead held out his open hand and gestured toward my luggage.

"Here are your things. Please unpack your clothing and place them in the wardrobe over there. Your bathroom is through that door there. I've started a fire, which should warm up the room in a short while. You might need to add firewood throughout the night if it gets too cold."

"Oh, thank you. I think it will be all right. I'm fairly tired from the long trip, and I'll most likely sleep soundly throughout the night."

"I expect so. The house is quiet at all hours of the day and night. The exterior brick walls and windows are thick. I don't believe you'll even be woken at dawn by the song of the birds."

Mr. Newstead bid me goodnight and departed.

I unpacked my things, put on my sleepwear, and freshened up in the elegantly styled bathroom. I placed another log in the fire, parted the silk bed drapery, and collapsed onto the bed. The comfort was heavenly. I had just enough energy to slip beneath the bedding, and with that, my eyes quickly closed. Even the soft crackle of the fire offered to make my transition to sleep a simple one.

A single thought raced through my mind as I felt sleep approach.

How had the Usher family acquired such wealth?

The morning was glorious, as golden sun rays cast glimmering streams across the bed and floor. I slipped from the sheets, stretched, and moved to the window. The view reached across the estate grounds, the forest, and the mountains beyond. I retrieved my watch and checked the time. I was appalled to discover that it was nearly a quarter past nine. I had always been an early riser. I thought of

Ratigan telling me that breakfast was at 7:30 sharp. I hoped I hadn't insulted my guest so early in my stay.

I quickly washed, dressed, and left the room. I was startled when I stepped into the hallway to find Mr. Newstead standing against the wall beside the bedroom door.

He greeted me with a smile and said, "Your breakfast is waiting for you in the dining room. Please, follow me."

"I'm so sorry. I hadn't planned on sleeping so late. I hope I haven't upset Mr. Usher," I said as we went down the hall to the stairs.

"It's quite all right. Mr. Usher is aware your day was long. I told him I would wait and prepare breakfast when you were ready. Mr. Usher has gone for a walk around the estate grounds."

I felt terrible that my oversleeping had inconvenienced both Mr. Usher and Mr. Newstead. The man must have stood beside my bedroom door for well over an hour, waiting.

The dining area was a modern elegance of priceless artwork, a large marble fireplace, and a mahogany table and chairs that nearly traveled the room's length. I settled in one of the chairs at the farthest end next to the fireplace. Mr. Newstead appeared moments later, pushing a silver cart with covered plates and bowls. He removed the stainless steel covers and began placing the dishes around me. I could only imagine consuming an eighth of the offering. I felt up to the challenge. I loaded my plate with eggs over easy, hash browns, bacon, sausage, toast with strawberry jam, a bowl of oatmeal, and a tall glass of orange juice. I had ample time to eat and relax, as my stomach felt comfortably full.

"I trust everything was satisfactory?" Mr. Newstead said as he entered from the kitchen.

"Yes, everything was wonderful. Thank you."

"You're very welcome."

He removed the plates and bowls from the table, placed them on the cart, and wheeled them away. I was left alone and wondered if Mr. Newstead would return and instruct me on what I would do next. Just as I was about to excuse myself and return to my room, Ratigan entered the dining room.

"I trust you slept well?"

"Yes, better than a baby."

"Wonderful. If you're up for a different kind of experience, I would like to show you something and receive your honest opinion on my artwork collection I keep in the lower level."

"Of course. You've been a gracious host, and I would be honored to see."

We briefly toured the mansion's east wing before descending a concrete spiral staircase and arriving in a subterranean area. This place instantly held an eerie sense as I had little trouble envisioning ghosts wandering the dark corridors and terrorizing all those daring enough to journey into this part of the mansion.

Ratigan produced two candles from a small wooden box at the foot of the staircase and lit them. The shadows slightly receded. Ratigan led me by candlelight. The basement was nothing more than large blocks that made up the floor, walls, and ceiling. The blocks were primarily covered in mold, as the substructure was incredibly damp and dark.

We reached an intersection that had three other corridors veering in various directions and stretching into blackened abysses. We stayed to the left and followed the corridor until we entered a great room that reached farther than my candle's strength. I thought the ceiling must have towered twenty feet over my head. I felt an emptiness penetrate my body like a spear. It seemed to consume me and pull me deeper into its silent dread. I couldn't shake the sense of terror down here.

Ratigan told me to wait as he walked along the walls and lit mounted candles. As the light filled the room, I felt my tension ease only a little. I was able to observe strange objects filling the room. Ratigan took my elbow and led me to the first mysterious structure.

"The basement is not equipped with electricity. I planned to have electricians oversee the development, but then I decided the basement's ambiance needed to remain. I feel that candlelight gives more depth, more realism, to what I have here. This one was my first attempt at the world of art. If you observe close enough, I believe you will understand its meaning."

I held my candle steadily in front of me and accepted my first notion of what it was.

It was a brick formation designed into a cube. The bricks were not large like the substructure in which we stood. Instead, Ratigan had used small, smooth stones for the structure and intentionally left it unfinished. There were half a dozen stones yet to be set into place. Behind that empty slot was a desolate blackness. A small pile of unused stones lay before the structure and hardened mortar and a used trowel. I understood its meaning.

I could feel Ratigan's devilish grin upon me. He must have known the wheels of my mind were rapidly turning. Yes, this was yet another mysterious puzzle piece of my host's purpose.

A recreation of "The Cask of Amontillado", a famous work of fiction by Edgar, was sitting before me.

"Charming," I said with obvious disgust.

"Oh, that's not all. I want you to close your eyes and listen closely," Ratigan said excitedly.

Although I was hesitant to close my eyes even for a moment in this place, I did as he suggested. It took a bit of time, but I finally heard the distinctive sounds of rattling chains and a lonely moaning coming from within.

Please, Lord, tell me this man has not lost his perception of reality and concealed someone within the hideous tomb, I thought.

"It's... strange." It was all I could manage to say.

Ratigan didn't seem offended by this, but pleased by my uncertainty at his dismaying work.

"If this delights you, then I think you must see this."

I had a fear he was right. Deep inside me, I wanted more of the madness.

It was madness I received. Should I place it on such an unqualified pedestal, the following art masterpiece was that of "The Tell-Tale Heart". It was another one of Edgar's stories. There were three lifelike wax mannequins. Two mannequins dressed in policeman attire stood before a third man buckled down upon his knees with his hands clamped over his ears, his face twisted by insanity. Again, I listened for the sound that was only fitting for this creation. Ratigan no doubt thrived for me to hear the sound of the beating heart. It was there, rhythmic and maddening, the constant drumming heart of the murdered old man buried beneath the floorboards. As Ratigan already mentioned, there was no electricity in the basement, so I knew not how he created his artworks' sound effects. Honestly, I didn't want to know.

Two heartbeats played in my ears, the stage sound effects and that of my own thundering heart. I felt the overwhelming need to buckle upon the brick floor, much like the mannequin before me. I could not take much more.

Ratigan had cracked my mental ability to withstand his devilish intentions.

I wanted to grasp him by the collar, pull him close to my face and scream a fury of questions and demand the answers. I felt this was what he desired, but I would not allow him to win this wicked game.

Ratigan thankfully brought me the relief I needed. He said, "You're looking slightly pallid. I think that's enough show for now."

Ratigan left the candles to burn out as he turned and led us back the way we had come. As we walked from the remaining projects I had yet to view, I thanked him repeatedly under my breath. We found the staircase, headed back toward daylight, and distanced ourselves from the horror Ratigan had taken from words on paper and given a life of their own.

I spent the remaining hours of the day wandering the mansion and estate grounds. The weather outside was warm and refreshing as the sun shone brightly on this dark house that contained sinister visions hidden within.

I asked myself many questions during the long walk and received no definite answers. There was an agenda somewhere in Ratigan's twisted mind. I suppose the man had left me no choice but to either pry the information from him or to leave this estate in my rearview mirror.

One other thing that pecked away at me was that I noticed my car no longer sat beneath the portico. Someone relocated it. I could only assume Mr. Newstead had taken the liberty of parking it in one of the garage's stalls adjacent to the house. I would have to inquire about it at our next meeting.

I was feeling deflated as Ratigan's demented artwork had raised my anxiety levels. The journey across the grounds had also sapped my strength. I decided to retire early tonight, and hopefully, tomorrow, Ratigan would be more forthcoming.

It was the soft fall of footsteps that awoke me the second night. I did not shift my position in bed, but remained utterly still. I suspected it was only Mr. Newstead checking on me during this late hour.

The footfalls approached my bed. I struggled to focus my eyes in the darkness. I saw no movement, even with the aid of the moonlight coming through the curtains. I was confident that someone was in my room but had somehow managed to avoid me seeing them.

I was reaching the edge of panic. I went to the lamp on the nightstand. As my fingers found the switch, the earth began shaking. It was an earthquake, and of that, I was sure. Books spilled from the shelves. The lamp on the bedside table pitched forward and fell to the floor with a jarring crash. Next, the bed heaved up as if the mouth of Hell were opening below me and prepared to swallow me whole.

The quake lasted perhaps ten agonizing seconds. When everything ceased movement, I shifted from the bed. As I went to the door to click on the light switch, I bumped into something unseen. I paused and tried to focus my eyes in the darkness. A fallen book suddenly slid across the floor as if kicked by someone. The bedroom door opened. When I reached the light switch and turned it on, I found myself alone. The door beside me was ajar. Whoever had entered my room was now gone.

A few moments later, Mr. Newstead came in to make sure that I was all right. I assured him that I was. I had decided to hold my tongue about Ratigan being in my room. Yes, I was sure that it was him who entered my quarters.

Mr. Newstead excused himself, as he was most likely off to find out if his employer was all right.

I was left alone to consider the strangeness of what had taken place. Why had Ratigan been in my room while I slept? Had he been watching me in some sort of disturbing way, or had he been searching for something? The other thing I thought about was the earthquake that had rocked the estate. I had never been aware that this part of the country was prone to such quakes. The quake, thankfully, was minor on the grand scale of things, but where there was one, more would most likely follow in due time.

The following day, Ratigan was nowhere to be found. Mr. Newstead assured me that my host was alive and well and unscathed by last night's quake.

Around noon, I discovered the main study. I quickly found the key resting on the threshold casing. It was an immaculate library indeed. The collection of literature found in this room was overly impressive compared to the collection found in the den that I saw during my arrival. I imagine that someone could find any desired subject in these volumes.

I browsed a bit and read the spines as I made my way from one end of a shelf to the other. I desired to find some sort of journal or ledger that contained important information about the Usher heritage. During our first conversation, Ratigan said he kept the family documents in the library. I had to know the mysterious secrets of the Usher family.

I searched the bookshelves with a few keywords in mind to assist with my endless struggle. I had discovered no logbooks of business or personal affairs. After nearly half an hour passed by and I turned up nothing, I sat at the desk and searched each drawer. I couldn't imagine what Ratigan would have thought if he walked into the library at that moment and found me rifling through his private property. The bottom drawer was locked, so I used a letter opener and worked it around until the drawer lock disengaged.

I smiled as I uncovered just what I hoped to find. There were five thick leather-bound volumes within. As I opened the first book and rapidly thumbed the pages, I realized that these weren't business journals but a collection of diary entries by various members of the Usher family spanning back to 1818.

At the beginning of the first journal, I found a rough sketch of a simple two-bedroom house. The entry read:

Here is the first page of what I will claim to be a great and lengthy documentation of my explorations to a universe I simply cannot fathom at this point. It's become an exciting time in our lives. Helen is proud of our little cottage among the secluded landscape, but she's concerned by the fact that we share our lives and property with such a strange creation.

I indeed chose this exact location to build our home because of this entity of light.

For future reference, I will refer to this phenomenon as the Hypergate. I will do my best to explain what it is. The Hypergate is a doorway to unlimited dimensions and places in time. It is possibly the only portal known to man that allows one to travel across infinite gaps in time and space. I have seen my birth and death many times. It is perhaps insane to claim such things, but I assure you that this proclamation is factual.

I am unsure how the Hypergate operates. I am also uncertain of how or when the thing came to be. I can only assume that a creation far more remarkable than mankind manufactured it through some divine nature. I'm only speculating that no one will understand this marvelous doorway of light. There is only one thing I am sure of—I am the first human to discover its magnificence.

I stepped through the Hypergate for the first time on March 2nd and entered a realm of the unimaginable. At the time, I held no particular destination in mind but instead had a heart full of fear. I honestly believed I would step into that brilliant shimmering light and terminate my life instantly or perhaps journey boundless through the world within for all of eternity.

It was such a strange sensation. It began with a tingling feeling that enveloped my entire body. It was like a warm light that penetrated my flesh and bones and pulled me toward my most fascinating desires.

The next moment, I was on a beach of such wondrous beauty. An ever-expanding ocean lay before me. I was utterly alone. As I turned about, I realized that a portal was here as well.

I had not wandered far, for I feared the Hypergate would forever close and leave me stranded in this place.

When I journeyed home, Helen was not aware of my return, for I discovered that there is one strange side effect to traveling through the portal. There is a duration of time in which the traveler becomes invisible. Although I was very much there in our house, Helen could not see me at all. Thankfully, the effect only lasted half of a day. Helen described to me that I slowly returned to my former self. She claims that it was at first like looking through a pane of glass, as she was aware that I was only slightly there.

As the hours passed, my body became more visually apparent. This unexpected situation had caused Helen to become afraid of the Hypergate. Before, I had almost convinced her to travel with me. However, now she refuses to discuss the incredible creation at all. She has tried to make me swear that I will no longer journey the brilliant pathway of light. I can never promise such a thing, for I am the only one to study the object and document my discoveries.

Here is my deduction of why one appears invisible after traveling through the Hypergate. I believe the Hypergate breaks down molecules when one passes through it. The molecules of a person or object then move across space and time to another destination. Here, everything is rearranged in perfect order. The molecules right themselves, as reconstruction has become a large-scale puzzle. During these twelve hours of transparency, everything finally finds its proper place and becomes whole again.

Of course, this is all theory and speculation. I need to take another fortnight to analyze my far-fetched idea and study the Hypergate further.

The first entry ended. I was in complete confusion. I could not comprehend if the writing before me was science fiction or based on facts observed through the writer.

I was sure any person not bearing the Usher name has ever read these volumes. I was more to believe that the journal was a creation of the imagination and nothing more.

I turned to the next entry that was dated precisely two weeks later.

The Hypergate works through the brain patterns of the individual. The images of the mind create the destination point. I have traveled great distances at what I believe to be instantaneously. I project a picture in my mind of a place and step into the light. Incredibly, my body transports to an almost identical place that is very much real. At every point I arrive, a Hypergate stands at my back. I've concluded that my stepping into the portal creates a similar portal at my destination.

Helen has become frantic that one day I'll step into that beautiful stream of light and never return. She is pregnant with our first child. I understand her concerns, but I simply cannot cease my investigations of the Hypergate.

I leaned back in the desk chair. *It has to be true!* I thought as I skimmed through the following pages. Was this so-called Hypergate Ratigan's hidden secret? Had Ratigan called me to the estate for reasons that dealt with this phenomenon?

I closed the volume and briefly thumbed through the other four. I realized that every generation of the Usher family kept documentation of their travels. The fifth volume was Ratigan's accounts of his journey into the light.

How marvelous to say that the same family had traveled through this dimensional gateway for the last one hundred and twenty years! No one outside the Usher family had been aware of its existence except, of course, the head caretaker of the estate. I was sure that Mr. Newstead must know of the Hypergate.

If I could just —

My trail of thoughts quickly ended as I heard footsteps approaching from down the hallway. I promptly placed the five volumes back in the drawer and closed it. I worked the letter opener in the lock like a master thief until the lock engaged. I stood from the chair and hurried to the bookshelves. I clasped my hands behind my back and leaned forward as I studied the infinite supply of literature.

If either Ratigan or Mr. Newstead entered the library, I hoped that my appearance would seem harmless, as if I were simply searching for some light reading.

I caught my breath as the footsteps paused outside the library door. Although the door never opened, I was sure someone was outside waiting for a noise to come from within the room. After a long moment, the footsteps traveled down the hallway. I released a sigh of relief.

As I left the library and headed to my room, I wondered if I should be brazen enough to inform Ratigan of my knowledge or let the subject's discussion be his decision.

If this Hypergate did exist, where on the estate grounds would such a thing be contained?

As it turned out, Ratigan approached me the following day. However, it was not in the manner I had assumed.

"Mr. Poe, I hope you don't mind me calling you that. I wish to show you something. You could say it's my most prized work of art. Of course, I can't truly take credit for the piece of work you're about to see. As you have already discovered, the creation dates back to at least the early nineteenth century."

Ratigan's accusation chilled my blood. He must have been the one who passed by the library as I was reading the Usher journals.

I held my tongue in protest. I felt no need to deny Ratigan's claim. I had searched a locked room, obviously without his permission, and I was glad that he was aware. Now I might be able to get to the bottom of his intentions of bringing me to the estate.

Ratigan directed me through the mansion by the same path leading to the mazelike substructure we had toured the other day.

With lit candles, we reached Ratigan's peculiar art collection. He didn't pause to show me the remaining pieces, but only continued forward into the unknown reaches.

We approached a massive steel door and halted. As we stood in the near blackness, our candles flickering in a ghostlike breeze, Ratigan revealed all of my unanswered questions.

"I know that you took it upon yourself to rummage through the library. I also know that you found my family's private journals. I'm not angry with you. I understand your curiosity. You've learned some secrets so far, so I will tell you what you don't know. I had to learn nearly all the information about the Hypergate from the books you uncovered. You see that my father passed away when I was six. My mother passed away a few years later. Mr. Newstead raised me like a son, but he always managed to keep his duties a priority. My father never revealed any eccentric secrets about the Hypergate to Mr. Newstead, only that it exists."

Ratigan leaned forward in the darkness and placed his hand gently on the steel door, as if embracing the cheek of a lover.

"My great-great-grandfather was a man who altered events in time. Of course, most of them were so small that the ripple in time was seemingly unnoticed. You see that he became a great thief. He traveled to points in history and stole a fortune at the most opportune times. There are newspaper clippings in the library that documented great sums of money gone missing. There were many places around the world where he easily appeared in a bank vault, collected all the cash, and transported back to the estate. He became obsessed with building the mansion. He wished to construct the mansion as a massive monument to the creation of the Hypergate. The mansion also hides the gateway from the outside world. Unfortunately, he needed money and lots of it. He became greedy, and it was this greed that eventually drove his wife away. Of course, the Usher line would continue as well as grow stronger and richer. We are a family that never accepts defeat. That is the reason I've brought you here."

"I still don't understand where you're going with this subject line," I said.

"I unraveled the allure of the Hypergate simply by testing my theories and making my journeys. A few nights ago, there was an earthquake. It was a terrible shock to the mansion. They are growing more intense. Inevitably, these quakes will be the downfall of the mansion. Before the earthquake, you heard me in your room, didn't you?" Ratigan didn't wait for a reply. "Of course, you had no idea that there was actually anything there, but I certainly was. I had just returned from a journey through the Hypergate and was still in the stages of transparency. I watched you sleep, curiously trying to figure out what makes you so special. I believe you're the key to my ultimate triumph. You will be the savior of my precious home, for it is your blood the Hypergate desires most of all."

Ratigan's insane statement completely dumbfounded me.

He reached past me, unlocked the steel door, and slowly pulled it open.

"Now, Mr. Poe, I give you the greatest creation since the dawn of mankind."

I couldn't avert my sight as the door parted to the warmest and most brilliant light I had ever witnessed. An array of colored ribbons of light filled the room as they constantly swirled with the pulsing energy of the Hypergate.

With my sight focused on the light that I hadn't noticed when Ratigan stepped behind me, and with an intensity of strength, he violently shoved me into the room and toward the reaching light of the Hypergate.

"Nevermore!" Ratigan croaked like the raven from Edgar's poem.

The true face of Ratigan's insanity had reached the surface. With a deafening boom, the steel door slammed behind me, sealing me inside. Of course, Ratigan's sudden act was the furthest thing from my mind. My sight refused to pull away from the tangle of beautiful lights.

The room was circular and constructed of large blocks that matched the rest of the mansion's substructure. However, the center of the room was void of foundation. Instead, it was a large pit in which the Hypergate pulsed like a massive heartbeat.

I was so intrigued by the dancing lights that fear had yet to find the surface. My feet involuntarily moved forward. I reached the edge of the pit and gazed down with glassy, unblinking eyes. The light stretched toward me like hands promising a warm embrace.

I heard metal scraping against metal. I turned from the Hypergate and saw the gleeful eyes of Ratigan Usher peering through a slot in the door.

"I'm sure by now you've come to understand why I wished for you to come to the estate. I believe that the Hypergate desperately wants you. I had told you before about Edgar staying at the estate. Edgar had spent that time touring the mansion and poking his nose in places it didn't belong. Edgar has been the only person besides you outside of the Usher family to lay eyes upon the marvel of the Hypergate. Ever since Edgar departed the estate, the earthquakes began. Of course, it really isn't the earth causing the tremors, but the Hypergate itself. The quakes were minor at first, but they've become much stronger and damaging to the mansion over the years. I believe the Hypergate wants revenge because your family knows of its secret. Since you are the last remaining Poe, it's your life that the Hypergate desires. It needs your blood. It's the only way the gateway will be satisfied, and the quakes will cease."

"That's insane!" I shouted.

I pressed against the steel door with Ratigan on the other side of it. I desperately searched his eyes for mercy, for some reason to this madness, as Ratigan searched mine for judgment, for vengeance.

I couldn't believe this phenomenon held triggering needs like revenge. Part of me felt that in some strange way the Hypergate was alive, but not in the sense that it had logical thoughts and emotions.

"I'm never going to step into that thing, Ratigan. Open the door!"

"Oh, you see, that's where you're wrong. I have one more presentation I've prepared especially for you. I do hope you can at least appreciate the irony of it."

A second later was the sound of Ratigan throwing a lever. Next came the disheartening sound of a mischievous whoosh of air as a giant pendulum began its sinister descent from the darkness.

As I shifted away from the door, I saw the gleam of the metal. I quickly dropped to my knees. However, I wasn't fast enough. The razor edge of the pendulum came cleanly across my right shoulder and parted flesh. A blinding pain erupted in my mind and body as I grasped the wound and fell against the wall in an awkward crouch. Warm blood seeped between my fingers.

The Pit and the Pendulum! Does your insanity know no bounds, Ratigan?

The pendulum had quickly disappeared. Dozens of thin vertical slits running from floor to ceiling filled the room. I suspected the blade began its descent from behind the walls as well as returned there. I heard the sound of turning gears.

The pendulum fell again. It hadn't exited the slit in which it had disappeared moments ago. This time it had nearly caught me full force, but I had managed to spin away at the last second.

"It will do you no good to stand in one spot, Mr. Poe. The pendulum rotates at random. Eventually, it will cover the entire room and find you again," Ratigan shouted and then offered a maniacal laugh, as if this was some sort of entertainment for him.

Dear God! What can I do?

The answer seemed so obvious. I decided that my only chance of survival was a faithful leap into the Hypergate. If I traveled to wherever my thoughts desired, I might increase my life span instead of taking my chances with a giant wielding blade.

Gears were turning again.

Damnit! Hurry and decide!

I quickly lay flat on my stomach and crawled toward the Hypergate.

The blade fell, slicing the air, and nothing more.

I honestly didn't know if this portal worked as described in the journals. If I did make a journey, I was sure that I would instantly die and satisfy the Hypergate's thirst for so-called vengeance, or it would pull me to some other place in time.

I reached the edge of the pit and stared into the brilliantly glowing abyss. Something happened that immediately changed my decision before I could muster all of my strength to hurl myself into the light. The wound on my shoulder bled into the swirls of light and disappeared. The ground heaved with furious rage. The quake was tremendous, nearly twice the magnitude of the one several nights before.

The pendulum swung again but couldn't withstand the Hypergate's wrath. The blocks supporting the giant blade gave way, collapsed into the portal, and the pendulum vanished from this existence.

My God! The thing is truly alive!

The Ushers hadn't built this mansion as a tribute to the Hypergate. They had constructed walls around it to confine the incredible creation as a means to control the unquestionable force of the portal.

The Hypergate had tasted blood. It was my blood that had awoken a sleeping giant who longed for life, too.

I gave it what it desired most. It wanted to be alive!

I dug my fingers in the flesh wound and desperately tore at the laceration. Pain flared. Tears stung. Hope rose.

Blood spilled into the light, making it pulsate with excitement. It seemed to grow with the life I was feeding it.

Another quake began, causing the block foundation to fragment. The walls containing the Hypergate fell away. The steel door came undone from its brick support and crashed into the corridor.

I saw my opportunity and dashed through the open doorway. Ratigan was in the corridor, pinned beneath the fallen steel door. I kneeled and checked for vitals. He was still alive, but unconscious. With great effort, I pulled him free from beneath the door and quickly tried to revive him.

After a moment, he came around to the earth rumbling underfoot.

"We need to get out of here immediately. The whole mansion is coming down!" I screamed at him.

"No! Not my house!" he yelled back. "Please, go into the Hypergate. It needs you. The quake will stop if you go."

I didn't have time for his nonsense. I grasped his arm and led him down the blackened corridor, but he quickly slipped from my hold and ran into the darkness alone.

"Usher, wait!" I yelled in panic.

Left alone, I felt along the corridor walls to steady my footing. I couldn't see anything, but I felt and heard everything. Bricks gave way and crashed into the corridor. A cloud of dust and debris filled the area. I used the collar of my shirt to help ventilate the air. Ahead, the passage collapsed, cutting off my only means of escape from this hell. As I reached the obstruction, I kneeled and blindly searched the rubble.

There was no opening that I might be able to squeeze through, but my blind search found Ratigan Usher. I touched his hand but could not uncover the rest of him, for a mountain of blocks had crushed the life from him.

Oh, Lord, where on earth could I possibly go?

I had answered my own question. The Hypergate was a doorway to unlimited possibilities, and it was the only chance I had.

I quickly made my decision and journeyed back through the darkness. After a moment, the brilliant glow of the Hypergate showed me the way.

The ceiling was coming down all around. Blocks fell into the Hypergate and traveled to an unknown destination.

Where in the world would my thoughts end as I leaped into the light? In the journal, Darius Usher explained that his thoughts would be the choice to his destination. I could not steady my focus on a single thing. I tried to envision home, but there were endless possibilities in which I could travel.

Then I remembered that I could do just that. I could travel as far and as often as I desired. A Hypergate would always be at my place of destination. I would own a teleportation device whenever I so wished.

One last thought entered my mind as I leaped from the edge of the pit and into the sheer brilliant light of the Hypergate.

What if Ratigan Usher was right, and the Hypergate wanted nothing more than to consume my life to save its own?

Neither Ratigan Usher nor William Poe remained part of this world long enough to witness the town of Endsbrook gather at the perimeter of the Usherland estates. They were drawn together by an earthquake tearing the heart and soul from the Usher's mansion.

Drawn by the magnificent glow of a sun born on earth, the spectators united in awe as light flared with intensity through every window of the mansion. Each person expelled a breath of unsettling wonder as the mansion began to fold in on itself. Mysteriously, the estate reformed as it journeyed through the portal to a parallel universe, crossing time and dimensions not so unlike our own. The mysterious mansion would reach to the stars and beyond humanity's most comprehensive images of what lay beyond those distant stars and distant worlds.

The house of Usher had indeed fallen, perhaps indefinitely this time, as a doorway swallowed it to a wonder that held no bounds.

The Hypergate would find another home, another world. Traveling within the spectacular pathway the doorway created, the destination was that of its own choice.

It's that Thing about Death

"What year was it your husband passed away, ma'am?"

The woman stared at him plainly for a moment, briefly considering the lost years.

"It was 1998, I believe. I remember it was autumn time."

"You reported to our magazine that he's still with you, in spirit, that is. Right?"

"Yes, dear. We do our daily routine just as we always have. We get up in the morning, take a warm bath, cook breakfast, read the newspaper, and walk three miles, and so on."

"What about communication? Since he's unable to vocalize human speech, how do you know what he's saying?"

"You don't know much about the afterlife, do you?"

"I'm afraid I can only define my knowledge of that subject through years of speculation from eyewitness accounts and interviews, just as we're doing now."

"Well, let me tell you about my husband so you can have your story."

Will Craig leaned back on the sofa, settling deep into the folds of the cushions. He retrieved his notebook and a pen and waited for the clarifying details this woman was willing to disclose.

"When my husband died in 2014, I swore to myself that I didn't have the courage or strength to continue without him. Following the funeral, I suffered from true heartbreaking agony. Every minute I prayed that the good Lord would take me from this world. I prayed for that great relief for many weeks. They had gone unanswered. I reached the point at which I decided that suicide was my only option. I just felt the need to die. I longed for death, actually. I went to the medicine cabinet and found the bottle of sleeping pills I had been taking for those restless nights. Just as I was about to swallow the entire bottle, something made me glance up, and there I saw my late husband in the mirror's reflection. With a start, the bottle of pills slipped from my grasp and spilled across the floor. I could only stare at that familiar face without uttering a single word. I was sure that I had completely lost all my senses. So finally, I turned around to face the illusion. It wasn't an illusion at all. My husband was standing right there, smiling softly. I nearly screamed out in both terror and joy. I was certain that he would evaporate at any moment. Then he spoke in that calm voice I knew so well. He said, 'Darling, what are you doing to yourself? I always told you that nothing could divide love, not even death.' He had said those words to me on many occasions. Since that time, we've always been together."

"So is the experience like sensing a presence or seeing an aura figure?"

"Neither, dear. I see my husband as he always was."

"Human figure, I see." Will jotted down several lines in the notebook. "Can your friends or family also see your husband?"

"You tell me, Mr. Craig. Do you see him here with us now?"

Will glanced suspiciously around the room, detailing every object.

"I'm afraid I don't, Mrs. Rasmussen. Is he here now?"

"Please, call me June. Yes, my husband is with us."

"Where is he standing?"

"He isn't standing. He's sitting right beside you."

Will quickly turned to his left as if he suddenly felt thousands of volts charge through him. There was empty air between him and the arm of the sofa. Although he knew he was acting idiotic, he waved his hand in the vacant space but did not contact the ghost.

"Can he make an appearance to me?"

"I think it only works with loved ones. You have no idea what Frank looks like, so your mind can't possibly project the image of his features," she said and casually folded her hands onto her lap.

Illogical crap, Will thought.

"Would you mind if I smoke, Mrs. Rasmussen?"

"Please, go right ahead."

Will produced a pack of cigarettes from his shirt pocket, shook one loose, and lit it.

I hate this job, he sarcastically thought. *Why I ever convinced myself to report for this crap paranormal magazine is far beyond me. It just goes to show you that I should have listened to my mother and become a cutthroat lawyer instead of a writer. At least I would have had the education to hack through the mounds of trash of everyday life. It certainly would have been better cash, too.*

Will raffled through the questions he was obligated to ask when sent on assignments.

"Why do you believe he's still here on earth? Is there some unfulfilled purpose he wishes to accomplish before he leaves?"

"No, he just wants to keep me company."

Will wrote.

"Does he ever leave for a while? Perhaps conjuring miracles for the unfortunate? Anything like that?"

"No. Frank is always here with me."

"Does he do anything?"

"I told you that he keeps me company."

"But does he do anything *special*?" Will said irritably.

"He helps me with the housework and in the garden."

Will closed his notebook roughly and tucked it away in his coat pocket.

"I'm afraid this is not the sort of column *Chase the Light* wishes to publish, Mrs. Rasmussen. You see, our publication wishes to write about paranormal activities that reach into the bizarre. If you are indeed telling the truth and your husband is here now, we would need to receive information that he's possibly haunting this house or terrorizing the neighbors and so forth."

"Well, that doesn't seem very nice to me. I guess you could say Frank is a polite ghost."

A polite ghost? That's a new one, Will thought.

Will hadn't noticed that his cigarette had burned down to the filter, and the tip of ashes was ready to fall to the carpet. The glass ashtray in the center of the coffee table suddenly slid across the wood surface and stopped in front of him. Without taking in the full effect of the movement, Will put out his cigarette with a stabbing motion, retrieved his jacket, and stood. The strange occurrence finally penetrated his mind. He gazed down, stared dumbfounded at the ashtray and the cigarette, whirls of smoke rising.

"Did—did your husband just do that?"

"Of course. Frank never cared for smoking but tolerated it because I used to smoke for many years. I told you he was polite."

Will settled on the sofa again. He was unable to pull his sight from the glass ashtray. He reached for it, carefully picked it up, and turned it around in his hands. He was unaware that the cigarette butt and ashes fell to the table. His eyes searched suspiciously over the ashtray, trying to discover a thin fishing line or thread taped to the bottom. He didn't find either. He replaced it and stared at his host.

She drank from the teacup and watched him doubtfully over the rim.

Without giving it much thought, he blurted out, "May I use your restroom?"

"By all means. It's straight down the hall, the last door on the left."

What the hell was that? The goddamn ashtray slid right to me. I know I saw it. I couldn't have imagined it.

He closed the bathroom door, turned on the faucet, and splashed frigid water in his face. As he used the hand towel to dry himself off, he gazed in the mirror and half expected to see the livid face of Mr. Rasmussen staring balefully back at him.

There was nothing behind him.

He stepped to the toilet, lifted the seat, and relieved himself. As he tucked his shirt back in, the toilet flushed by itself, and the lid closed over the bowl.

He propelled backward against the wall hard enough to crack the plaster and send a thin crease snaking up and down the bright yellow wall. The gushing sound of water roared in his ears as the tank refilled.

An unsettling silence followed.

The door handle turned by an unseen force, and the bathroom door opened. The hallway beyond was utterly empty. Will cautiously stepped through the threshold and into the hall. He moved quickly back to the living room with a fear that a ghoulish ghost was hovering over his shoulders with hideous twisted claws ready to pierce his flesh and tear out his—*Stop it!* he yelled at himself. *Quit psyching yourself out!*

The living room was empty. Will turned the corner and started to call out for the woman when they collided. June lost hold of a plate of cookies, and glasses of milk went hurling through the air and crashing to the floor.

"Jesus, I'm so sorry!" Will never hesitated with his momentum as he stepped to the sofa, grabbed his jacket, and said, "I can't stay here. I just can't. I apologize for my rush, but this story hardly seems like our type of material."

As he grabbed the knob of the front door, he heard the deep grumble of some ungodly creation. He abruptly turned around and expected to be devoured by a monster from the greatest depths of Hell. His arm shot up to cover his face, his knees nearly buckled in fright.

There was nothing behind him.

Mrs. Rasmussen stared at him with a horrid look. She twisted her face with a cruelness not drawn by the incident of spilled goods but by his quick retreat.

"He doesn't want you to leave. He wishes for you to hear what I have to say. You must stay!"

Will turned the knob just as the deadbolt suddenly engaged. He reached up and tried to turn it, wanted to distance himself from the insanity of this damnation, and needed to sprint toward freedom. The lock wouldn't disengage. He was trapped.

Think! Do something! he thought as desperation ran through his mind.

Then it came to him like a bright flashing revelation. He briskly stepped to the old woman, reared his fist back, and struck her as hard as he possibly could. He could feel the brittle bones of her cheek give way under pressure, and the horrible sounds of splintering followed. She pinwheeled back into the kitchen, struck the counter edge, and collapsed with a violent gush of breath to the tiled floor.

Will ran to the door again, quickly turned the bolt, and yanked open the door. The entity was no doubt consoling its injured wife and allowing Will to escape. He ran with every bit of motivation he could find. Will slipped in his car, jabbed the key in the ignition, and revved the engine to life. He slammed the car in reverse and stomped on the accelerator. The car jutted into the street, nearly sideswiping a man on a bicycle. The man threw up his fist and lashed out with a fury of profanity.

As Will shifted in drive, the passenger door flew open, the seat creaked with movement, and the door slammed shut. Will's foot came down on the accelerator without his permission.

The car started forward with fierceness, racing down the block with little consideration of obstacles. Bushes, mailboxes, and garbage containers quickly vanished over and under the vehicle. After a moment, Will regained control of the steering wheel and centered the car on the street. He applied both feet to the brake pedal, and with all his strength, pressed down. A raging pain shot up both his legs, almost making him believe that he was stabbed repeatedly in each leg. He screamed out and retracted his feet from the pedal. The car only continued to rush forward. In another moment, the steering wheel left his control and locked straight ahead.

People glared and yelled for him to slow down as his car shot down the block, topping out at seventy-five miles an hour. The vehicle approached the crest of a large hill. Will reached for the door handle and yanked. He was ready to tumble from the speeding car before chancing a death-defying aerial stunt. He thought he could make the edge of the grass if he leaped hard enough.

Will pulled the door lever, but the door held shut. He yanked the lever again in a flood of panic until the lever broke off in his hand.

The vehicle hit the hill with such velocity that the wheels entirely left the pavement. A high-pitched wail escaped from Will as he continued to watch the iridescent sky rapidly change to a clouded horizon, to the peaks of commercial buildings, to a flat tone of gray concrete. A shower of sparks covered his field of vision. The groaning twist of metal filled his ears. As the entire vehicle came to the ground once again, the impact caused Will to pitch forward. He instantly felt the sickening crunch of his nose breaking over the rim of the steering wheel. His vision blurred by blood, and a well of tears was spilling from his eyes.

The vehicle's direction never faltered as it barreled down the San Francisco street and headed directly toward a parked cement truck where half a dozen men were working.

"Please, I'm sorry for what I did. I panicked! Please stop this!" Will yelled.

Will jerked the wheel, stomped the brake, and neither reacted to his demands.

He reached over his left shoulder and grabbed his seat belt.

The front of the car had just missed a pedestrian.

The seatbelt wouldn't latch.

A stop sign blurred past.

Fifty yards.

The road crew ahead of them scattered in all directions.

Will screamed as loud as he could, his throat burning with irritation.

"Please, Mr. Rasmussen! You're a polite ghost! You're a polite gh—"

Red Hour

Calvin flicked Genghis Kahn on the nose. He gently massaged Cleopatra's breast. He even traveled across the red plains of Mars without a protective suit.

Each night, Calvin Westcott did the same boring routine. The night watch guard duty at the museum was one of the dullest occupations he had ever subjected himself to do. He had tried nearly every bottom-rung job the city offered, but the solitude of working at the museum was almost enough to drive him mad.

To prevent dying of boredom, Calvin moved artifacts around in the back room, yet to be displayed. He could only imagine the near panicked state the day shift staff worked themselves into while searching for misplaced items.

Calvin thought about taking something valuable out the back door, placing it in his car until his shift was over, and then hocking it at the local pawn shop. Calvin knew that he would be the first person to pop up on the radar should something go missing. He could easily alter the security recordings and leave no evidence of his theft, but in any case, he wasn't ready to start job hunting just yet. The gig was easy. All he had to do was make hourly rounds by triggering sensors throughout the museum that recorded each security check. Otherwise, Calvin would find a comfortable chair, prop his feet up and sleep through his entire shift until he heard the morning staff clocking in.

Besides moving items around, Calvin had one other thing that got him through most nights: inspecting new items the museum received.

A few nights ago, a meteorite from Utah came in the door. Before the meteorite was the bones of a pharaoh, and before that was a sword from ancient Greece.

Calvin heard the news as soon as he clocked in that a spellbook was the museum's most recent acquisition. A recently deceased collector of unusual artifacts had donated the book to a local museum. The museum experts were still speculating about the book's authenticity, but they were certain the book once belonged to a woman deemed evil by a town judge and hung during the Salem witch trials.

Calvin patiently waited for the evening staff to exit the building. When everyone was gone, he locked the doors and made his first rounds through each wing of the museum. Calvin then headed directly for the back room, where they held new exhibits before being placed on display.

"Well, well, so this is where you're hiding," he said as he observed the tattered book under the protective Plexiglas. "It looks like you've been beaten to shit, left in a sewer for the last two hundred years, and then baked under a sun lamp for the last week. But yet you've got some possibilities still left in you, I think," Calvin said.

Even though Calvin knew the museum was empty, he looked over both shoulders to confirm he was alone. He unfastened the latch and flipped open the lid. Calvin carefully reached inside and stroked the brown leather cover with his forefinger. With the same finger, he slowly opened the book and touched the yellowed pages. The paper was incredibly brittle and made a crackling noise as he turned through each section.

The writing was severely faded and illegible in some parts. Whoever had taken quill to paper had exquisite penmanship as the words within had been written with a graceful hand.

Calvin gently pulled the book from the case, placed it on one of the cloth-covered tables, and spent the next hour reading. Calvin thought the book seemed more like a documentation of experimental herbal remedies instead of a spellbook. There were many areas where the woman mentioned a combination of plants and minerals to soothe achy muscles, stop headaches, have regular bowel movements, and stuff that Calvin cared little about at the moment.

"Come on. I can find any of these remedies at the supermarket. Give me the good stuff. Christ, if they hung you because you helped someone get rid of the shits, then gratitude was once a cruel son of a bitch," he said.

When Calvin reached the last dozen pages, he realized that what he found written was worth its weight in gold. There were sections titled: Rotten Breath, English Death Dance, Pandora's Secret, and even Hell's Fury. Beneath each title was a type of rhyme that sent an odd shiver creeping up his spine.

"Well, now we're talking," he said and began reading.

Finding a person to work the spells on was no easy task. Calvin wanted to cast a spell on someone who deserved it. On Wednesday morning, the target found him instead.

When the museum coordinator, Kenneth Stanton, asked Calvin to join him in the office just after he clocked out, Calvin knew from experience that bad news was rapidly on the way.

"I'm sure you're aware, Mr. Westcott, that the museum takes great pleasure in showing rare items to the public as they've never seen before."

"Of course, sir."

"Mr. Westcott, hiring you was certainly more for your benefit than mine. I'm sure you're aware that I did a background check on you before my commitment to bring you into our little family. I knew about your past and the trouble you've had with the law. Of course, these offenses were minor, and that's why I overlooked your criminal record. During our interview, you struck me as a man who wanted and even needed a second chance to find his place in society."

"Yes, sir. I greatly appreciate the opportunity you've given me. I do enjoy working here."

Kenneth Stanton leaned forward, placed his elbows on the desk and studied Calvin for a long uncomfortable minute, and then said, "I wonder if you really do, Mr. Westcott."

"Yes, sir. The hours are perfect. The job is rewarding. I love the responsibility of looking after priceless artifacts that have incredible stories."

Mr. Stanton retrieved the remote control from the desktop, swiveled in his chair, and pressed the PLAY button. The television centered on the mass of bookshelves behind Mr. Stanton began to play a video.

"This is what I will refer to as your greatest hits," Mr. Stanton said.

Calvin felt his face flush as he watched a video of himself handling items in the back room and shuffling them around. He hid a set of Roman coins in a small crate on the second shelf of inventoried items. He juggled delicate clay pots discovered in the Andes Mountains that dated back nearly a thousand years. He even removed a fragile mummy from a sarcophagus, placed it on the floor, and morbidly took an hour-long nap inside the mummy's resting place. One clip followed another until the video reached yesterday. Calvin saw himself removing the witch's book from the case and reading the material. The video ended a few seconds after Calvin tore twelve pages free from the back of the book.

"I would say that it's hardly inspirational material to watch. In fact, I would title it as a complete lack of gratitude and respect for what it is we do here, Mr. Westcott."

"I'm not sure what to say," Calvin said as he stared at the desk.

Mr. Stanton leaned back in his chair, folded his hands across his enormous belly, and watched Calvin with distaste.

"You must believe that I'm a complete fool. Did you honestly think that you could screw with my museum, and I would look the other way? Did you think that you could hide or ruin artifacts here and get away with it? I gave you a great opportunity to become a member of the family at this facility. I have to say that I'm greatly disappointed. I could have you arrested, you know? The book you destroyed was priceless. It's worth more than a pathetic twerp like you could earn in your entire lifetime. I want those twelve pages back, and I want them back right now."

"There's no excuse for what I've done here. Maybe it was out of boredom. Maybe disrespect because I feel I've never gotten the chance I deserved."

"Oh, you got the chance. I gave it to you. Give me the pages you took."

"I don't have them. I mean, the pages aren't here. I have them at my apartment."

"Get them, bring them back to me within the next hour, or the police will be informed of the destructive nature in which you live, Mr. Westcott. You have one hour. I recommend you start moving now."

What was it? How did the curse go? Calvin thought. *It was titled: Rotten Breath.*

Although he had only read the curse once, the strange words came tumbling back into his mind.

Calvin looked up and caught Mr. Stanton's eyes and said, "Of mouse paw and serpent spit, come germs of old which will not stall. Each will decay to a blackened pit, and with the next breath, they'll start to fall."

"Excuse me?" Mr. Stanton asked.

Calvin could see Kenneth Stanton's face twist a little. At first, the look was one given when someone felt a mild discomfort. Calvin could then see Mr. Stanton working his tongue around the inside of his mouth, probing areas.

"Something wrong?" Calvin asked with an amused grin.

"Look, Mr. Westcott—"

Something tumbled from Mr. Stanton's mouth and landed on his desk calendar on the 1st day of May.

Their eyes broke contact and slowly traced down. The tooth, which had been bright white, was now rapidly shading to an aged yellow, brown, and then as black as night. Before their unblinking stares, Mr. Stanton's tooth crumbled to fine black dust as if incinerated.

Mr. Stanton cupped his left hand over his gaping mouth.

Calvin reeled out of the chair and hit the wall hard enough to knock a picture loose. Calvin already pulled open the office door when the picture frame hit the floor and shattered. He ran past the secretary and tore off down the corridor for the front entrance.

"Impossible. It's just a stupid book. It can't do the things it says. There's no such thing as curses," Calvin said after he slammed his apartment door and sank to the floor. He held his head in his hands and stared at the dirty area rug. "Were his teeth already decayed, and it just happened to fall out at the right time, making me believe that I had performed a genuine curse?"

If there's one thing he knew, it was that Mr. Stanton had clean white teeth. The man was always smiling at the goddamn customers and employees like he was a jack-o'-lantern.

"It was all you, Calvin, old buddy. You just got back at the son of a bitch who fired you," he told the empty apartment.

Calvin started laughing, and he didn't stop until the neighbor began beating on the thin wall and barking for him to keep it down.

"It's not a crime to laugh, partner. You keep pounding and watch what will happen to you," he yelled.

Calvin retrieved the twelve spell book pages from beneath his mattress and searched through them. There were thirty-two curses in all. Reading through the pages again, he found most of them harmless, more of a nuisance than anything else to the cursed person, but a few of them seemed downright nasty.

There wasn't any explanation for what each curse would do to someone. It was the simple formations of the words that made Calvin believe that the curses could do physical damage. He decided to take a chance on an unwilling subject, someone fitting enough for such a cruel curse.

Calvin walked to the apartment window that overlooked 5th Avenue. The street was bustling with people.

Across the street was the basketball court where low-rent people played their low-rent games. Calvin knew drug dealers and whores hung out there at all hours of the day and night. If anyone deserved to be tortured by ancient curses, it was those people.

Calvin flipped through the pages until he found the proper curse. He memorized the lines and found one unwilling member of the park grounds. He was a shifty-eyed man with his pants hung low, his legs tensed and ready to take flight should a patrol car suddenly appear. Calvin locked his eyes on the subject.

As he spoke the first words, a fist urgently hit his apartment door.

Calvin lowered the pages to his side, turned from the window, and stared at the door. He instantly knew who it was. The landlord was relentless at receiving his monthly check on time. There had even been some months when the man would stand at Calvin's door and wait in the early hours until Calvin got home from his shift at the museum.

Calvin moved to the door while being cautious of the squeaking floorboards and gazed through the peephole.

"You unbelievable prick," Calvin whispered as he realized who it was.

Mr. Stanton was staring at the door as if he could see through it. His fist raised and hammered the door again with a half dozen raps.

"I know you're in there. Do you realize what you've done? Do you realize that you've passed the point of no return?" Mr. Stanton bellowed out with a slurred voice. He sounded drunk, as speaking with no teeth would take some adjustment.

Calvin needed to laugh at the man, mocking the bastard that had cost him another job. He wanted to open the door, grab the man by the collar, and release an uncontrollable chuckle of delight into the man's face. He wanted to do all this, but the gun in Mr. Stanton's left hand prevented him from doing anything at all.

"I've got something for you, Mr. Westcott. Why don't you come out? I'll show you what I've brought."

Mr. Stanton took a long moment to study the peephole. Calvin instantly crouched when he saw the man step back, raise his arm and place the barrel of the gun against the fish-eyed lens. Before a bullet could tear through the door, Calvin heard a familiar voice calling from the stairs.

"Just what in the hell do you think you're doing, mister?"

Calvin heard Mr. Stanton shift around on the other side of the door. Calvin stood and looked through the glass again. He saw his landlord, Frank Tipps, standing on the platform at the bottom of the stairs. Calvin could only see the landlord's head staring up at the museum coordinator at his front door.

"Are you his keeper? Are you his protector?" Mr. Stanton said.

"What the hell?" Mr. Tipps asked.

"Did you know that he's a descendant of evil? Do you know that he's the offspring of the witches that should have died out centuries ago? Why have you been hiding him?" Mr. Stanton said and raised the gun.

"Now, just wait a goddamn second," Mr. Tipps said. He received his one second just before the gun roared and the top half of his head splattered the cornflower wallpaper behind him.

Calvin's eyes were wide as he saw his landlord casually lean against the wall and slide down, almost as if taking a rest from extreme fatigue.

Mr. Stanton tapped the gun against the door and said, "It's just the two of us again. I'm sorry we were so rudely interrupted. I want to tell you something before I blow the lock off the door. I want you to understand that I have a passion for the Salem witch trials. I've always had this passion because it's part of my family's history. You see that my ancestors were part of the committee that passed judgment on those witches and had them executed. I know such evil could never really die. I suspect that perhaps some of them fled before capture and moved across the country. You must be a living relative of one of those evils. I want you to know that when the book first arrived at the museum, I had tried the curses, too. I had read them out loud to several people who I disliked, but the results delivered nothing. However, you rattled off a curse, and my fucking teeth fell right out. That means you're one of them. That means you must die, Mr. Westcott."

Before Calvin could mutter a denial, the deadbolt exploded in a shower of metal. The door caught a brutal kick, causing Calvin to fly back, hitting the coffee table and crashing to the floor. His elbow smacked the table's edge, and a pain thundered up his arm.

Mr. Stanton stepped inside the apartment and focused the gun between Calvin's eyes.

"I'm sorry. I'll buy you dentures. I'll do whatever it takes to make this right," Calvin pleaded as he held his arms in front of his face.

"Relax. I'm not going to shoot you because a bullet isn't fitting enough for unholy crimes. You're an abomination. I have something else planned for you," Mr. Stanton said and stepped back into the hallway. He retrieved a gas can and held it out so that Calvin would fully understand his objectives.

"The town's folk hung some of the witches, but the majority of the convicted witches burned. I can't even imagine the kind of screams someone makes while they're burning, but I'm confident people will hear you from blocks away," Mr. Stanton said.

"This is insane. You can't honestly believe I'm a witch. I'm a goddamn security guard. I'm nothing. I've never been anything important in my entire life," Calvin said and tried to stand.

"Stay where you are, or I'm going to blow your kneecaps off."

Mr. Stanton set the gas can down, unscrewed the cap, and then casually used his foot to tip the container. Gas gurgled out, covered the throw rug, and soaked the left leg of Calvin's uniform pants. Kenneth Stanton's eyes were gleaming with delight. His smile was broad and almost sadistic. His pink tongue slid out from that toothless mouth and slicked across his lips.

"Burn, devil," he said and removed a lighter from his trouser pocket.

"Police! Drop the gun!" someone called from down the hall.

"Help me! He's crazy. Can you hear me? He's crazy. He's trying to burn me alive!" Calvin screamed.

When Kenneth Stanton directed his attention toward the police, Calvin rolled away from the puddle of gas and reached for the dropped pages. He quickly found the curse titled *Hell's Fury*.

Gunfire filled the small space. Large pieces of wood tore free from the door as the police returned fire. Mr. Stanton fired three quick rounds and kicked the door shut. When he turned around, he saw Calvin was holding battered, faded, and ancient pages written by the spawn of

Satan. Calvin muttered the words as his eyes locked on Kenneth Stanton.

"What's that you say?" Mr. Stanton said and fired a round that caught Calvin in the right shoulder.

Calvin screamed and grabbed the wound.

The door violently came open as two police officers charged inside.

"Drop the gun, or we're going to take you down. Do it now!" one of the cops shouted.

It wasn't because of the order the police gave, but he dropped the gun out of sheer bewilderment. He held out his left hand and stared stupidly at the lighter. The metal collar of the lighter was growing incredibly hot, turning a cherry red, and the fuel inside began to bubble.

"What the hell is with this thing?" he asked just before the lighter exploded in his hand.

A torrent of fire shot up his arm like a fast-moving serpent and quickly consumed his jacket before the blaze nearly blinded him. The fire moved with intensity across his clothing. Mr. Stanton spun, and as he did, he screamed loud enough that people could actually hear him from blocks away.

Calvin felt a laugh rumbling from him as he thought, *I am a witch! You knew it before I did, Mr. Stanton. You brought it out of me, and I thank you for that. With these pages, I'll no longer be a pitiful doormat of society. I'm going to show people what I can really do. I feel sorry for all those who cross me from now on.*

Calvin collected the rest of the scattered pages, and in a frantic shuffle, he moved for the door.

The policemen only gave him a passing glance as he brushed by them. The burning man and his nearly hypnotic dance had seized their attention.

When Calvin hit the hallway, his foot caught the stream of gasoline running from the apartment. He went down painfully on his back, and his head bounced off the floor. With blurry eyes, he looked back and saw Mr. Stanton collapse as death finally grabbed him. His body hit the pool of gas, and with a *whoosh,* the fuel caught. The policemen and the apartment beyond disappeared in a bright orange flash.

Calvin opened his mouth and started screaming as the fire ran into the hallway after him.

"Is there a damn war going on?" an old man asked as he poked his head out his apartment door.

"Yeah, something like that. You should probably grab anything important because the building is on fire," Calvin said as he headed for the front entrance.

Fire engines rolled up to the building with a vicious wail. People crowded the streets and watched with amazement as Calvin's third-floor apartment windows blew out from the extreme heat.

Calvin brushed off a dwindling flame on the cuff of his uniform jacket.

One of the onlookers watched him with curiosity as he came down the front steps. With his uniform partially burned and black soot covering his face, he figured he probably looked as if Hell had just spit him out.

"Hey, man, is that your place?" the kid asked.

"Was," Calvin said.

"You're lucky as hell you made it out of there with your skin, man."

"Yeah. I never figured that particular curse would work. So you can bet that I doubted the counter curse could actually make me fireproof."

"Huh?" the kid asked.

Calvin was already on the move down the street.

As Calvin began tucking the slightly scorched spell pages inside his jacket pocket, a large man crashed into him and nearly sent Calvin pinwheeling to the ground.

"Watch where you're going, peckerhead," the man said with a scowl.

The man stopped after a few paces and gazed up at the fire consuming Calvin's apartment.

I'll show you who's a peckerhead, Calvin thought, and began shuffling through the pages. *You just keep standing there looking stupid, and that will be the look to permanently mark your ignorant face.*

Calvin found and read the curse titled *Medusa's Eyes*. As the last words left his lips, something knocked against the café window in front of him. Calvin couldn't be sure what had struck the inside window because the windows were mirror-tinted. As he looked up, he caught his reflection, and his appearance was appalling.

I'm going to need a doctor to fix my bullet-holed shoulder. I damn well need a bath to clean all this grime off my face. Then I think I'll sleep for a week. Performing curses is one exhausting trick in itself.

Calvin's sight captured his own tired brown eyes in the reflection.

He felt the pain start somewhere deep down in his core. Something solidified and spread like the fire that had consumed Mr. Stanton. Calvin tried to turn away from the window or even direct his sight anywhere else. He tried to open his mouth and call for help, but all the pedestrians watched the apartment fire. Their unblinking stares focused on the curse he had performed, but now they were missing his greatest and final curse.

As the pages fell from his stiffening grip and blew away in the breeze, Calvin thought he could hear Mr. Stanton's blackened corpse gurgling with laughter from somewhere in the apartment blaze.

Calvin's mind slowed like a dying clock. He thought about the witches who performed exceptional curses throughout history that were hunted down and defiantly hung or burned. Now he thought of the only witch in history who would turn to stone by mistakenly cursing his own reflection.

From Shadowed Places

"Colleen, can you look at the map for a minute?" I asked.

"The map? Don't even tell me that we're lost, Drew," Colleen Parsons said.

"No, I'm not saying that. I just want you to double-check that we're approaching Highway 75 North."

"We're supposed to be. That's the only highway that leads to the resort. I swear to God, if you took a wrong turn, I'm going to be severely pissed." Colleen closed her book and gazed out the window.

The snow had come lazily at first. The forecast had called for moderate to heavy accumulation throughout the afternoon. As the miles fell away behind us, the snowfall had dramatically increased. The road had become practically unbearable to maneuver.

"I agree with Colleen. If we're lost, I'm going to be severely pissed times two," Joel Lesser said from the backseat and then added a series of wet, hard coughs into his fist.

"Times three, for me," Ryan Gibson said.

"Yeah, I get it. You're all pissed at me. Not that it will do any of you any good. Besides, did I say I was lost? To my recollection, I believe I simply asked Colleen to look at the map. I just want to confirm that I didn't jump off route somewhere. With the snow coming down as hard as it is now, it's possible to get mixed up a little. It's bad outside, and I'm starting to worry a little because I haven't seen another vehicle in nearly half an hour."

"Dammit, Drew. You just had to go and say that you were worried, didn't you? Now you're going to get me all frantic and bug-shit crazy. I told you from the beginning that the weather called for heavy accumulation. You said we'd be fine. You said that we'd reach the resort long before the snow really came down. You promised," Colleen said as she began searching beyond the windows for some sort of life.

"I know. I guess we can all take from this experience that I don't know everything. Just look at the map, please. We left Highway 20 about an hour ago and merged onto Highway 26 East. We're supposed to come across Highway 75 North after the town where we gassed up. What was that town called? Fairfield?"

Colleen was closely inspecthe map, tracing the curving black lines with her finger. Ryan was leaning over the backseat, peering over Colleen's shoulder and squinting at the map.

"I don't believe it. Did you just say that we merged onto Highway 26 after we left Fairfield an hour ago?" Ryan asked.

"Fairfield, or whatever it's called. Yeah, why?"

"Because if that's the case, then we're on the wrong damn highway, that's why," Colleen said, her finger poised on the map at the point at which the highways split and began running in different directions.

"Drew, you weren't supposed to get on Highway 26 at all. We went too far. You shot past Highway 75 by a good forty miles. According to the map, we're heading to the other side of Idaho, which just so happens to be a long way from where we should be going," Ryan shouted.

"There isn't any reason to yell at me. I asked Colleen earlier if I was supposed to continue east at the last highway intersection we had. You told me I was."

"Don't blame me, Drew. You said you knew the way there. It's not like I knew for certain because the damn snow is covering most of the signs," Colleen shot back.

"Okay, let's all calm down. Shouting or blaming each other isn't going to solve anything. What we need to focus on is our next decision. We either keep heading in the same direction and lay over in the next town we reach, or try to turn around and head back to one of these small towns we've passed before we completely lose traction on the road. That is, if I can somehow manage to turn around," I said.

"You're right. I'm sorry. It's nobody's fault. According to the map, the next town along this highway is called Arco. So we're about thirty miles from where I figure we should be. Fairfield is over an hour behind us, and with the snow coming down as hard as it is now, our smartest choice would be to continue forward. I guess that's my vote," Colleen said.

"I can say that I'm not exceptionally happy with this outcome, but we have no choice. Let's head for Arco," Ryan agreed, and slumped back in the seat.

I glanced in the rearview mirror and watched Joel. His face was sallow and nearly drained of life. A slight fever began to hit him when we departed from Sacramento, but his fever dramatically increased, like the snowstorm raging outside. Joel was having a difficult time breathing and constantly released violent coughs that worried me. The four of us, maybe stranded in the middle of nowhere with a storm raging outside the windows, brought out the guilt in me. I was blaming myself for getting lost, and there was no getting around that.

"Joel, what's your opinion on this?" I asked.

Joel's bloodshot eyes found mine in the rearview mirror. "Um, yeah, if Colleen thinks the town in front of us is closer, that would be the wisest direction to go."

"I agree, too," I said. "I guess we're moving forward. Hopefully, we can find a motel in Arco and sit out this storm. It might take a day, or maybe even two, before the roads are cleared. I couldn't even estimate when this storm will end."

Traveling the highway became more of a challenge as we moved forward. The tires of my Explorer continued to lose grip and caused a slight skid before I could regain control. I gazed at the speedometer and saw that we were only going thirty miles per hour. If Arco was thirty miles ahead of us, as Colleen predicted, I honestly didn't think I could negotiate the road for another hour in these conditions.

The windshield wipers were having a hard time keeping up with the snowfall. The snow not brushed away from view was packed tight at the lower half of the windshield. I feared that the gears of the wiper blades would strip from being unable to complete their full motion. I also worried that I wouldn't start forward momentum again if I took a minute to stop and clear away the obstruction.

"What are we going to do if we don't make it to Arco, Drew?" Colleen asked.

"How about we try being optimistic? Let's keep focusing on a town right in front of us. Before you know it, we'll be there," I said.

"I'm not trying to, but we need to prepare for the worst possible scenario. We only have a half tank of gas. If we get stuck, we can still run the engine for a little while, but what would we do then if no one comes along?"

"Colleen, I really don't want to think in that frame of mind right now. Joel is getting worse, and we need to get him somewhere warm. Let's not worry about anything until there's something actually to worry about. All right?"

"Okay, sorry. I'm just getting a little scared, that's all."

I was trying to stay calm. I had the same fear creeping inside me. I didn't want the others to know that I was worried. I didn't think it would help matters. Colleen was right about our current situation. A half of a tank of gas would most likely get us to Arco, and if by some unfortunate chance we become snowbound, we have enough gas to last a little while and keep the interior of the vehicle warm. Maybe someone else would pass by. Maybe someone wouldn't.

I shook away the thoughts. I wasn't taking my own advice. I had told Colleen not to worry until there was something to worry about. At this point, things were all right. We had few problems, and I needed to keep my focus on the road ahead.

The plan had been simple at first. Four college friends compiling part-time earnings and reserving a private cottage in the Sawtooth Mountains of Idaho. It was supposed to be a pre-Christmas holiday vacation filled with skiing, drinking, hanging out by the fire, and enjoying each other's company. Even the best-laid plans couldn't predict the wrath of Mother Nature.

I kept the vehicle centered on the highway. I thought that driving down the middle of the road would keep us from catching a slick patch, skidding off the pavement, and becoming stuck in an accumulating snowdrift.

Colleen glanced over her shoulder and quietly watched Joel trying to sleep in the backseat. She tugged on my coat, and I chanced a quick look at her. There was concern on her face, and she nodded toward Joel. I peered in the mirror. There was a sheen of sweat on his face, and he seemed even paler than the last time I had looked at him. He was going to need something to bring his fever down. The problem was that there wasn't a pharmacy or grocery store anywhere close. I thought that there would have to be at least a local grocery store in Arco, even if it were a small population town.

I offered her a concerned look and put my focus back on the road.

The rear wheels slid a little to the right. I automatically spun the steering wheel in the opposite direction and gently applied the brakes. Our momentum slowed, and the vehicle straightened out on the road. As we centered on the road again, I gave it a little more gas.

One long, slow mile crept after another until I finally saw lights to our left. There was a farmhouse partially hidden in the blanket of white. I was amazed that the power was still on. I figured the power lines would have been taken out by the wind or under the weight of the snow unless they were running a generator.

A moment later, I said, "There's a lot of country out here, and I'm hoping there's another small town before Arco that we can bunk in until this storm blows over."

"I hope so. Just don't run us off the road until then," Colleen said.

It's funny how words can curse a situation. All things had been all right. They had been good. When Colleen, God love her, had said that, the back end fishtailed a little and then picked up momentum and went haywire. The rear end slid slightly to the right, then to the left and back again, like some strange solo dance. The steering wheel spun in my grip as I tried to regain control. Then, with little resistance on our part, my SUV headed for the shoulder, plowed through the snow, barreled down the embankment, and stuck like an arrow.

"Shit. I told you not to do that," Colleen said and watched me.

What the situation didn't need was a fury of yelling. I kept my comment to myself and looked in the backseat. "Are you all right?"

Joel nodded. Ryan gave me a thumbs up and said, "Can we back out?"

I shifted gears to reverse and gently pressed the gas. At first, I thought the vehicle would back right up the grade with little problem, but then the wheels started spinning. I let it roll forward and punched the reverse again. This time, we didn't go anywhere. We only spun in place. I worked at it for ten minutes before I angrily threw the vehicle in park and turned to the others.

"We probably packed down the snow so much that it's now a sheet of ice. Ryan, I need you to help me try to clear some of it away so we can try again."

Ryan and I stepped into the torrent of snow. The wind caught the door and nearly tore it from my grip. I managed to get the door shut, but then lost my footing and went down. In any other situation, I would have found this funny, but not today of all days.

We worked at using our feet as makeshift shovels and kicked the snow clear from the wheels. We used our heels to break up the packed snow down the slight embankment. When my toes and fingers felt repeatedly stuck with hot needles, I yelled for Ryan to get back in the car. I wasn't sure if it was enough, but we had to make another go of it.

I took a minute to hold my hands in front of the heater vents. The numbness had eased, and the blood flow was going a little more steadily. I put the vehicle in reverse and tried again.

We made it halfway up the hill before spinning and sliding forward again. I thought about trying to get turned around and going up the slope that way, but the fence in front of us prevented that maneuver. I didn't have a choice of going out rear end first. I worked at it for nearly twenty minutes. The ground beneath the tires had become deeply grooved mud slicks. We weren't getting out of here any time soon.

I slammed the vehicle in park and stared out the window. I felt stupid, tired, and defeated. We were at a loss for this situation. There was only one thing I could think of doing from this point. We had to find shelter.

Everyone was watching me, waiting for an executive decision. I had made a choice, but I didn't think the others would agree, especially with Joel in his condition.

"We're going to have to abandon the vehicle. There's a farmhouse I saw about a mile back. The lights are still on, so that means they have power and heat. We can't stay here and hope that someone comes by because I don't see that happening," I said.

"That's crazy. A mile in this wind and weather will make it seem like ten miles," Colleen said.

"The wind will be at our backs, so that will help quite a bit. Look, I know you don't want to go out there. I assure you that I don't either, but we have the only chance with all of us leaving together. If I went alone or took Ryan with me, and they didn't have anything to pull us out of here, then we'd have to walk back to get you," I said and watched the falling snow that had nearly doubled accumulation.

Colleen said, "But what if no one is home and we have to walk back to the vehicle? It just makes more sense if you—"

"If no one is home, then I'll kick the damn door down! We're talking about our lives, Colleen. I'll buy them a new door if that's what it takes. Don't say anything else, just get your stuff," I told them.

I could tell Colleen wanted to protest further, but she probably figured it would do little good. I knew her mind had accepted my idea as the only logical one at the moment. We gathered our things, bundled our clothing, and stepped from the vehicle.

Colleen was right about the journey that seemingly stretched to ten miles, even with the wind at our backs. I figured it was a little over a mile to the farmhouse driveway. The snow was nearly a foot in some places, and trudging through it was exhausting.

Joel staggered in a sort of trance. He looked like a zombie trying and failing to catch fresh meat. We paused every so often for him to catch up and then moved forward again. It was slow going, but step after step got us closer to heat and food if the homeowners were gracious enough.

I didn't know how long it had taken us, but we finally hit the open gate of the driveway. Unfortunately, the beginning of the driveway was nearly a quarter-mile to the actual house.

I was sure that all of us were ready to collapse when we found the front door. I looked down the driveway we had traveled and could see that our approaching path had already disappeared in the blowing snow.

Ryan rang the bell and pounded with an urgent fist against the screen door.

"Hello? Is anyone home?" he called out.

The porch light flicked on, a curtain pulled aside, and the face of an elderly woman appeared. She studied us for a few cautious moments before deciding to open the door.

"Yes? What is it I can help you with?" she asked.

"We're sorry to disturb you, but we got caught in this blizzard, and our car went off the road a mile back. We've got a friend here that's very sick, and we didn't know where else to go. Would it be all right if we came inside until we could get someone to pull our vehicle out?" I said to her over the blowing wind.

She studied us again. She looked at Joel's pale features and the way he slumped against Colleen for support.

This woman isn't going to let us in and tell us to go away. She's going to say that there's another farmhouse a few miles down the road, and we should try there. She's scared that we only have intentions of harming her, I thought.

"I don't suppose it would be Christian of me to send you off in a storm like this. Come on in and get yourselves warmed up," the woman said, and stepped aside.

"Thank you so much. That's very kind of you," Colleen said as we moved inside.

We walked into the welcoming blast of heat. The woman closed the door and followed us into the moderately sized kitchen. This place was welcoming shelter from the storm, and I was gracious about that.

We volleyed a series of "thank you," and she replied with a "don't mention it." She showed us to the living room with a roaring fireplace. The area was also a trophy room for previously living creatures. There were several buck heads, a few ducks, a goose, and even a bobcat, holding pose beside the couch.

As we walked in, Colleen cringed and pressed against me. Her eyes switched from one almost lifelike animal face to another. Her arm wrapped around me as we stepped closer to the fire.

An older man in a wheelchair was beside one of the wingback chairs. A cigarette hung from his mouth, and a book lay closed on his lap. He was watching us with curious eyes as we approached.

"Found yourselves in a bit of a bad spot, did you?" he asked in a grainy voice, probably roughened by countless years of smoking.

I wasn't sure if he meant our vehicle getting stuck or a situation that I wasn't even aware we were in yet. By the look of the room, I fully expected that we were next on his hunt list. He would give us a ten-minute head start, and somehow the man would push himself from the wheelchair and follow our tracks in the snow until all of us were targeted and brought down on the hunt. I shook my head at the stupid, paranoid thought and offered him a warm smile.

"We sure did. I can't thank you enough for helping us," I said.

"Of course, think nothing of it. I suppose we'll be together for some time by the look of things outside. I'm John Harris, and this is my wife Norma," he said.

I pointed and said, "This is Colleen, Ryan, Joel and I'm Drew. We're pleased to meet you."

Joel delivered a series of fitful coughs, followed by a sneeze and a whine of his lungs as he drew in a breath.

"Oh, dear, you really aren't well, are you?" Norma asked.

"No, ma'am," Joel said.

"Well, get on over here and take a rest beside the fire. Norma, get some hot tea to warm their bones. Norma's brand of tea will fix you up quick as you like," John said, and stabbed his cigarette in the ashtray.

Joel took a seat in one of the chairs, and Colleen took the other. Norma disappeared into the other room and quickly returned with a wool blanket and draped it over Joel. He thanked her and held his hands closer to the flames. She moved into the other room again, and I could hear the clanking of pots and then the facet running.

"I wonder if we might be able to use your phone so we can call a tow truck out here to get our vehicle back on the road," Ryan said.

"Sure you can, but I couldn't say if it will do much good. The nearest town is Arco, about twenty miles down the road. They've got a small auto shop there, but I wouldn't imagine anyone would be insane enough to stick around the shop in a storm like this. Frank, he's the guy who runs it, is probably home now waiting out the storm just like everyone else. Even if you manage to get ahold of him, I couldn't figure he'd drive all this way in a blizzard to pull a car back onto the road. But you can give it a shot if you like. The phone is hanging on the kitchen wall beside the refrigerator," John said and lit another cigarette.

Ryan moved to the kitchen, and I could hear him asking Norma for the auto store's phone number and then dialing an old rotary phone.

I don't know why I kept shifting my gaze from John, sitting in his wheelchair smoking another cigarette, and then to the fire. I thought it was the discomfort of the situation we were in. The four of us were unfortunately stranded and taken in by two people that seemed good-natured enough. Maybe it was the dead animals lining the walls and my philosophy of live and let live. Whatever the reason, I felt out of place.

"I had a stroke earlier this year. It was a pretty bad one, actually. That's the reason for the wheelchair. I saw you looking and figured you'd want to know," John said and watched me through his rolling cloud of smoke.

"I'm sorry, I didn't mean to stare," I said as I suddenly felt like an ass.

"Think nothing of it. My speech has improved since the stroke, but my left side doesn't want to work like it used to. I haven't given up sleeping in my bed since it's upstairs. It's good therapy to work that staircase every night. But I've been having a bastard of a time trying to take care of other things around here. Norma tries to do it all and grumbles when I try to help out. We're both getting up there in years, and it's damn near impossible for two old fools to run a farm anymore."

"What type of farm is this?" Colleen asked.

"Wheat farm. Ain't too much to it. The stuff mostly takes care of itself. This year since I had the stroke, I hired someone to harvest. Of course, there are lots of other things that need tending to around the farm."

"Sounds like you've got your hands full," I said and sat on the hearth and immediately felt the warmth of the fire on my back.

"Sure, that's until we harvest, and then I get plenty of time for reading and watching my programs."

Norma walked into the living room with a tray of cups, a kettle, and cookies. I got up and helped her with the tray. She poured the tea into the cups, and I handed them out. Norma passed around a tin of sugar cookies, and everyone took a few. We ate and drank in silence. I was still feeling a little awkward about our intrusion, and I couldn't think of a thing to say.

"Where were you heading before you got stuck?" Norma asked.

"Oh, we were on our way to one of the Sawtooth Mountain resorts. We thought we'd be able to make it through until we got a little lost and then went off the road," Colleen said.

Even though she hadn't looked at me during her explanation, I felt the accusation directed toward me. Drew got us lost, and then he developed a severe case of poor driving skills and stuck us right in the fucking ditch, is what Colleen meant to say. It didn't seem like a fitting time and place for an argument, so I let it go.

"The phone line is down," Ryan said as he came back into the living room.

"Down? We've never had the phone go down before. We've lost power plenty of times, especially in storms like this, but never the phone line," John said.

"I tried several times. There's no dial tone whatsoever," Ryan said and poured a cup of tea.

"Well, I guess that means you'll be staying put for a while. We're certainly not a bed-and-breakfast, but I don't see any other way around it. We've got a few extra rooms for you to sleep in," Norma said.

The four of us looked at each other. I think we understood that our options had hit an impenetrable wall. We were staying the night whether we liked it or not. Our trip to the ski resort would have to wait a day or more until the damn blizzard blew itself out and we could get our vehicle pulled free.

"That's very kind of you," Colleen finally said.

"I say this all the time, so you'll have to get used to it, but think nothing of it," John said.

Something hit the front of the house with a jarring rap that made all of us jump. We turned and looked at the kitchen as if a bear had hastily come through the front door and had ass-kicking business to consider.

"Was that a tree branch that hit the house?" I asked.

"Couldn't have been. We don't have any trees close to the house," Norma said and headed for the kitchen.

Ryan joined her as they inspected what the disturbance was all about. I heard the front door open, bang against the wall as the wind grabbed hold of it and then heard Norma say something I couldn't understand.

"Drew, get in here and give us a hand, will ya?" Ryan called.

I was on my feet in a second flat and running for the kitchen. I was expecting several things, but what I saw wasn't one of them. There was a man lying face down in the snow on the front porch. Norma and Ryan each had a grip on an arm, and they were trying to pull him inside.

"What in the world?" I asked as the situation completely caught me off-guard. I hurried to Norma's side and took the man's arm.

When I first touched the man, I was sure he was dead. In fact, I would have put down a sizable amount of money on it. I didn't feel a bit of warmth coming from him. The only thing that convinced me the man was still alive was the wisp of his white breath.

Norma moved out of the way. Ryan and I were able to drag the man inside and across the linoleum like a sack of grain. As we carefully rotated him on his back. He was breathing all right, but each intake was labored and slightly gurgled. Norma closed the front door, and the blowing snow fluttered to the floor and melted.

Everyone from the living room came into the kitchen or lingered in the doorway. The group watched us as if the man's appearance had been some divine magic trick that contradicted all logic.

I pressed my fingers to his throat. I knew he was alive, but I wanted to feel his pulse and get some idea how close to death this man was. His pulse was weak, barely a gentle tap on my fingertip.

He moaned something, and those unintelligible words made several of us pull back. His eyes slowly opened, closed, and opened again. His glacier blue eyes gazed at the ceiling for a long moment before his sight fixed on the faces hovering over him.

"Can you hear me?" I asked.

He moaned again, then must have decided that his voice just wasn't there, and nodded.

"What's your name?" Colleen asked. She had taken his hand and was briskly rubbing it to get the blood flow working again.

"Lewis Thorson," he said, and I think all of us understood him that time.

"You must have got caught up in the storm just like these four," John said from his wheelchair in the kitchen doorway.

Lewis nodded.

"It wasn't such a smart thing to be traveling alone in a blizzard. We'll get you fixed right up. Norma, draw this man a hot bath," John said.

Norma started for the bathroom but immediately halted when she heard what Lewis said next.

"Wasn't traveling alone. There's another. My patient, he tried to kill me," Lewis said. He closed his eyes, and his body went slack.

Ryan and I undressed the man and gently dropped his unconscious body into the warm bathwater. I thought the hot water would immediately revive the man, but his eyes remained closed, and his body kept sliding forward and deeper into the water. We held him from going head under and taking a lung full of water.

We soaked him for twenty minutes. I constantly checked his pulse until I was satisfied that his heart rate was steadily kicking again. Instead of trying to redress a two hundred pound wet man, which would have been a trick in itself, we draped John's bathrobe around him and carefully moved him to the couch. Once there, Colleen covered him with a wool blanket and tucked the edges under him like she put down a child for the night.

"While you guys were in the bathroom, we went out front to check if this other man was anywhere outside. We didn't see anyone or other tracks in the snow, but we found this on the porch under the snow," Colleen said, and held up a brown leather case.

I took it by the handle and studied it. It seemed odd that a man fighting for his life in one of nature's more devious acts would drag along this case.

"He didn't have gloves with him, but he managed to bring this up to the house?" I said.

"I know. It's a little strange," Colleen agreed.

"Did you look inside?" I asked.

"No, it's locked. I wouldn't have searched through it, anyway. Whatever is in there is none of our business," Colleen said.

I put the case on the floor next to the couch and watched it for a minute, as if the thing held sinister secrets.

"The reason I asked was that Lewis said that someone else was with him and that this other man almost killed him. If that's true, we need to start worrying that this unknown man might show up at the front door. What if this other man is crazy? We can't predict what this guy will do if he manages to get inside the house," I said.

"So if someone else shows up, we're just supposed to lock him out in the blizzard and let him freeze to death?" Ryan asked.

"I didn't say that. I'm just saying that we don't know the whole story, so we need to be extremely cautious if someone else comes around," I said.

"When this fella comes around, I suppose we'll have some pretty interesting questions for him," John said.

"I don't like this at all," Norma said.

At the back of the living room was an oak gun case with glass doors. Inside were several shotguns and half a dozen hunting rifles. I said, "As a precaution, I think we need you to unlock the gun case, John."

"Let's not panic. This guy barely made it from his car to the house without freezing to death. It's been an hour since he arrived, so if someone else is out there, then they're probably already dead," Colleen said as she looked from one face to another.

"Maybe," I agreed.

"Well, we don't know how far away his car got stuck, which means that maybe the car is much closer to another farm. Maybe this man came here when he could have gone to another house much closer, and the other guy went another way. We've also got a heated barn we keep the animals in. Maybe he stumbled in there," John said.

"I don't think we can even guess at this point. Maybe this guy here was able to kill the other for whatever the circumstances were," I added.

Ryan went to the front window and peered out. I could see around him. Outside was a blanket of white. I couldn't figure on how anyone could make a path through a blizzard that had doubled its momentum since we'd been here.

"It's your house and your guns, John. I just think we need to have a gun ready in case something unexpected happens," Ryan said.

We all watched John. John watched his wife. Even though it was clear that he was the man of the house, John obviously respected his wife's opinion. I didn't think the matter would go any further, but then Norma nodded to indicate that she agreed.

"Well, here's where I find myself. I just met your group, and I'm usually a pretty good judge of character, but the truth is that no one knows what's truly in someone's heart. As it stands, I wouldn't trust any of you as far as I could throw you, and being that I'm in this wheelchair, you could say that my toss wouldn't be very far. Except for this man who has barely mumbled a few words since he arrived, I think the rest of you are stand-up individuals. However, part of me agrees we need the protection. The other part of me disagrees. The gun case has a glass front, so it wouldn't take much for any of you to break in there if you got it in your head. I will tell you that the ammunition is locked up in the drawers, and the wood and locks are solid. It would take a lot of work to get the drawers open. I suppose you're right, and we need protection if things suddenly get stirred up," John said. He then maneuvered to a row of cabinets in the dining area, opened one of the drawers, and dug in the far back until he produced a ring of keys.

John moved to the gun case, opened the door, and removed both shotguns. Ryan took one, and I took the other.

"Those are twelve-gauge shotguns. I'm going to give you buckshot rounds which will tear a man's guts right out of his back. I want you to keep the safety on and your fingers off the triggers until something gets out of hand. We don't want anyone accidentally injured. If someone gets wounded badly, then they may die right here in this house," John said. He opened the bottom drawer, removed a box of shells, and handed it to me.

"I promise that we'll be careful. No one is going to get shot that doesn't deserve it," I said as I loaded the shotgun.

Ryan loaded his gun, and then we moved to the windows and studied the outside like a couple of sentries. I thought that Colleen was right by saying that anyone trapped outdoors in this weather condition was surely dead or dying. But there was a small part of me that feared what John had said. If there was a deranged man on the loose and holed up at another farm, then, unfortunately, that was a situation we couldn't contend with for the time being. The phone was out of order, and there was no way for John to contact his closest neighbors and warn them of a possible psychopath trying to find shelter. I also worried about the heated barn John mentioned. If the man that had tried to kill Lewis had situated himself in there, then he could very well wait until nightfall and attempt to get inside the house when the rest of us were sleeping. I thought that we'd have to take shifts during the night. Someone was going to have to stay awake at all times. Someone would have to listen for the faintest sounds of an intruder.

Of course, nightfall was a long way away, and no one could tell what might happen between now and then.

A few hours later, Colleen pulled me off to the side in the kitchen. She wore an expression of worry.

"Joel's getting worse. I just checked his temperature. It's reached 103 degrees," she said and watched me and waited for an answer I didn't have.

"I know. Norma gave him some flu medicine earlier. It'll take time until we figure out if it does any good. We'll have to wait it out. In case you didn't notice, there's an endless path of deep snow to the nearest hospital."

"I'm aware of that. I hate it when you talk to me like I'm a complete moron," she snapped.

"I'm sorry. I didn't mean to do that. I'm worried, too. I have to admit that the other guy worries me as well. We don't know anything about him. We also don't know anything about his companion and what happened to him," I said.

"Do you think this other guy tried to kill Lewis?" Colleen asked.

I shrugged and said, "Who knows? I've been thinking about Ryan and I going out to the heated barn John has and making sure there isn't someone hiding out in there."

"Do you think that's smart?"

"I think I'd feel better knowing either way. If he's in there, then we can capture him. Maybe we can keep him locked in a room until we know the whole story of why he tried to kill Lewis. Maybe he isn't in there at all. Maybe he's frozen to death on the side of the road. We need to check that barn. I don't want any surprises during the night," I said.

"I understand. I'm just a little scared about someone in the barn surprising the both of you and getting the upper hand."

"We'll take one of the shotguns and leave the other here. We'll be extremely cautious," I said and looked out the kitchen window to see how much snow had accumulated since I'd last checked. The snowfall was steadily blowing. A deep drift had built up against the north side of the house. If Ryan and I were going to attempt to reach the barn, we had better do it soon.

I wrapped my arms around Colleen. I hadn't realized how scared she really was until I felt her tremble in my arms. "Hey, everything is going to be all right. Try not to worry too much. You'll see that this storm is going to blow past us by nightfall, and in the morning, we'll be able to get a tow truck out here and get our vehicle back on the road. Before you know it, we'll be at the resort, hitting the slopes and having a great time."

"You better be right. I can't take much more of this tension," Colleen said.

We moved into the living room. The others were watching a hazy picture of the local forecast on television. The meteorologist told the viewers that the blizzard moved southeast from British Columbia and hit a major portion of Washington, Idaho, and Montana as it continued to pick up strength. He was anticipating a snowfall of more than thirty-six inches by morning.

"That's just great. What the hell are we going to do?" Ryan asked.

"We'll hunker down, as the man said to do. We've got more than enough supplies to outlast this storm," John said.

I looked out the window again and said, "I've decided that Ryan and I are going to head over to your barn and check out things in there."

"What's in there you're looking to find? The animals will be just fine as long as the power lines hold out," Norma said.

"Well, I've been thinking about this other man our friend here spoke of before he passed out. We've had this discussion before. We need to make sure this guy isn't waiting for the opportunity to come after us," I said.

"We can't even be sure there is another person. This guy has suffered from a traumatizing experience. Maybe he wasn't in his right mind when he said those things. Maybe he was traveling alone, and under the bad weather conditions, he could have imagined that someone was after him," Colleen suggested.

I looked over my shoulder and watched the sleeping man. He hadn't stirred since we had placed him on the couch and covered him with several blankets. Although we had given him a warm bath and brought him back from the edge of death, he hadn't consciously come around.

"I don't know the man, but I'm going to take his word for it. I believe what he told us. We have to make sure the barn is clear," I said.

"All right, I don't have a problem going with you," Ryan said.

John looked at his wife and shrugged. He said, "I suppose you've got it in your head that you have to do this. I don't figure any of us are going to stop you."

"No, probably not," I agreed. I looked at Ryan. "Let's get bundled up and head out before we can't get ten feet in this stuff."

Colleen continued to protest as we went out the front door, and her calls after us were taken away by the relentless wind.

Our trip from the abandoned vehicle to the farmhouse was with the wind at our back. The wind now was coming at us with a ferocity unlike any I'd experienced before. To further add to our insane journey, the accumulation of snow nearly doubled. Since the early afternoon, the snow had risen almost mid-calf in some areas. Our progress was slow and downright exhausting. I did my best to drag my legs through the snow. Not only was I trying to cut an easier path for Ryan to follow, but I also wanted to make sure that our path back to the house was as clear as possible.

The barn that housed the animals was over a hundred yards south of the farmhouse. I couldn't see the barn very well, but only a silhouette of the building that John assured me was there. I stopped around the midway point and turned to Ryan.

I leaned in closer so that he could hear me over the howl of the wind. "I'm going to rest a minute. Making a path in this damn snow is killing me. It's cold as hell out here, but my legs are on fire."

Ryan was wearing his ski goggles and face mask. He pulled the mask below his chin. "How about if I take the lead? You can stay behind me. I want to get there as quick as possible and get this over with."

I nodded, and we switched positions. Staying behind Ryan was a great deal more manageable for me, but my leg muscles still burned in protest. I thought that once we got to the barn, cleared the area of any intruders, we'd still have to take a good five-minute break to catch our breath before heading back.

As I followed Ryan and tried to keep my balance, I kept shifting my sight to the surrounding area. No other foot tracks marked a path to the barn. I thought of this mystery man who accompanied Lewis. I figured that his course to shelter would be noticeable if the man had managed to get to the barn. Then again, as I thought more about it, it had been hours since Lewis arrived, which meant that if the other man was close behind his companion's lead, the snow would have long since covered his trail.

There's no doubt that I worried over the information about another man, a man who attempted murder, hiding out here somewhere close. I wasn't sure if I had jumped the gun and decided if the search in a blizzard was a great idea or not. This whole situation was part of my personality. I hated not being in control and facing circumstances I hadn't planned far in advance. I also hated the idea of something happening to my friends. I didn't think I'd forgive myself for getting us stuck in the first place if something terrible happened. I'd be the first to admit that being snowbound was my fault, and now I was trying to make sure that nothing else unfortunate found us until we could safely get to the ski resort.

There was no lock on the barn door, but Ryan and I spent five minutes clearing the high drift of snow away from the door so it would swing it open enough for us to squeeze through. A blissful blast of warmth welcomed us as we went inside and closed the door.

John and Norma didn't have many animals, but all of them gave us their attention. There were two horses, a dozen chickens, a rooster, and a goat.

I removed my gloves, rubbed my hands together, and flexed my fingers. There was sharp tingling throughout my hands as the blood began moving more steadily through them. We spent a moment looking around, observing the animals, and searching for someone who didn't belong. Ryan was holding the shotgun in front of him with his finger on the trigger.

We searched the horse and goat stalls. The chicken coop was too small for a person to hide inside. We looked in the area John kept as food storage for the animals. When we were sure the barn's main floor was clear, we moved to the ladder leading to the loft. Ryan went first as he still had the shotgun. When he reached the third rung from the top, he swung the gun up and around the opening, perhaps anticipating a sudden attack. Ryan moved up like a fired piston over the edge and propelled himself into the loft area. I stayed a few rungs below as Ryan shuffled around the loft as if he was a soldier under fire. I heard him shifting around, the creak of floorboards, and finally, Ryan called out the all-clear. I moved up the ladder and into the loft. There were bales of hay, a shelf of tools, and nothing more.

"No one here," Ryan said.

"I can see that. Well, at least we know this other man didn't make it this far," I said.

"He's probably a Popsicle on the roadside."

"Do you think we should feed the animals while we're here? There's no telling when they'll get fed again with this blizzard on top of us. I think it's the least we can do for John and Norma since they took us in," I said.

Ryan agreed, and we got to work. We rummaged through the food storage and dished out extra helpings as well as refilled water bowls. When we finished the work, we bundled up again, moved outside, and closed the barn door. Our approach path had already started to cover over, but the walk back was much easier since I had the idea to plow through the snow instead of taking giant steps.

Our walk back took half the time. We entered the kitchen, stomped our boots clean, and began peeling off layers. Norma was already preparing a pot of coffee to revitalize us. Colleen and John came into the kitchen and watched us.

"Well?" Colleen asked.

"We didn't find anyone. There wasn't any indication another person was out there," I said.

"So all of that was for nothing?" she said.

"Well, I wouldn't say it was all for nothing. We made sure that no person was hiding in there. We also fed and watered all the animals, since it might be a long time until their next meal," I said.

"I appreciate that. You're good men," John said.

"You're welcome. We thought it was the least we could do," Ryan said.

After I took off my winter clothing, I sat beside the fire and enjoyed a cup of strong coffee.

I was watching the sleeping man on the couch when Colleen said, "He woke up. It was only brief, but he came around for a moment before going out again."

"He did? Did he say anything?" I asked.

"No. Lewis barely opened his eyes. I didn't even get the chance to ask him a question," Colleen said.

"Too bad. I think we have some serious questions for this man. Where's Joel?"

"He's lying down in one of the bedrooms. He isn't getting any better. The medicine Norma gave him isn't doing much," she said.

"I didn't figure he would get better anytime soon. As long as he doesn't get worse, that's what I'm worried about," I said.

I'm curious by nature. I suppose we all are to a certain degree, but when I get curious about a particular thing, there's no stopping until I'm satisfied. The man on the couch had my curiosity in overdrive. We knew his name, and we knew he was traveling with another man. We knew this other man tried to kill him. At least, that's what he claimed. Of course, I didn't know the full extent of the circumstances between the two men, but I found it rather odd that this unknown man would try to kill Lewis when both of them were trying to find shelter from the blizzard. Perhaps Lewis meant that the other man wanted to kill him long before they took the trip, and the statement was a simple memory from so long ago that it came to the surface with no rhyme or reason. Maybe Colleen was right, maybe there wasn't another man, and Lewis was fighting delirium as much as he was fighting the severe storm.

What piqued my curiosity the most was the locked satchel Lewis brought with him. He had carried it through a curtain of endless white snow until he reached the farmhouse. I wondered what was so important that he couldn't leave behind until the storm passed and he could get back to his abandoned car.

It was nearly ten o'clock when Norma and John wished us goodnight and retired to bed. Norma had made up the beds in the other vacant rooms for when we decided to call it a night. Joel had taken one of the guest beds on the main floor. I decided to check on him in a little while, but I wanted to do something first.

I went to the fireplace, which was now more glowing embers than flames, and threw a few logs on. I looked at Ryan and Colleen. They sat in the armchairs in a similar pose, with their bodies slumped, arms crossed over their chests, and heads lulled to one side. Their eyes were closed, and they deeply breathed as sleep had a firm hold on them.

My eyes shifted to the man on the sofa who hadn't moved in several hours. He was still fast asleep. I watched Lewis for signs of waking as I walked to the couch, leaned down, and seized the handle of the satchel. I practically tiptoed to the dining room table and set the case down. Lewis's coat was hanging on the back of one of the chairs, and I searched the pockets for the key. A minute later, I came up empty-handed. After removing Lewis from the bath, we used one of John's bathrobes to cover him. We had bundled his clothes and left them on the dining room table. I searched the pockets and couldn't even find a wallet or car keys. His only possession in this house was the damn satchel.

I took the case to the kitchen and spent several minutes searching the drawers, looking for something to work the lock open. I figured I would come up with nothing again until I saw several letters fixed to a corkboard beside the refrigerator. A pushpin held the letters in place, but binding the letters into a stack was a paper clip. I pulled it loose and sat at the small kitchen table.

I worked diligently for nearly ten minutes. I'm not a master thief or even a thief with a relative clue. I wasn't sure if a simple paper clip could open a lock like this. Ten minutes turned into fifteen as I struggled. I kept my ears tuned for the sounds of someone getting up and moving toward the kitchen. I was afraid of getting caught. I was more fearful of getting caught by Lewis. I'd have no explanation of why I was searching through his personal property. I didn't know the man at all. I had no way of knowing how he might react to finding someone digging through his personal property.

I was about to give up the effort when the latch popped open. Much to my disappointment, the case was full of papers. I peered in and fingered through the files. It wasn't a mystery. It wasn't a secret satchel that held answers to my much-needed questions. I couldn't really say what I was expecting, but I didn't figure it would be a bundle of papers. I pulled out a yellow folder, placed it on the table, and opened it. Inside were handwritten notes on white paper. The top sheet was dated yesterday. I flipped through the stack until I reached an entry dated at the beginning of September. I pulled out this two-page note and began reading.

After spending an hour reading, I sat there for a few minutes, lost in thought. I had reached only one conclusion. The man Dr. Thorson was traveling with was his recent patient in which the file spoke about. The case file of Dr. Thorson's patient was disturbing, to say the least. If I understood everything in the files, then I had every reason to be paranoid from the beginning. If Dr. Thorson's patient was alive and somewhere on the farm, then the situation was even more troubling than I first suspected. We were battling a nasty blizzard. We were also fighting a deceptive man who was mentally ill, and there was no telling what someone like that would do given a chance.

A firm hand fell on my right shoulder. I felt the blood flush from my face. My voice caught in my throat as silent terror ran across my nerves. I knew it was Lewis. I knew the man who was near death all day was now fully recovered. His fury would hit the ceiling as he saw that I had picked open his satchel and gone through confidential files of his current client.

"What do you think you're doing?"

I swiveled my head and looked at Colleen. Even though it wasn't Lewis, I still felt a great deal of shame in what I had done.

"Christ, you scared the hell out of me," I whispered.

"Did you break the lock open?"

"No, I picked it open."

"What the hell for?"

"I'm curious about why he went through a hell of a blizzard dragging this thing along with him. I wanted to know why it was so important," I said.

"You're completely mental. It's none of your damn business. Why would you do that?" Colleen whispered.

"I'm sorry. I'm not proud of it. What I really wanted to know is if there's some sort of information in here that can tell us about who this other guy is, the guy Lewis said tried to kill him."

"Whoever he is, he's most likely dead. I want you to relock the case, put it back and let this whole thing go, Drew." Her eyes were unwavering as she spoke to me like I was a child who was seconds from throwing a tantrum.

"You should read this file. The guy's name is Simon Crane. I couldn't say for sure if that's the person Lewis was referring to, but if he is, then I think we're in serious trouble if he's still alive."

"I'm not reading anything. I don't care what it says. Put it back, Drew. I think you need to get some rest," she said and lovingly squeezed my shoulder.

"I know. I'm tired, but this file is damn interesting. Our friend in the other room is a psychiatrist, and Simon Crane is one of his patients. Simon Crane has one hell of a life story. He had quite a few traumatic experiences as a child. Lewis believes those experiences split his personality. He thinks Simon has as many as five personalities. All but one of those personalities is extremely violent," I said as I ruffled through the pages again.

"Drew, I don't care about this Simon guy. Lock the damn case and forget this thing."

Reluctantly, I did. I replaced the files exactly as they were and spent more than five minutes working the paper clip around until the lock gave a distinctive snap of engagement. I returned the satchel to the couch, retrieved the shotgun from where I had left it leaning against the wall, and peered out the window.

It was no surprise to see that the snow hadn't relented. It hadn't worsened, either. The snow fell with steadiness as defiance to our plans for a winter resort getaway. The moon reflected off the snow of the farm's landscape and offered a strange eeriness.

Colleen had returned to the chair beside the fire and had already fallen asleep. I don't know how long I stared out the window as my thoughts ran over what our next move would be. Someone entered the kitchen. I turned to face Norma as she walked toward me. She almost appeared to be sleepwalking, as her face was pale and her eyes fixed.

"Is everything all right?" I asked.

She spoke in a whisper. "I couldn't sleep. I just checked on your friend. He's gotten worse. I took his temperature. It's at one hundred and four degrees now. The medicine isn't working to bring down the fever. I don't know what else to do."

My entire body sagged. I had earlier thought of one measure to bring Joel's temperature down. It was a method that wasn't only dangerous, but one Joel certainly wasn't going to like.

I said, "All right. I'm going to have to wake the others to help me with something."

I went to the chairs beside the fireplace and gently shook awake Ryan and Colleen.

"What is it? Is something wrong?" Ryan asked, as he was suddenly alarmed when he noticed the shotgun in my hands.

"Joel's burning up pretty bad. We've got to take drastic measures to bring the fever down. I'm going to need your help."

Norma flipped on the hall light, and Colleen, Ryan, and I moved into the bedroom where Joel was currently staying. He hadn't been asleep as his eyes reflexively pinched shut from the bright light.

Colleen sat on the edge of the bed, tenderly stroked his sweat-covered forehead, and said, "How are you doing, sweetie?"

His voice was raw from the countless hours of painful coughing. "About the same. I'm sweating quite a lot. I think the fever is going to break soon."

"Norma said your temperature is now 104. That's making all of us nervous," I said.

"I'll beat it. You don't worry about it."

"You're going to start frying brain cells before too long, and you can't afford to waste any more of the good ones," Ryan said over my shoulder.

"I'd kick your ass if I could stand up," Joel said.

I spoke in a whisper now. "Hey, I think we're at the point at which we have to take extreme measures. We don't want to do this to you, and I'm sure that you'll be unwilling to have it done, but we need to knock that temperature out. As you know, we're a hell of a long way from any hospital."

"What are you talking about?" Joel asked.

"I have an idea that if we take you outside and put you in the snow for a few minutes, it should knock your core temperature down some. I don't see any other way around it," I said, and studied his face.

Joel looked one step beyond horror-struck. He searched one face after another, confirming that our intentions were genuine.

"That's insane," Joel said.

"Not if it works. I've heard of this before. The temperature outside is more than enough to cool your body temperature in a short time. The only thing I fear is that doing this might put you in shock," I said.

"No, I'll take my chances of fried brain cells before I do something that crazy," Joel said, and gave a racking cough into his fist.

"I'm sorry, Joel, but I don't think you're going to have a choice in the matter. This is the best thing for you right now, and we'll do it forcefully if we have to. You know you're too weak to offer much of a fight. I don't want to make you do this, but we'll drag you out the front door kicking and screaming if need be," I said.

"You're an asshole. I always knew you were," Joel said in a somewhat playful voice that I read as defeat.

Thankfully, we weren't going to have to force him because he was willing to go with our plan.

The three of us helped him up from the bed. Slowly, we made our way to the kitchen and then to the front door.

"All right, before we go out, you might as well do it inside," I said.

"Do what?" Joel asked.

"Strip. Take all of your clothes off. Not only will your clothes stay dry, but the cold needs to be right on your skin."

"I know you've always had a thing for me, Drew, but this is one hell of a method you're using to see me naked."

"I've seen you naked before. I'm sure I'll still be unimpressed."

"All the way?" he asked and glanced at Colleen and Norma.

"No, you can keep your skivvies on," I told him.

"I don't like this one bit," Joel said as he started to shrug out of his layers of clothing.

He was having a hard time getting his tired and sick body to move, so I helped him. I pulled his shirt over his head. The back of my hands went against his skin, and I thought I had touched a flame. Joel's skin was pale, slick with sweat, and about the temperature of the sun.

Colleen whistled appreciatively as her eyes roamed the bare parts of Joel's body. We all turned to look at her smiling face.

"That's nothing. You should see me when I'm feeling good," Joel said.

"All right, enough with the fun and games. Let's get this over with," I said as Ryan and I assisted Joel to the front door.

The door nearly tore out of my hand as I turned the knob, and the wind came screaming inside. For a moment,

I thought this was a terrible idea that we could just let Joel stand there, exposed to the frigid elements of the wind and snow, to drop his temperature. Then again, I didn't want to sound like I had no idea what I was doing by telling Joel to do something completely different. I decided to stick with the original plan.

Colleen and Norma stayed behind. Colleen closed the door, and the both of them watched through the window as our mad quest progressed into the front yard.

As Joel reluctantly sank in a four-foot-deep drift of snow against the house, I saw a horrid expression find the surface of his features. A scream also found the surface, as if he were settling down in molten lava instead of snow. Then the cold shock stole Joel's breath, and he released a series of groans, as all his muscles were no doubt painfully contracting from the massive temperature drop. His breath returned a moment later, and he began gasping in stuttering whispers.

Seconds seemed to last minutes as I kept time. I had figured three minutes would be enough, but it was all guesswork. I didn't even know if it would work or if I was torturing one of my closest friends for the sheer hell of it.

"You're enjoying this, aren't you?" Joel asked as he resentfully eyed Ryan and me.

"It's no picnic," I assured him.

"I think it will work," Ryan said.

After three minutes ticked by, Ryan and I helped Joel out of the snowbank and into the welcoming heat of the farmhouse. Norma quickly wrapped a large bath towel around his shoulders, and Colleen used another towel to dry his bare legs.

"Come on. We need to get you in the bathroom, out of the wet underwear, and into some dry clothes," I said.

"Still trying to see me naked. It never ends," Joel said through chattery teeth.

We left the bathroom and helped Joel to a chair beside the fire. Norma stuck a thermometer in his mouth and then checked the reading.

"It's gone down. One hundred degrees now," Norma said.

"You see? Now wasn't it worth it?" I asked.

Joel simply offered me his middle finger and then an apology to Norma.

"I think just because your temperature is down now doesn't mean it will stay down. I'm not trying to jinx anything here. The cold brought it down, but that doesn't mean your body won't crank it back up. We'll have to wait and see," I said.

"Whatever happens, I won't be doing that again," Joel said, and closed his eyes.

When I turned around, I discovered eyes carefully watching me. The man named Lewis, who had come from the cold of the blizzard, was looking at us.

"Hey, you're finally awake," I said in stunned surprise. I figured the man had slipped into a coma and wouldn't come out of it for years down the road when this entire experience was a distant memory of my life.

He cleared his throat and said, "Did you find me in the snow?"

"Sure did. You banged against the front door. When we answered, we found you face down on the porch," Ryan said.

"I don't remember finding a house. I remember walking through the snow, and I guess blacking out," he said in a raspy voice.

"Norma, could you get him something to drink?" I asked.

"Of course. Where are my manners? Would you like some tea or coffee? Something to warm you up?" she asked.

"Some warm milk would be fine. Thank you."

Norma went off to fetch a glass. We watched the man with fascination. I thought we were waiting for the man to reveal the ending to his brief story during our introduction.

"Is something wrong?" he asked as he studied us.

"We're just curious, that's all," Colleen said.

"Curious in what way?"

"You said something when we pulled you inside. You said something that spooked the hell out of all of us," I told him.

"I did? I don't even remember meeting you, and I certainly don't remember saying anything," Lewis said.

"Well, you did. You told us your name was Lewis Thorson, and that you were traveling with another man who tried to kill you," I said.

Lewis closed his eyes as if trying desperately to remember the events that led him to this secluded farmhouse in the middle of a blizzard.

Lewis nodded and said, "Yes, I remember now. I was traveling with one of my patients."

Norma returned with a glass of warm milk. Lewis thanked her and drank half the glass in several loud, relishing gulps.

"Are you a doctor?" Colleen asked, even though she knew the answer from my snooping through the man's belongings.

"I'm a clinical psychologist. I was taking my patient, Simon Crane, to a special facility outside of Langdon. Mr. Crane has multiple personality disorder, suffering from five separate personalities."

"Wow. I've never known anyone like that," Ryan said.

"He's a distraught man who desperately needs any help I can provide."

"Did he try to kill you?" Colleen asked.

"Yes, he did. When we got caught in the worst part of the storm, my car couldn't stay on the road, and our situation became tragic. His personality changed as a method of self-defense. The strongest personality, known as Dominic, came to the surface. Dominic is extremely violent. He tried to choke me to death. I managed to strike him several times over the head with my case, and I ran down the road. I don't know how, but I ended up here."

"Incredible. What do you think happened to him?" Colleen asked.

"I couldn't be sure. The blows were pretty hard, and I know I had cut his forehead open, but I'm sure it wasn't enough to kill him. I certainly didn't want to kill him. I just wanted to get him off me long enough so that I could get away. It wasn't his fault. He's a sick man that needs serious help. I only hope that he's somehow able to survive out in the blizzard. Are there other farms around here he could go to for shelter?"

"A few houses. I suppose it depends where you broke down," Norma said.

"I couldn't say. We were heading northeast. I remember seeing a grain silo with a tree growing through the middle of it near the road. After we got stuck and had our confrontation, I continued to go northeast on foot. I'd say a mile to a mile and a half if I had to guess," Lewis said.

"Sure. Actually, Richard Stanton's farmhouse would be closer to where your car is. It would be only a quarter mile or so from where you were," Norma said.

I told Lewis about our paranoia about this other mysterious man and an unseen danger about him. I told him our attempt to call the nearest neighbors and warn them of a potential threat from a stranger, but the phone lines are down. I also told him about our journey to the barn to check the area if the other man had found refuge there.

"I think the blows to the head had knocked him out. I know he went down, and that's when I started running. If he was knocked unconscious, then he could have frozen to death if he was out very long. I don't know," Lewis said and drank the remains of his warm milk.

"Whatever the case, it's out of our hands. If you barely made it here, then I'm certain he couldn't have with head trauma and all," I said.

"Why were you taking him to a facility in Langdon? Is it an insane asylum or something like that?" Colleen asked.

"No, not at all. It's a clinic that has a revolutionary new method for treating people with multiple personality disorder. They've found a way to isolate a single personality, the original personality, and drive the others to a deep recess of the mind in which they'd presumably be unable to resurface. The original personality of the individual would be the only one to survive. It's a cutting-edge advancement that will help thousands once the methods are open to the public. Right now, it's in the trial stages, and I received permission to introduce Mr. Crane into the program."

"That sounds pretty interesting. It's too bad you couldn't get your patient there before the blizzard came in," I said.

"Yeah, it's a shame Mr. Crane won't get the help he needs," Lewis said.

Let's play a word game. Let's link words.
Death: expire, deceased, departed.
Mutilate: maul, cut, gouge, maim.
Murder: kill, kill, kill.

Dr. Thorson tried to kill me, didn't he? Yes, he claimed he was going to take me to a special clinic that would give me the so-called help I need. I don't need help. I don't need help. He said that something was wrong with me. He said the clinic had a special program that would make me feel much better. I don't feel sick. I feel fine. Dr. Thorson is the sick one. He tried to kill me. He tried to end my life for the thrill of it. Dr. Thorson is the one who needs help.

Simon felt a deep shiver rattle across his nerves. His head was throbbing and pulsing like a drum as he placed his palms against his temples and squeezed. He thought the act would crack his skull and release the built-up pressure. He thought the tension in his head needed to dissipate or his entire head would explode.

Then the darkness came again and was quickly followed by the light.

My God! Why won't the pain stop? Why does it hurt so much? I don't have my medication to make the pain go away. The only other way to ease the suffering is by doing the bad thing. Dr. Thorson said that I wasn't allowed to do the bad thing anymore. He said that doing the bad thing would send me to Hell. He told me the Devil would take my soul, and I would forever burn in the cruelest pits of Hell if I did it again. He said I'd get good help if I went with him. I don't want to go to Hell. I don't want to kill. I don't want to kill!

Yes, you do, someone in the blackness said.

Someone was shaking me. My eyes snapped open, and I looked up. I saw Colleen leaning over the recliner. Her sweet face was close to mine as if she were moving in for a kiss. She smiled as I looked at her in surprise.

"Sorry to wake you," she said.

"It's all right. Is something wrong?"

"It's Joel. His temperature has shot back up. I woke up and decided to check on him. He's shaking and badly sweating, and his temperature is back up to 104. I don't know what to do."

"Christ. Will this night never end?" I said and slid out of the chair.

Colleen and I stood in the doorway of the guest room and watched Joel. The hall light was on, and I could see him shivering and a gleam of sweat covering his face. He was mumbling something in his sleep.

We went back to the living room, where Ryan was asleep in one of the armchairs, and Lewis slept on the couch. We woke Ryan and told him about Joel's worsening condition.

"Okay, so what do we do?" Ryan asked as he rubbed his eyes.

"Well, medicine isn't working, and trying to drop his body temperature by putting him outside didn't work, so what other options do we have?" Colleen asked.

"A hospital is the only way, but there's no possible way to make contact with any emergency personnel. With our cell phones not having any signals or the landline here being down, we can't get in touch with anyone from a neighboring town," I said.

"I have an idea, but I don't think you'll like it," a voice behind us said.

We quickly turned. Lewis was still lying on the couch but now propped up on his elbows and watching the three of us.

"I really wish you'd stop startling us like that. First, it was the pounding on the front door, and now scaring us half to death when we thought you were asleep," Ryan said.

"I'm sorry. I was sleeping, but your conversation woke me."

"Well, then I guess we're sorry for waking you. You said you have an idea?" I asked.

"Yes. It's a long shot, but worth a try if it can get help out here for your friend."

"All right, I suppose we're all listening," I said.

"Well, my car has a CB radio. I should think that someone could get in touch with someone else in one of the nearby towns which might have one. I was going to use it myself when I got stuck, but I had the confrontation with my patient that sent me off running for my life," Lewis said.

"I didn't know people still use CB radios," Ryan said.

"The car was left to me when my father died. He spent a lot of time on the road for work and needed a way to contact someone if an emergency happened," Lewis told us.

Colleen, Ryan, and I all looked at each other. It was certainly one hell of a long shot. The trek Ryan and I had taken to investigate the barn had been treacherous. The barn was only one hundred yards or so from the house. Not to forget that the snowfall accumulation had grown since then.

"How far away was it you said your car got stuck?" I asked.

"I think it was a mile to a mile and a half," Lewis said and retrieved a glass of water from the coffee table and took a long swallow.

"Impossible," Ryan said.

"I can't imagine how deep the snow is right now. You'd die of exhaustion or freeze to death if you even attempted it," Colleen said, as they were all watching me now.

I shook my head at their attempts to bring out the negative side of the plan. In fact, it was all negative. There was only one positive thing about the whole idea: the possibility that it worked. If Ryan were to join me on another harrowing quest, we could very well die out there and only be found after the spring melt. However, if we did nothing, the flu would likely kill one of our best friends. I didn't see any other way around this dilemma.

"I've got to try," I told them.

"Whoa, you're not heading out in this shit alone. Against my better judgment, I'm going out with you. Someone will need to carry you after you collapse," Ryan said.

"I don't think that will happen, but it will be slow going. Thanks for volunteering," I said.

"Think nothing of it. I'm fully aware Joel needs medical help and that he would do the same if it were me in his position," Ryan said.

"Right. Let's bundle up. We've got a long road ahead," I told Ryan.

Just as Ryan and I were preparing to head into the never-ending snowstorm, Norma stepped into the kitchen. She asked us just what in the hell we thought we were up to at this time of night. I told her the plan, as incompetent as it sounded, and she insisted that if we had it in our heads to do such a foolish thing, then she wouldn't stop us. Norma did insist that we hold off a few minutes and follow her into the attic. There were a few things she had in storage that she knew we'd want and need.

"We've held on to these since our boys were young. They left them behind when they moved off. I didn't see any need to throw them away because you never know when something might come in handy," Norma said as she folded open the flaps of a cardboard box covered with a heavy layer of dust.

I smiled when she pulled two pairs of snowshoes from the box.

"They're old but still in good shape. These should work out fine for the both of you."

I couldn't help it, but I hugged Norma.

"Well, it's not exactly a snowmobile, so I don't see why you're excited," she said, and laughed.

"You've saved us a load of trouble and effort. These snowshoes will make the walk a lot easier," I said.

Twenty minutes later, Ryan and I were battling the blizzard again. Norma had also dug up coveralls to help us deal with the undeniably cold-biting wind. The snowshoes had worked wonders. It had taken a small amount of time to get adjusted to walking in them, but I think both of us were handling things pretty well now. We sunk some, but not nearly as deep if we had tried the walk without the snowshoes.

I had major doubts that we'd even be able to journey to the car. If we did make it there, I hoped the battery would have enough juice to operate the CB radio and call for help. As I said before, I couldn't imagine sitting around the house and doing nothing and suffering the possibility that Joel could die from our lack of effort.

As we reached the road, we discovered that a snowplow hadn't yet been able to travel down this stretch of road. I only knew it was the road because of the partially covered signs in the distance heading northeast. We followed the road southwest.

One foot landed in front of the other, and our journey became an event that only the Devil could have thought up. My legs were burning, my breath labored, and the rest of my body riddled with cold exhaustion. Ryan had dramatically slowed his pace as well until I closed the marginal lead he had on me.

It was hard to judge the distance out here. Ryan and I couldn't fixate on a marker with visibility at a minimum, as the landscape was masked in white. All we knew was that Lewis's car was south of the farm a mile or more. He had told us that it was on the side of the road. Even though the snow accumulation was plentiful, I didn't think we'd simply walk past a massive snow-covered lump without a second thought.

Ryan and I were now side by side, trudging through the snow in a sort of wobble but managing to make our way with relative quickness. Norma also supplied us with flashlights to guide us through the night, but neither of us had yet to turn them on as the snow reflected the moonlight and gave the landscape an almost twilight appearance.

Even though we were tired, I felt like talking to help take our thoughts off the circumstances we'd faced on the last day.

"It's going to be all right. We'll be able to get help out here," I said.

"You don't need to talk like that. I'm not Colleen. There's no need to try to ease my mind from the problems we have. I know the score," Ryan said.

"I know you do. Maybe I'm just trying to ease my mind. I'm scared as hell right now. I don't know what's going to happen to Joel, and that terrifies me. The three of you are like family to me, and I get worked up when something bad is happening to any of you."

Ryan clapped me on the back. "I know. That's why I'm out here with you. There was no way in hell I was going to let you make this trip alone. We watch each other's back. That's the way it's been since grade school, and that's the way it will be until we're all in our graves."

"Hopefully, that's a long time from now. Don't forget that there's still the possibility of a madman hiding out here somewhere. Hell, he might even be hiding in the car."

"That's why you brought the shotgun. If anyone comes at us with crazed eyes, you blast the psycho to hell. I don't care if the guy is sick in the head. When it comes down to it, our lives are more important than his," Ryan said.

"I don't like the idea of killing anyone, but I will if the situation arises," I said.

Ryan slipped and almost went down, but I instinctively reached out and held him until he could find balance again.

"Careful. If you slip again, you might sink deep enough that I'll never find you."

A moment later, I pointed to what I was sure was a car covered in snow. We had gone more than a mile, and so the only vehicle it could belong to was Lewis. Ryan and I quickened our pace. While trying to catch our breath, we hurryingly ran our hands over the car and started clearing the mountain of snow. It was a four-door maroon Buick, the kind of car Lewis told us he owned. I looked through the passenger window. It was incredibly dark inside the vehicle with snow-covered windows. I tried the driver's door after finding the passenger doors locked. The latch clicked, and the door swung open.

I sat on the cold leather seat and searched the interior. There was a CB radio below the dash. My body sagged in defeat as we saw Lewis' patient had smashed the radio to pieces.

"Son of a bitch!" I screamed loud enough that anyone in this vast countryside probably heard it. The sight of the destroyed radio lit the fire of my rage.

Ryan was leaning in and looking at what I saw. It was a pointless journey. The radio was our last hope, broken and inoperable.

"Lewis said the guy was a nut, but I didn't think he'd destroy something that might save his life. Maybe he tried to reach someone after Lewis took off, couldn't get anyone on the other end, and lost his composure," Ryan suggested.

"I don't give a shit why he did it. We just came all this way for nothing," I said as I tried to figure out what we would tell the others when we got back to the house.

Ryan reached in and unlocked the rear driver's side door.

He said, "I'm going to see if there's anything in here we can use."

Ryan cleared the snow away and opened the door. I sat there staring at the broken CB radio and tried to consider any possibilities from this point. Even if I tried to start the car, the snow wouldn't let us get anywhere. My SUV had a hard enough time handling the roads, and I was sure that a Buick sedan wouldn't have a chance.

"I don't think we need to worry about Lewis's patient suddenly showing up and creating problems for us," Ryan said from just outside the car.

I turned and looked over my right shoulder. What I saw propelled me from the car faster than a rocket. I stood in the blowing wind and torrent of snow, staring through the window at a man lying in the back seat of the Buick. I had automatically trained the barrel of the shotgun at the back door and turned on my flashlight. I remember Ryan saying that if the man came at us with crazed eyes, I should blast him to hell.

"Sweet Jesus!" I said as I watched for the man to make a move.

Ryan stood beside me, and we waited.

"I think he's dead," Ryan said.

"Or he's waiting for us to check so he can surprise us," I whispered.

"I'll hold the gun while you check," Ryan suggested.

"My ass. I already have the gun. You check."

Ryan slowly and carefully leaned in as I directed the flashlight beam on the man's head. Ryan reached for the man's collar and a second later said, "Shit, the guy's an icicle. Yeah, he's dead all right," Ryan said and stood up again.

"What do we do?" I asked.

"Well, I don't think there's any chance of reviving him."

"That isn't what I meant. Obviously, we can't call the police. So do we just leave him here?"

Ryan looked at me for a long, confused moment and then said, "I'm not going to lug a two-hundred pound corpse on my back all the way to the farmhouse. I can't think that there's much we can do. The guy is dead, Drew. I think he can stay refrigerated until we can reach the authorities."

I didn't know what to expect from my question. I understood everything Ryan had said, but I was hoping for some sort of revelation that would erase the last sixteen hours of my life.

I said, "Sorry, I've never seen anyone dead before. I panicked a little. I guess I already realized that we'd have to leave him here, so forget I said anything."

"I think this ski vacation is becoming more and more of a bust. Come on. I'm freezing to the core. Let's get back to the house. There isn't anything more we can do out here," Ryan said.

As Ryan started to close the back door, I said, "Wait, maybe he has a good cell phone that might get a signal out here."

Although I had no desire to search the pockets of a dead man, I knew I would regret it later if I didn't. I handed the shotgun to Ryan and slid partially inside the back seat. I practically straddled the body as my hands quickly roamed his coat pockets. As Ryan had said, the man was frozen, and it was like sitting on a log.

It was challenging to get in his pants pockets. I figured I'd have to turn him over to gain access. I gripped the backside of his coat and rotated him. I remember how moments ago I was squeamish about being in the presence of a dead man, but now my uncomfortable state had taken flight. My hope of finding a working cell phone had overpowered all mental roadblocks.

I don't know what I expected, but I received the appearance of a very ordinary man. With his ruffled black hair, trimmed mustache, and fair complexion, he seemed to be the kind of person I'd passed on the streets a million times. I suppose the adage of "looks can be deceiving" applied here. A person's appearance was one thing, but the inner workings of one's mind were an entirely different story.

There was a deep gash above the man's left eyebrow. There was a trickle of blood that ran down the side of his face and was frozen in time until a mortician's touch would clear it away. Lewis had struck the man with his satchel to fend off the attack. Lewis had escaped death, but this man had shaken hands with Death personally.

My search turned up very little. I uncovered a tube of lip balm, a small tin of breath mints, and a wallet. I searched the backseat, hoping a cell had fallen from his death grip and lay hidden. I found nothing else worth attention.

Something popped into my mind. Earlier, I had read Lewis's case files on this man. Now I couldn't remember his name. We shouldn't forget those who recently passed, even if the man was a lunatic. I know I don't want to be forgotten when I'm gone.

"Didn't Norma say something about Lewis breaking down pretty close to another farm?" Ryan asked as he studied the surrounding countryside.

"Yeah. I think Norma said it was around a quarter mile or half a mile from where she figures Lewis got stuck."

"Why don't we try to find it? Maybe their phone works, and we can call for help."

"That's not a bad idea," I said.

I shined the flashlight on the wallet and opened it. The driver's license photo was recent. Five-foot eleven, black hair, brown eyes, birth date March 11th, 1968 and—

It wasn't from the howling bite of the wind, but I felt a terrible cold shiver course through my body as veins turned to rivers of ice. Everything about the situation had gone from bad to worse in a matter of moments. I stepped out of the car, looked at Ryan, and dropped the wallet.

She's beautiful, and I want her. She's the kind of woman only a lucky man could have. I'm lucky. I survived an attack from a psychopath who tried to kill my voice. I survived the damn blizzard that desperately tried to kill me as well. I'm immortal. I'm invincible. I'm unstoppable. I'm the luckiest goddamn person on the planet.

The girl desires me. She's falling in love with me. I think I love her, too. The gentle way she looks at me. Her precious, heavenly blue eyes are watching me with admiration. She wants to be with me forever and ever. I went her, but not forever because nothing lasts forever, sweetheart. Love comes and goes. I've been loved before. I've been hurt. I've been pushed aside like a used item and left in the gutter to rot. My love is only brief, and then I must discard it before it has the chance to walk away from me.

Someone is trying to talk to me. It isn't the girl, but another voice, a voice coming from a long, dark tunnel. What is it saying?

I'm getting tired now. I've had such a long day. The hour is late, and I've got to rest. The girl is watching me. She looks concerned. She's saying something, but I'm not sure what it is because the other voice coming from shadowed places is getting louder. It's drowning out all other sounds. It's been such an awful day, and I can't keep my eyes open. I'm sure I'll feel much better after a bit of rest, goodnight my beautiful girl. I'll see you in the morning when the snow has stopped, and the sun finds the land. It's going to be a beautiful day.

I thought my energy was depleted when Ryan and I had finally reached the car. Now the reservoir was pumping out adrenaline as we followed the partially covered path back to the farmhouse.

After I had dropped the wallet, Ryan had immediately picked it up and discovered what I had.

The body in the car was not the patient of Lewis Thorson, but the doctor himself.

The man at the farmhouse was the patient described in the files.

The man had killed his doctor, taken the satchel containing his personal files, and assumed Lewis Thorson's identity.

"He had me fooled. I would never have thought the man on the couch was disturbed," Ryan said.

"I think the man we saw was one of the submissive personalities. I'm goddamn afraid that the worst of his personalities will come out. The violence he's capable of is downright scary," I said as we did an awkward run down the deserted highway.

"I wish a damn plow would come through so we can catch a ride and call for help. We needed help before, but now we need it more than ever," Ryan said, out of breath.

My entire body wanted to rest, but I didn't want to waste precious minutes. The man on the couch had sent Ryan and me on a fool's quest. He had shattered the CB radio into pieces. He purposely sent the two most vital individuals from the house in order to do something that terrified me to even think about.

Nearly fifteen minutes later, Ryan and I had found John and Norma's driveway. Instantly, things didn't seem right. The driveway entrance was a long stretch to the house, but neither of us could see it at this point. Although I knew Colleen and perhaps Norma were still awake and awaiting our return, no lights shone through the house windows.

"Come on. Hurry!" I said to Ryan.

"The power must have gone out," Ryan said as we found even more strength from the nearly depleted supply.

"Yeah, it went out, but I don't think it was the storm that caused it."

Even though the man on the couch hadn't shown any signs of hostility up to this point, I had a feeling that a switch in his mind had flipped, and he was no longer the docile man we knew from before. The house without lights had only intensified this new feeling of mine.

If exhaustion had tried to overwhelm me, I hadn't noticed. My focus was strictly on the people inside the house. Ryan and I trudged up the drive and across the porch to the front door. I gripped the handle only to find the home tightly locked up. I beat my fist against the glass nearly hard enough to crack it. I called for Colleen, Norma, John, or even Joel to answer the door. My calls went unanswered.

"Should we break the glass?" Ryan asked.

"I want to, but not yet. I don't want to break anything until we know for sure what's happening. Let's go around the house and check the other door."

Snow had accumulated in great drifts along the north and west sides of the house, and Ryan and I had to make a wide circle to reach the back door.

They're coming for you now. They know what you've done. They're going around the house to another locked door. They will get in. They will discover what you've done since they've been gone.

So? I can kill them. I can destroy them. I can hide in the deep shadows. I have all the time in the world to wait for them. I'll catch them off guard, and I'll plunge this knife deep into the recess of their hearts. The beating will stop. The life within will simply slip away. Close your eyes, gentlemen, because it's time to say goodnight.

"Shit," I said, pushing on the locked back door.

"I'm freezing my ass off, and we don't have time for this."

"I agree."

"Damn, look at this," Ryan said and grabbed the end of a gray wire running from a small green box fastened to the side of the house.

"Well, I guess we got our answer on why the phone line went down," I said.

"That son of a bitch yanked it loose before he even went to the front door. Now that really pisses me off."

I drove my elbow through the pane of glass. Shards shot through the curtain and tinkled to the floor. I reached inside, half expecting a knife to drive through my searching hand, and disengaged the deadbolt. I turned the knob and slowly pushed the rear door open. A dark, silent laundry room greeted us. I flipped the light switch several times, but the light failed to come on.

"I've got a real bad feeling about this," Ryan said.

"I've had that since finding the dead body."

We took a quick moment to remove our snowshoes. As we moved through the laundry room, I let the barrel of the shotgun guide the way. I tried to keep my finger from tensing on the trigger. I didn't know if someone would suddenly step out in front of me in the flashlight's beam. There's only one person in this household I could imagine releasing all of the buckshot at, and I had to be sure before my finger went into action.

"Stay close behind me, and try to remain quiet."

"I'm a church mouse," Ryan whispered as we left the laundry room and took a right into one of the back bedrooms.

As soon as we entered the bedroom, I could hear the unsteady rasping sounds of Joel trying to breathe. I stepped to the bed, kneeled, and gently gripped his forearm. His skin was on fire. A thick sheen of sweat covered his face and had soaked the pillow. In response to my touch, Joel muttered something unintelligible.

Aside from the severe illness, Joel was unharmed.

"Hey, can you hear me all right?" I said in a volume just above a whisper.

"Huh?"

Joel's eyes fluttered. His sight shifted around the darkened room until he found Ryan and me in the glow of the flashlight.

"I'm all right. Stop worrying about me so much," Joel said loud enough that I cringed.

"Shh, don't talk so loud. Look, something has happened," I said.

"The lights went out."

"Yeah, the power went out. We're not sure if it's from the storm or something else. Do you remember the man who came to the house?"

"Uh-huh."

"Well, he isn't who he says he is. Ryan and I went to his car because he said there was a CB radio in there that we could call for help. We really needed to get a medical crew out here to help you. The only thing is that the man is actually the patient of the psychologist. We found the doctor's body in the car. He smashed the CB to pieces. When we got back to the house, the lights were out. We had to break in the door because no one answered."

"Shit, man, I knew this whole vacation was a bad idea," Joel rasped.

"It's going to be all right. Ryan and I will take care of everything. Has Colleen or Norma come to see you recently?"

"I don't think so. Christ, my head is on fire."

"Just sit tight. We're going to look for the others, and then we'll come back for you," I said.

"I'm not going anywhere."

I prayed that if his fever was going to break, it would soon because he appeared nearly defeated.

I patted his shoulder and said, "If you have to cough, cover with a pillow. I'm hoping the guy out there forgot you were in here."

Joel gave us a thumbs-up, and we left the room. We followed the hallway to the kitchen and then the living room. The light from the dying fire offered us a visual of the empty space. The couch that had been occupied by the man now only held a wool blanket and a pillow. Both armchairs were vacant as well.

Ryan went to the gun cabinet. The key hung from the top-drawer lock.

"Son of a bitch. The ammunition isn't in here," Ryan said as he peered into an empty drawer.

"He must have taken it," I whispered.

"Now we're up the creek."

"We still have at least one gun. Come on, let's get you a knife from the kitchen."

Ryan selected a carving knife from the block that was probably long enough to skewer the man if the opportunity came. After a second thought, Ryan also grabbed a sharp steak knife before we left the kitchen.

We went back into the living room, and I nodded toward the stairs. We had cleared the main level, and now we had no choice but to head up to the second floor and, room by room, find out exactly where everyone else was.

I had an overwhelming terror that everyone, except Joel, was murdered and heaped into a morbid, bloody pile. Meanwhile, a mentally ill patient was crouched in a corner, rocking back and forth, covered in blood, and talking to himself.

It was an old house, and the stairs squeaked under our weight. We stayed close to the wall to minimize the sounds where the strength of the boards was much stronger. I felt my heart hammering hard enough that my eardrums echoed like a bass drum.

I stopped on the top landing and peered around the corner. To my left was a hallway with three closed doors. To my right was a single entry. I moved to the right, gripped the doorknob, turned it, and gently pushed the door open. I shined the flashlight inside and swept the beam around the room. I figured the room had once belonged to one of their sons. While in the attic, Norma said they had two sons all grown up and moved away. The furniture, wall art that showed snapshots of mostly '80s rock bands, and shelves loaded with trophies probably hadn't changed in the slightest since he had gone off to college.

Ryan and I quietly searched the closet and beneath the bed. We found no one hiding in this room. We went down the hall, opened the first door on the right, and revealed an empty bathroom. The next door was another bedroom, much like the previous one. We searched the room and also found it deserted.

My hand paused as I reached for the final doorknob. I leaned closer to the wood, pressed my ear to the door, and tried to slow my breathing so that I could hear the slightest sounds from within. There was no noise of whispering, shuffling around, or even breathing.

I pushed the door open and the hinges squealed. Ryan and I moved inside. I had the gun ready, and Ryan held the flashlight. John lay in his bed. His eyes were wide open, but his body was still. Crimson covered his white nightshirt.

I held my breath as I stepped to the bed. John's eyes were blank, lifeless and forever fixed on something above. At least a dozen vicious wounds covered his chest.

"Oh, my God," Ryan said.

If ever there was a time to worry during our entrapment on this large acreage estate, now was that time. Horrified, I wondered if Colleen had suffered the same fate. For that matter, I wondered if everyone in the household would find death in the winking gleam of a blade wielded by a madman.

"Where else could they be?" I asked.

After a moment of thought, Ryan and I moved back into the hall. We had forgotten that Norma had earlier led us up the retractable stairs and into the attic to find the winter supplies we required for our journey into the blizzard.

I gripped the hanging string and pulled the stairs down. Despite our slow pace of searching the house, I wanted to get through this. We charged up the steps with no intensions of concealing our assault. Our flashlights quickly traced bright scars across the blackened attic. There were racks of old clothes, shelves overloaded with odds and ends of things that no longer held interest but were unable to be thrown away. The attic was a maze of objects where anyone could hide.

Carefully, Ryan and I moved through the narrow paths with our flashlights illuminating every dark nook. Half-sized doors opened to recessed areas of the attic. Each space was void of life, except for maybe mice nesting in the insulation.

Ryan and I looked at each other and shrugged.

"Now what?" Ryan asked.

My mind was already running down that road.

"They couldn't have just vanished. I didn't see any tracks leading away from the house at either the front or back door," I said.

We spent time backtracking through the house. In the hall near the bedrooms on the main floor was a door leading downstairs into a type of storm cellar. I couldn't figure out how we missed it the first time.

The steps popped under our weight. As we moved down, my thoughts fully expected to receive a sliced

Achilles tendon from the maniac hiding under the staircase. The air was drastically colder, and a breeze was driving through the basement. When we hit the bottom step, I immediately saw two things.

Norma was on the floor and leaning against the cinder block.

Beyond the ascending concrete stairs, the storm cellar doors leading outside were open.

Colleen and the insane man were gone.

Ryan and I crouched beside Norma. She was breathing slowly, and her hand was clutching her left side. Her tear-filled eyes were on us.

"Are you all right?" I asked.

Norma sniffed, drew in a stuttering breath, and said, "He did something to John. Did you find my husband? Is he all right?"

Ryan and I exchanged a glance that said everything. Watching us, Norma began crying harder. Without words, we had confirmed her worst fears.

I squeezed her shoulder and said, "I'm so sorry, but we need to worry about you right now. Are you having a heart attack or something?"

She shook her head and said, "No, but I acted like I was. He was going to drag us outside. I don't know where he's taking your friend. I thought if I managed to stay behind, I could warn you when you came back."

We helped her up.

"How long have they been gone?" Ryan asked.

"No more than ten minutes."

"I'm going after them. Ryan, I want you to secure this door after I leave and get Norma upstairs.

"I can help you. I think it will take both of us to bring this bastard down."

"No, take care of her and Joel. They need you more right now. I'm going to find Colleen and do anything else I need to do to end this."

I think both of them understood what I meant by that. I certainly wasn't a killer by nature. However, there are times in a person's life when such actions are justified. Right now seemed to be one of those times.

I moved up the concrete steps and back into the blizzard. The wind immediately bit hard. I hadn't thought to ask Norma if Colleen was wearing a coat when he forced her from the house. If she wasn't wearing one, severe frostbite or possible death would be the only outcome.

Two sets of footprints were easily traceable. Ryan and I had removed our snowshoes when entering the back door, and I hadn't thought of strapping them back on. Now I was sinking up to my knees and even deeper in some places. There were several areas where either Colleen or the madman had gone down. Body prints were pressed in the snow as they had lost balance.

It was exhausting, but I trudged through the snow at a steady speed. The tracks led to the forest behind the house. Although the sun was a long way from making its rise, I could see enough by the light of the moon's reflection off the snow. I followed the path of tracks with an eager desire to finish this deception and bring my friend back to the house safe and sound.

My speed quickened when I heard a scream in the thickness of the forest ahead. I could see several silhouettes in the night. Somehow, I had managed to catch up with them. I couldn't understand where the man was taking her. Was his purpose, his delusion, fulfilled only by allowing himself to freeze to death and taking Colleen's life as well? I couldn't be sure, but I was almost positive that there would be no other buildings this far from the farmhouse. I didn't think the man had any particular destination in mind as he attempted to escape. He was simply mad, and there was certainly no other way of making that statement.

Simon had taken the key to the gun cabinet, removed the ammunition, and hidden it. I couldn't be positive if he armed himself when he took Colleen and ran from the house. I remembered that John was stabbed to death, not shot. Of course, I didn't know the circumstances leading up to that moment. Perhaps he had done the act covertly not to alarm the others before he could make his next move. I thought that even a madman would take one of the guns in preparation for any conflict. It was this thought that stopped me from calling out Colleen's name.

I could tell that Colleen was having a difficult time keeping upright in the snow. It was Colleen's struggle that had slowed their momentum and allowed me to catch up so easily. My gain was slow, but the gap was undoubtedly closing. I wanted my advancements to remain secret. Neither of them looked back as the three of us drew farther into the woods.

"Please," Colleen was saying, "I can't go on. I can't force myself to go on."

"You will go on, or I'll cut your throat here and now and leave you to bleed to death in these woods. You should cut her. Cut her and be done with it," he said.

The last part came in such a different voice. A personality switched so well that I looked around for another man hiding somewhere in the woods. It took a moment to understand that it was Simon speaking. Had another one of his personalities surfaced? Had they exchanged places so rapidly that one had finished another's thought?

"Just stop it! It doesn't have to be this way. Cut her. Cut her now. We've got to keep moving. There's another house just beyond these woods. I'm sure of it."

Although I desperately tried to keep my attention on closing the gap, keeping my balance, and preparing myself for the possible execution of a man, I couldn't help but draw my eyes toward Dr. Thorson's patient.

If I had been scared before, then now I was absolutely terrified. The man's multiple personalities were fighting for control. One wanted to kill, another to flee the area, and still another longing to find reason in this situation of madness. I was sure that the triangle of the fight wouldn't last much longer. The dominant personality would prevail, and that outcome could lead to Colleen's death.

I didn't see a gun in Simon's hand, but I did see a knife. He was wielding it madly in the air as if battling creatures or people that only he could see. I knew that I had been right. His personalities were colliding on an epic scale. Simon's hand quickly flashed out, and the knife raked across the bark of a tree, leaving a clean scar on the surface.

I had to end this now. I moved even faster, closed the gap as much as possible before raising the shotgun and getting Simon's attention.

"That's enough! Let her go, and this will all be over!" I yelled.

Simon whirled around, spinning Colleen with him. His eyes found me and the business end of the shotgun aimed directly at him. He didn't appear scared, but ecstatic at the new development of his questionable plan.

"Good," he said in a long, slow breath. "I had hoped you'd follow. I'm sure this young woman didn't want to die alone."

"No one needs to die. It can stop right now."

Simon's expression rapidly changed. His eyes searched around as if confused about where he was and what was going on. Then there was another fast transformation.

"I'll cut her throat and turn the snow a wonderful shade of red. You can shoot me, you can kill me, but I'll have time to do that. You are only one, but we are many," Simon said as he tapped the tip of the blade against his temple.

As if to provoke me, he then pressed the knife to the exposed back side of Colleen's hand and pulled the blade across. Her skin parted to a flow of crimson. Simon's eyes locked onto the blood seeping from her hand. He appeared to relish the sight with an almost orgasmic delight.

"I know you don't want to die. No one really wants to die. There is still time to redeem the terrible things you've done." I had no idea what I was saying. I was trying any means necessary to end this thing peacefully.

"No more time! It's too late to take it all back!" he shouted and thrust the point of the knife in my direction.

Colleen saw her brief chance. Her right hand balled in a fist and struck bluntly across his gripping hand. The connection quickly broke as Colleen spun, lunged forward, and collapsed into the snow.

I pulled the butt of the shotgun to my shoulder and squeezed the trigger. A brief, hollow clack ran across the stillness of the woods as the shotgun's firing mechanism went into action. The eruption of a shell didn't follow as it should have. Confused, I pulled the trigger again and received the same result.

Simon laughed madly.

I looked dumbly at the shotgun. Although I didn't know much about guns, I knew the safety was off, and the weapon should have torn the man in half.

Simon reached inside his coat pocket and removed two shotgun shells. His laugh was maniacal and colder than the bite of the winter wind. His arm quickly shifted to the left, and the red shells flew from his grasp and disappeared in the torrent of falling snow.

My heart sank. I fully understood that Colleen and I had no more hope of walking out of this forest alive.

"I removed the shells when you took the doctor's case into the kitchen, and the others were sleeping. Of course, I don't like guns. I never have. Guns are impersonal. Anyone can use a gun when it comes down to it, but using a knife is an entirely different matter. A knife is very personal and used face-to-face. You can feel their breath on you when you slide it in deep, and the blood squirts from the wound. You can see the light slip from their eyes. You can't get any of that from a gun. No, a knife is always the way to go," Simon said while holding up his knife and admiring Colleen's blood on it.

Even though I had no shells, I could still use the shotgun as a weapon to batter his skull apart. By the confidence in his eyes, Simon was probably pretty good at using a knife. I would need luck and timing to get close enough to make the first strike without spilling my guts across the snow.

Colleen had backed up to a tree and, with panicked eyes, watched the conflict unfold.

Simon came forward with his arm raised and a maddening shriek. His eyes were wide and insane.

I turned the shotgun in my hands and gripped the barrel. I was going to have to use the thing like a bat. I backed up a few paces and desperately tried to keep my footing. If I went down, it was all over.

"I'm gonna cut you real bad. Time to bleed," he chanted, and the blade sang through the air.

The knife bit into the breast of my coat, peeling the fabric, and cotton fibers flew out. I had spun at the last second and prevented the blade from going deep. My flesh was thankfully untouched.

I swung hard, but the shotgun butt traced a path over his head as he was falling forward from a loss of balance. Before Simon went down, he tucked his head and did a summersault onto the powdery snow and was quickly on his feet again. The blade arched but had just missed my stomach.

I swung and connected the shotgun with his left shoulder. He screamed in pain, and in a fury, he sliced the blade quickly a dozen times but again missed.

Colleen was on her feet and coming at him. She had pried a large branch from the frozen ground and held it high above her head as if she were about to swing a battle-axe. Simon dodged to the left as she swung. The branch whistled and smashed into the ground. Simon threw his arm back and smacked Colleen hard enough across the cheek that she pinwheeled to the ground.

I came forward, and Simon's knife reacted. The blade dug this time, cut through my coat sleeve, and parted the skin and flesh of my right forearm. This time I screamed a long, bellowing cry that echoed across the bleak forest.

Simon stepped back a few paces and smiled gleefully. His tongue slicked out and ran across the flat side of the blade.

"You see? The knife makes it so personal that I feel much closer to you now that I've seen your blood. I can even taste your cowardice. Come on, let's see how much more I can get to flow."

Simon took one step forward and then quickly halted. His eyes were wide and staring in the distance behind me.

"That isn't fair," he said so low that I was positive he was talking to one of his other personalities.

"Step aside, Drew," Ryan said.

I turned and saw that Ryan was holding a shotgun of his own. Only he had no intentions of using it like a baseball bat. The two black eyes of the barrels pointed in our direction. Ryan must have found where Simon stashed the ammo back at the house.

I moved to the left.

"Wait," Simon said in a frail tone.

"No, not one more second," Ryan said.

The shotgun went off with a thunder-cracking eruption. There was a strange moment in slow motion as fire flowed from the barrel in rippling orange waves, and the buckshot left the gun.

Then time hastily caught up to its normal rhythm.

Simon violently pitched back as his coat opened up into a shower of red and shredded fabric. His face twisted to a look of utter surprise and pain. He landed on his backside and nearly disappeared in the depth of the snow. I could see his right hand, but not much more. I stared at that hand for a long moment. A spatter of blood covered the palm. The fingers were still for a long moment. I was sure he was dead, blown back to whatever part of hell he came from, but then I saw the fingers twitch a little. I didn't think it was simply reflexive nerves of a corpse, but that he was somehow still alive.

The three of us slowly came forward. Our eyes fell upon the man that had created one of the most horrifying memories any of us would ever come to know. Simon was alive, but barely. His body hitched as his lungs drew in bloody breaths. His eyes swam back from whatever distant place they had been and focused on us.

The look on his face reminded me of a time when my car struck a deer on a dark highway. Under the glow of the headlights, the deer gave me a pitiful and yet terrifying look that eerily matched Simon's. Part of me felt sorry for the long road this mentally disturbed man had endured. But sometimes situations come around that leave someone believing that it was truly the only option to take.

Colleen pulled in close to me and began crying. I think that look got to her the same way it did to me.

"Mama," Simon said in a voice almost childlike.

Ryan lowered the gun to his side. There was another shell remaining, but we all knew the fight was over.

"Mama, I don't want to go to school today. They make fun of me. How come they're so cruel to me, Mama?"

Then Simon's mouth quit working. His eyes focused on something far beyond the tree line. His chest rose and fell, rose and fell, and then simply stopped.

His final question went unanswered.

Colleen turned away and pressed her face into the crook of my shoulder, and cried some more.

Ryan and I looked at each other, waiting for one of us to verbally justify what we'd done. We both wanted reassurance that the death of this man was the only choice. I had thought so, and I'm sure Ryan did as well, but sometimes questions never receive answers, at least not answers that help you sleep at night.

We made the long walk back to the house in silence. I didn't know what we were going to do once we got there. Norma needed comfort. Joel needed to see that we were still here for him. I was pretty sure I could repair the damaged phone line at the back of the house. Even in the cold and darkness, I was going to give it one hell of a try. These were several things that would keep us occupied for a little while. The three of us needed to put our minds somewhere else until we could reach the authorities. I figured the rest of the night was going to continue to be the longest of my life.

The house lights were back on.

"Joel's fever broke just before I headed out after you. He was so sweaty I thought he just stepped out of the shower. I could tell just by looking at him that he was feeling a great deal better," Ryan said.

I smiled. After all of our worrying and daring efforts, Joel had fought and won his fever battle. Joel refused to give in. He refused death. I guess we all had on this night.

"That's wonderful news," I said.

"How about that? The snow is slowing down," Colleen said when we reached the storm cellar doors.

I watched the night sky. The snowfall had only slightly decreased, but it was thankfully slowing.

"Yeah, looks like the storm is finally passing," I said and wrapped my arm around Colleen just a little tighter.

Made in the USA
Monee, IL
15 September 2022